The Haunting on Palm Court

Stephanie Edwards

ISBN: 978-1-7351691-1-8

This is a work of fiction. Any references to historical events, real people or real places are used fictitiously. Other names, characters, places and events are products of the author's imagination, and any resemblance to actual events or places or persons, living or dead, is entirely coincidental.

This novel contains some violent acts, abuse, adult language and mature situations. Discretion is advised.

Thank you to all of my friends and family who have supported my writing. I'm especially grateful to Ron, Darlene, Lia, Kelly and Linda. Each of you has spent countless hours helping me brainstorm, edit and make this dream a reality. Thanks for your tireless support and love.

Prologue

Julia

Standing in front of the window inside her island home, Julia Caroline Mason watched her granddaughter, Blake, step out of her car. Illuminated by the moon and streetlights, Blake's long dark curls fell onto her face. She swept them back, revealing the tears that were streaming down her cheek. Julia bit her lip and clenched her hands. *That wasn't a good sign.*

Blake was an upbeat person. She had worked hard to find her place in life, and nothing had set her off course until she met her fiancé, Parker Sutton. He'd captured her interest at what Julia had considered an unhealthy pace. Was Parker was responsible for the tears in her granddaughter's eyes? Julia had never trusted him.

The slamming of the front door caught Julia's attention. She ran down the steps to console Blake, who was sitting on the living room sofa with her head in her hands.

Julia sat down next to Blake and put her arm around her. "There, there. Please, honey, tell me what happened."

"I don't understand," Blake whispered. She pulled out her cell phone and looked at a picture of her and Parker standing on the beach. "Why would he cheat on me?" She continued sobbing.

"He did what?" Julia demanded. She stared at her granddaughter in disbelief. Blake had inherited every attractive trait in the family line. Even filled with tears, her hazel eyes sparkled. Her bronzed complexion even made her white t-shirt seem glamorous.

Blake didn't answer. She curled up on the sofa and cried herself to sleep. Julia let her rest, trying to figure out what to do to help her feel better.

Julia's best friend Nancy had always had a way of cheering up Blake when she was younger. Maybe Nancy could help distract her. It was worth a try.

The next morning, Julia walked over to Nancy's house and let herself in through the kitchen door.

"Nan, you home?" No answer, but she'd wait.

A few minutes later, Nancy burst through the door, almost dropping two grocery bags full of produce. She balanced herself, set everything down on the counter. Red-faced, she drew a deep breath. "What's the matter?"

Julia sighed. "Blake's here. Parker couldn't behave himself. She's hurting. Can you talk to her?"

"I never trusted that son of a…" she started, but Julia waved her hand.

"Don't waste your curse words on the likes of him. He's not worth it."

"I couldn't agree more. Let me wash my face, and I'll be ready to head over to your place."

Julia nodded and sat at the table, waiting for Nancy. Thank goodness Nancy was free to help today. That child may have grown up into a woman, but she still needed her family, blood-related or not, to support her through this predicament. Julia feared that in a moment of weakness, Blake might return to Parker to give him a second chance, but infidelity should be the end of the narcissist's reign in her granddaughter's life. She deserved better—the best.

"Are you ready?" Nancy asked.

Julia hadn't noticed her reenter the room. "Let's chat before we leave."

"Honey, I know what you're gonna say. We need to keep her away from that—ahem, this ain't the word I want to use—loser." Nancy put her hands on her hips and snapped her head from side to side.

"Exactly. Blake doesn't know much about my past or what's coming in her life. It's better if you explain it to her after her heart has recovered from this affair nonsense. After you do, I'll find the right time to approach her and say my piece."

"Are you sure the child's mother shouldn't talk to her first?" Nancy stared at Julia.

"No. Susan doesn't understand the first thing about that part of my life, and, even if she did, I doubt she'd want to share it with Blake. She's never...believed." Julia looked down at her folded hands, which were resting on the knotty pine table that had once sat in her own kitchen.

"Very well. I love Blake like family, as I do all of your kinfolk." Nancy placed her hands over Julia's and smiled. "It's my honor to help watch over her and make sure the *loser* leaves her alone."

"Thank you. Us blood sisters gotta stick together." Julia winked at Nancy.

"Amen to that. Our friendship makes the world go 'round." Nancy smiled.

Nancy had bailed her out of a pickle so many times she couldn't count them on one hand. They had been friends since their youth, seeing each other through marriages, the births of their children and the deaths of their husbands. She trusted Nancy more than almost anyone.

Nancy grabbed her purse off a cast-iron hook on the wall and looked over her shoulder at Julia. "Okay, let's go talk to that granddaughter of yours."

Julia nodded and stood up.

They made the five-minute walk to the cottage in silence. Nancy didn't need to say anything. Julia knew she was planning out what to say to Blake to convince her to stay on Isle of Palms long enough to make her forget Parker's indiscretions. She hoped her granddaughter would be receptive to Nancy's firm but nurturing ways. It would be a delicate dance. Blake embodied the powerful, modern woman, except when it came to Parker. When he snapped his fingers, she came running. If anyone could keep her from making that mistake again, it was Nancy.

When the cottage came into view, Julia's heart fluttered. This weathered beach home was still a beauty. The memories of her life with her family flooded her heart. Now her granddaughter needed the solace this house had once provided Julia when her husband of 40 years had died. Its comforting, sun-filled rooms had warmed her soul and provided a nest for rebuilding her life and heart. She sighed. *Thank you, old house.*

Julia turned to Nancy and asked her to wait for a minute. "Let me go check on her. I don't want her to think we're ambushing her…even if we are."

Nancy nodded. Julia entered the cottage and looked through the first-floor rooms, but she didn't see Blake. *She must be upstairs.* Julia found her granddaughter fast asleep on her childhood bed. She bent over to kiss Blake on the cheek and slipped back out of the house.

Julia found Nancy standing under the willow tree. "Blake was asleep. I couldn't bear to wake her. She'll come to you when she's ready, and I'm betting it will be sooner rather than later. I think you'll be able to convince her to stay here and as far away from him as she can."

"I agree. If she was in that big of a hurry to leave Knoxville, she must have plans to stick around for a while. I'll do what I can to make her think it's her idea." Nancy grinned, but her smile faded and her eyes narrowed. "You remember her as the girl who wore her curls in pigtails. Blake is an adult now. She deserves to learn her family history, what you did, your book…what she's capable of herself."

Julia agreed, in part. She wanted to appear to Blake and explain everything now, but the news would shock her granddaughter. Being on the Other Side of the grave carried disadvantages, despite Julia's gifts. "Nan, I trust you to break the news to her at the right time."

Nancy pursed her lips. “I’ll do whatever you need me to.”
“Thank you. I’m sure she’ll come by the restaurant soon.”
Julia planned to be there every step of the way.

Chapter 1

The Day Before

Blake Nelson was on a mission—tonight, she would persuade her fiancé, Parker, to set a date for their wedding.

Two candles cast their half-moon crescents onto the otherwise dark dining room ceiling. The rich scent of skillet-seared steak and her spicy perfume filled the air. Her slinky dress and the seductive jazz music playing in the background set the tone.

She checked her makeup in the hallway mirror, fluffed her dark curls and admired her curvy figure. Shimmery gold shadow gave her eyes a bewitching glow, and the pale pink gloss she applied added a subtle shine to her full lips. Satisfied with her appearance, she poured a glass of chardonnay and relaxed on an oversized leather chair while she waited for Parker.

An hour past his usual arrival time, Blake texted him to ask if he was working late, but he didn't reply. She'd mentioned cooking a special dinner for him that morning as they were leaving their downtown Knoxville apartment for work. She dialed his number.

On the fifth ring, he picked up. "What?"

"Hi, did you forget I was making dinner for us tonight? I made…"

He interrupted her, "I don't have time for this."

"But, dinner's ready. I made your favorite meal. I've been looking forward to spending the evening with you."

"Whatever. I'll be there when I'm there." The line went dead.

She slammed her phone down on the coffee table and crossed her arms. Before she met Parker, she wouldn't have stayed home on a Friday night. Blake needed to talk to someone. Her sister, Brittany, was studying for finals, so she'd be around. Blake texted her and asked her to video chat.

After opening her chat app, Brittany's face popped up on screen. "Hey, what's up?" she signed in American Sign Language. Brittany had lost her hearing at the age of two, following a high fever. In addition to signing, she read lips and spoke vocally.

Blake waved and signed, "Do you have a minute?"

"Definitely. I'm ready for a break." Brittany laughed.

Blake clenched her jaw. "I'm so effin' mad right now. I'm trying to chill. Parker stood me up for dinner tonight."

"Oh, my God. Weren't you planning to set the date tonight?"

"Yep." Blake sighed.

"Um…why are you with him? You deserve better."

Blake paused. "Well, he's been going through a lot lately. His job has been stressful, and his sister just died. Things will get better again." *She'd called Brittany for support. Her sister was right, so why was she defending Parker's actions?*

"I hope so," Brittany signed.

"Sorry I bothered you while you were studying. I'll let you get back to it. Good luck with your exams." Blake ended the video chat.

She shouldn't have called her sister. Brittany was engaged to her high school boyfriend, Ryan. Their love-at-first-sight relationship was next to perfect. She wouldn't understand.

Before Blake met Parker, marriage had not been a priority. She had intended to spend her downtime traveling to experience the world. However, that changed when her boss, Sharon, the owner of the McKinley-Johnson Marketing Firm, moved his family's account to her.

After just two meetings, Blake had found herself mesmerized by his piercing green eyes and perfect smile. Parker always got what he wanted with a smooth demeanor, something that had captured Blake's attention. She was confident she had captivated him, too, as he lingered at meetings longer than most clients.

Her heart jumped each time he *accidentally* touched her hand or shoulder. When he asked her out, Blake had accepted. As their relationship had grown more serious, Parker had made it clear her priorities needed to change. Flattered by his affection, she had put plans with her friends and family on the back burner, attending social events where he'd demanded her presence instead. Blake had emphatically accepted his marriage proposal after one year of dating.

Now, almost two years after their engagement, Blake couldn't help but feel his focus had shifted from her to something else. Late nights apart were becoming commonplace. When she'd tried to ask him if everything was okay, he'd told her how busy he was with work.

Parker's twin sister, who had lived overseas, had disappeared almost a year ago. Blake never had the opportunity to meet Maggie, a successful maritime lawyer, who rarely took a day off from work. The couple had planned to visit Maggie the week of her disappearance. The news had come as a shock to Parker. He had slipped into a deep depression for the first few months. Eventually, he recovered, but his relationship with Blake wasn't the same. She was happy to be patient and supportive, but she hoped that by setting a date, he would find a renewed passion for being with her.

She had been oblivious to the ever-shrinking candles on their dinner table. Perhaps their relationship had met a similar expiration date, but Blake was not a quitter. She had to give it one more shot to flourish. Blake blew out the candles and changed into yoga pants and her most comfortable tank top. After putting away the steak, she received a text from Parker. *I'm working overnight.*

Long workdays weren't unusual for him. Blake fought back the tears as she flipped through her saved streaming shows and scrolled through her social media pages. No one was posting anything of interest. She thought about walking to Preservation Pub on Market

Square to see if any of her friends were there, but Parker didn't like her going out on the town without him.

The last time she had met up with some work friends for a happy hour, he had given her the silent treatment for a week and slammed the heavy oak doors in their apartment every time he left a room. Parker had refused to talk to Blake until he pushed her into the granite countertop in their kitchen, bruising her hip.

After the *accident*, he'd apologized, saying it would never happen again. He'd sent a dozen roses and a black pair of Louboutin pumps to her office the next day. It could be worse.

She gritted her teeth but decided it wasn't worth the frustration of having to live with his passive-aggressive bullshit. If he was working late, she might as well be productive herself. Her boss, Sharon, had mentioned a new prospective client before they left the office that day, so she called her to get the details.

Blake paced the dining room floor, waiting for Sharon to answer. She started to hang up, but Sharon finally answered.

"Hi," she said, breathless as if she'd been running. "Don't you have plans tonight?"

Blake bit her lip. Parker would be angry if she discussed their relationship, so she glossed over the subject. "No. Parker had to work late, so I thought I'd start prepping for our meeting with the new client. What do you know about them?"

Several seconds of silence passed. Blake pulled her phone away from her ear to make sure the call was still active.

"Sharon? Are you still there?"

"Oh, yeah, sorry…shh, stop it." Sharon giggled. Blake heard a man whispering to Sharon. Bryce, Sharon's husband, was out of town, but she had a reputation for having other *friends* stop by while he was away.

"Do you need to call me back?" she asked.

"Sorry, I just got distracted for a second. Next year, the owners will open several restaurants in Chattanooga and Knoxville. They want us to help rebrand their business and web presence and build a social and PR campaign."

As Blake and Sharon discussed the client further, more texts from Parker rolled in—*I will definitely be here late. I'm sure you're upset. I'll take you shopping for a new purse this weekend. If you still have my credit card, buy yourself whatever you want.* She responded to him a few times. With each response, she heard his text notification, the sound of a banging gavel, over the phone.

Was Parker with Sharon? No, he couldn't be.

"Hey, Sharon, I need to go. Someone's at the door." She tried to maintain the illusion that she was okay. But pacing back and forth on the creaky hardwood floors of their apartment, she had to be honest with herself.

After she hung up the phone, Blake gave in to paranoia and searched the house for Parker's tablet to verify his location through his connected devices. When she didn't find it, Blake needed to put her mind at ease. She grabbed her keys and purse and drove to Sharon's house.

Why do I have an overactive imagination?

But she couldn't lie to herself when she rounded the corner to Sharon's house, and there sat Parker's blue Italian sports car with its customized plate, 8URLNCH.

Blake trudged to the front door, determined to confront them. As she peered into the bay window from the front porch of Sharon's Parkridge Victorian home, she saw everything she needed to confirm her suspicions through the crack of the curtains.

There lay slender, dark-haired Parker and curvaceous, redheaded Sharon, naked by the fireplace. He was caressing Sharon's face like she was his entire world.

Tears stung Blake's eyes, and her heart sank. She leaned in closer to the window to snap a picture of the scene with her cell phone, planning to send a copy of the photo to Parker, break off their relationship via text and leave. But her adrenaline and emotions got the best of her, and an uncontrollable rage built up inside her.

What a cheating asshole! She kicked the foundation of the house, but the lovers didn't stir, and Blake's anger multiplied. She picked up a small but heavy decorative planter and hurled it through the window, shattering the glass into hundreds of pieces.

Sharon and Parker looked at the window, but it was dark. As Blake ran away, she heard him yelling, "Who's there?" She had some lead time while he found his pants but needed to leave before he discovered she was the one who had disrupted his indiscretion. She was unsure of how he would react.

Without so much as going home to pack a bag, she ran back to her car and mindlessly drove to the one place where she would be safe, her late grandmother's beach cottage on Isle of Palms. Although her grandmother had passed away more than a decade ago, the family had maintained the property as a vacation home. The cottage was a vault for happy memories for Blake and her family. With the current state of her life, it was the only place she could find comfort.

After the six-hour drive, she parked her car and stood in the driveway taking in the weathered but gorgeous cottage. Tiny white flower petals swirled in the wind, collecting like snow at Blake's feet as she walked across the sand and shell driveway. A pair of fireflies led the way, dancing across the wide front porch to the double-door entrance. She inhaled the salty air and sighed, running her hands through her long, dark curls, matted from being windblown during the drive.

Upon opening the front door, her grandmother's loving presence washed over her, welcoming her home. She could almost smell her granny's homemade biscuits baking in the oven and had to fight the urge to find and hug her. She dropped her purse and keys on the kitchen table and crashed on the living room couch. Tossing and turning, she woke covered in sweat.

Blake walked to the bedroom where she had spent her childhood summers and holidays. Memories of her granny teaching her how to swim in the ocean, fry chicken and, most importantly, love with all her heart flooded her mind. She smiled, but then the image of Sharon and Parker together disturbed her.

She collapsed onto the mattress and stared at the gold-flecked popcorn ceiling above her bed. With tears streaming down her cheeks, she flipped through old pictures. Images of their special moments filled her phone screen, including hiking in their beloved

Smoky Mountains, European and beach vacations, and gatherings with their family and friends.

All the pictures had one thing in common—his piercing green eyes looked determined to get what he wanted. For the first time, Blake saw him for what he was: a controlling, possessive egomaniac.

It was time to reclaim her independence and regain the strength she had lost during their relationship.

Blake shifted in the bed, and something sharp poked her hip. She reached into the inside pocket of her yoga pants to find Parker's credit card, which she had used for an online pizza order the previous evening. The bruise from the night he'd pushed her into the countertop was still blue and sore.

She screamed in frustration. Even in her haven, she couldn't get away from Parker.

Chapter 2

Blake's stomach rumbled, awakening her from a fitful sleep. It was lunchtime, and she hadn't eaten in almost a day.

A quick scan of the pantry made it clear none of her family members had been there in months. In her foggy and hungry state, she got into her car and drove to an Isle of Palms icon—the Sea Biscuit Cafe. Not only was their food deliciously comforting, but her grandmother's best friend, Nancy Parsons, worked there as a waitress and surrogate mother to her regular customers.

As Blake walked into the restaurant, Nancy's face lit up. She floated across the room and squeezed Blake, making her gasp for air. Nancy was strong for being a petite seventy-seven-year-old woman. Despite her white hair and wrinkled skin, she had a youthful exuberance that shined through her very core.

"Honey, I haven't seen you in so long! I wasn't expecting you this weekend. Let's sit for a spell. How's your mom an' 'em?" Clutching her signature pearls, she took a step back and looked Blake up and down. "Are you all right, hon?"

Blake was still wearing her faded yoga pants and the smudged remnants of yesterday's mascara. Before she answered, Nancy had disappeared to the kitchen and quickly returned with a stack of pecan pancakes and a pot of coffee.

"Spill the beans, child." Nancy poured Blake a cup. "What you've been through, not the coffee." She winked and sat down next to Blake, buttering a biscuit and hanging onto every excruciating detail she provided. Nancy wrapped her arms around her and wiped Blake's tears away with a napkin.

Blake sniffed. "I've wasted three years on a man who loves someone else. Last night, I saw them together, completely naked. I thought we had a future together. I feel so stupid."

"Now, now, don't be so hard on yourself. We've all made mistakes. After all, we're only human." Nancy patted her shoulder. "Anyway, Parker sounds like a peach gone to rot, and so does Sharon. I don't blame you for running away. When did you get here?" Nancy pushed more food in front of Blake.

"Late last night—I drove straight to the cottage right after I saw them together. Well, right after I threw a small ficus through her window."

Nancy bit her lip, stifling a giggle. "Bless your heart. They deserved worse, but you know what they say about karma. They'll get their just desserts."

Making her way through a stack of pancakes, Blake pushed up the sleeves of her long-sleeved T-shirt.

Nancy gasped, grabbing Blake's arm, examining four purple fingerprints and flipping over her arm to reveal a thumbprint. "What in Sam Hill is on your arm? Did that sorry S.O.B. do that to you?"

Blake shifted in her seat and looked at her plate. "I'd rather not talk about it."

"Well, that's too bad. If your granny knew Parker had hit you, why, she'd turn over in her grave and cut off his eel and oysters. You'd best not talk to him again. I'm gonna send Clint to talk to you. You need to file a police report."

Nancy's grandson Clint, who she'd raised, was the Isle of Palms Police Chief, and Blake had dated him throughout her teenage years. Other than Parker, Clint was the last person she wanted to see right now.

"Parker hasn't ever hit me. I pulled my arm away from him when he didn't want me to leave for work one morning. He just doesn't realize how strong he is."

Nancy shook her head. "That's still abuse. You need to protect yourself."

Blake sighed. "Seriously. I'm okay. He doesn't know I'm here."

"If you hear from him, call me," Nancy said. "I'll be there in a heartbeat. Speaking of which, I want to get together with you. How does dinner tomorrow sound?"

"That works for me."

"Great, sugar. I'll swing by to pick you up at seven. I've got to get back to my customers now. You rest up, and we'll talk more tomorrow." Nancy hugged her.

Blake thanked her for the meal that warmed her stomach and soul. When she reached for her purse, Nancy clasped her hands over hers. "It's on the house, hon."

"Thank you. See you tomorrow."

Blake slid out of her seat and walked toward the row of souvenir shops and the beach access that lay ahead. This section of the island had been the backdrop for her childhood summers. The rocky road ice cream from her favorite vendor called her name. She ordered a heaping scoop for old times' sake, paid the cashier and began walking to the expansive sandy beach.

The March wind pierced her skin, but she forgot the chill in the air when the sparkling grayish-blue water came into view. Blake stared at the horizon. The ebbing tide pulled her problems to the surface, and as it retreated, took them away. She spread out a towel and allowed the beach book she'd brought along to transport her to its pages.

As the sun began setting, she shivered. It was time to go home. She pulled herself up off the sand and re-engaged with reality. A dozen shorebirds chattered in front of the beachfront hotels and homes as she walked to her car. The evening traffic offered little resistance as she parked under the oak-draped canopy that framed the roofline of her grandmother's cottage.

She had never stopped to appreciate the unique setting. On one side lay the entrance to powdery sand and shimmering waters, the other to an old Charleston-style homestead where the Spanish moss waved in the wind. Stars peeked through the canopy, glowing like spotlights on Granny Mason's prized rose and azalea bushes.

The next morning, she woke to the doorbell ringing. Blake yawned and stretched, padding down the steps. Who would visit at eight a.m.?

Blake opened the front door. Nancy's grandson, Clint, was clutching a small red cooler. His police uniform fit his muscular body to a "T." She diverted her gaze. The last thing she needed was Clint thinking she wanted to rekindle their old flame.

He smiled but didn't maintain eye contact with her. "Long time, no see." He shifted his weight from one foot to the other.

Blake's eyes widened. "You've gotta be kidding me! That's what you have to say to me after ghosting me and not talking to me for 15 years?"

Clint put his hands up. "Hey…can we call a truce? We were just kids, and I didn't know better. Besides, I'm just dropping off some food from Gram. She has company and couldn't get away, so she asked me to come by."

Indeed, Nancy would do that. Although Clint was her grandson, she had raised him and his brothers. They couldn't do any wrong in her eyes. Even Nancy had faults.

Blake glared at him, grabbing the cooler out of his hands. "Thanks for bringing the food, but you can leave now. Do I need to show you the way out?" She motioned toward the door.

He waved his hands at her and laughed. "Hey. No need to get feisty. I'll manage on my own. Enjoy your breakfast."

As she closed the door, he called out to her. "Hey. Gram said you needed to talk to me about your fiancé. If you want to file a report, stop by the station anytime, and I'll call the Knoxville PD."

Blake leaned against the partially cracked door and drew a deep breath. He stared at her as she opened the door a smidge wider.

"Thanks for the offer," she said. "I'm fine now that I'm here. I just needed to get away from Parker."

Clint nodded. "The offer doesn't expire. Just text me," he said. "Me and some of the guys from the station play at the Windjammer twice a month. We usually go on at seven. You should stop by sometime. It's a good crowd."

Blake bit her lip and simmered as he walked away. When they were younger, Clint had broken up with her without explanation. He still made her blood boil, but she checked out his sculpted body again as he climbed into his Jeep Wrangler. A flashback of him playing guitar and singing on the beach came to mind. Maybe she would stop by the beach bar to see him perform at some point, but for now, Nancy's comfort food was calling her name.

The intoxicating scent of comfort food seeped out of the cooler. Blake's stomach growled. Opening the lid, she found fried chicken, biscuits, peach cobbler and a small bottle of homemade sweet muscadine wine, along with a note: *Take care of yourself, hon. Love, Nancy.*

"Aww—how sweet! Too bad your grandson broke my heart. He's still pretty cute."

She sighed, filled a plate and a wineglass, and walked to the luscious garden, surrounded by colorful blossoms and her grandmother's loving presence. Comfort food was the universal language of love and hospitality in the South. Nancy embodied this concept wholeheartedly, just as Granny Mason had. Their similarities did not end there, including their love for the Nelson family. They were lucky to have Nancy's devotion.

Something rustled in the bushes, capturing Blake's attention. She grabbed a nearby gardening shovel with a tight grip and spun around. A beautiful child with dark curls jumped onto the old tire swing Blake and her siblings had enjoyed during their childhood. The girl locked eyes with her before turning away to jump off the swing and run behind the potting shed.

"You don't have to go. I won't hurt you. You just startled me," Blake called out while walking over to where the girl was hiding. But when she peeked behind the shed, the child had vanished.

Just as well. Blake sat back down to eat dinner, hoping that a second glass of wine would help her forget Parker and Sharon's affair.

She picked up her phone and a blanket and moved to a hammock where the ocean breeze and swaying tree canopy lulled her to sleep. Unsettling dreams interrupted her slumber. First, she dreamed of Parker and Sharon, getting married and toasting their nuptials, laughing at how they had toyed with her life. Then of Granny Mason's last month on Earth. She had refused chemotherapy, saying if it was her time to go, she was ready. Her late-discovered lung cancer had surprised the entire family. She'd always been their rock, their matriarch.

Just before her grandmother died, she had turned to Blake, squeezed her hand and whispered, "You will see hardship, but the way you rise from the ashes will be everything. I'll always be with you." Alone, Blake had sobbed and laid on Julia Caroline's chest until her grandmother drew her last breath.

Children's delighted laughter woke Blake from her fitful sleep. The girl had returned with a somewhat older boy, around nine years old. Blake grinned while they played and giggled. "You're welcome to stay and play as long as you'd like."

They smiled, nodded and went back to swinging.

Her phone rang in the cottage. She got up from the hammock and ran inside to answer the call.

"Hey, where are you? It's not like you to be late," Anna, her boss's assistant, said.

Blake wanted to tell Anna every dirty detail of Parker and Sharon's affair, but she bit her tongue. "I had to leave town last-minute on Friday for a family emergency. Please reschedule my appointments for the rest of the week."

"I'll be happy to take care of that for you. I hope things get better for your family. Call me if you need anything else."

"Thanks, Anna." Blake hung up the phone and looked out the kitchen window. The girl climbed onto the tire swing, and the boy pushed her into the air.

Blake turned away to reach into the fridge to scavenge some leftovers from Nancy's provisions. After she made her plate, the children's laughter had stopped.

Where did they go? Are their parents okay with them playing on their own?

Something hard hit the back of her skull. The room tilted, blurred and darkened as her body collapsed onto the floor. She attempted to scream, but no sound came from her vocal cords. Blake grasped her head. Warm blood oozed through her hands and down her neck as she lost consciousness.

Pivotal moments in Blake's life flashed before her—first as a child winning her first carnival game, then as a teenager performing the lead role in her school play, her college graduation and, finally, the night Parker had proposed. She was on a cloud, climbing up higher and higher into the sky until she eventually fell through the bottom and into the depths of the ocean.

She came to with the plush rug from Granny Mason's bedroom underneath her.

Who had moved her from the kitchen? Who had knocked her out?

Her head throbbing, she pulled herself up off the floor. On the four-poster canopy bed, sat Granny Mason.

Blake rubbed her eyes. She had seen ghosts throughout her adult life. There had been no rhyme or reason to when a supernatural being revealed itself to her. She'd always been too afraid to mention it to anyone. Some specters had appeared once for only a few moments while others had returned multiple times. But until now, her grandmother's spirit, the one she'd longed to see the most, had never appeared.

Trembling, she ran over to Granny Mason with her arms outstretched and teardrops falling. Her grandmother embraced her and stroked her hair. "My sweet Blake, you're alive, and you're stronger than you think. You must fight. Now go."

Granny Mason pulled away from her and pointed to the door.

Realizing she must still be unconscious, Blake pulled herself together and ran through the house looking for a door that would allow her to wake up and return to reality. She ran to open her bedroom door. Her look-alike-doll was suspended from the ceiling, hanging from its neck.

Blake screamed and ran out of the room, trying each of the remaining second-floor bedroom doors to find all of them locked. She ran down the staircase and opened the door to her parents' bedroom to see her mother.

"Thank God! Mom! You're here. Please help me!"

"Okay. Yeah. I'm listening. Tell me more." Susan scratched her head.

"Someone hit me over the head, and I'm having an out-of-body experience. I can't seem to find myself."

"Oh, no big deal. Don't worry about that at all."

"What?" Blake shrieked in desperation and threw her hands up in the air. Then, she saw Susan's hair had covered a Bluetooth earbud.

She shook her mother's body, but Susan didn't notice. She stood up and started putting away folded laundry. Devastated, Blake threw her arms around her mother's neck.

"Mom, it doesn't seem like you can hear me, but just in case I don't wake up again, I want to say I love you."

Crying, Blake walked to the kitchen and sat down to think. Something told her to exit and reenter the house. As she turned the doorknob to the front door, a jolt of electricity flooded her body. Her hunch was right.

Blake had to follow Granny Mason's advice. She had to fight.

Chapter 3

Blake came to on the blue-and-white-tiled kitchen floor. Light from the windows burned her eyes.

When her vision came into focus, she saw Parker sitting calmly at the kitchen table. In front of him was a landscaping paver, stained with blood.

"Parker?" she choked out while struggling to sit up. She assessed her injuries, alarmed by the amount of blood on the floor.

"Your granny had a nice garden." He tossed the landscaping paver from one hand to the other. He gazed at Blake. She gasped. "When you didn't answer my texts, I tracked the location on your phone. So, who are you here with, and where is he?" He puffed out his chest, rose from his chair and craned his neck to look into the living room.

"What are you talking about? I didn't receive any texts. I'm alone." Blake held her head while blood streamed between her fingers. Her stomach lurched.

"Yeah, right." He snickered while towering over her.

Maybe Parker's violence shouldn't surprise her. He'd always been controlling and arrogant. And when his sister had gone missing, something in him had broken. Her heart ached as she thought back to all the times he had been manipulative and controlling. The negative comments he had made, saying she didn't dress appropriately for a woman her size—a size eighteen to be exact. Worst of all, the bruises he'd left on her body and heart. Parker had done little to make her feel loved in the past year.

It made sense. Blake hadn't been the love of his life; instead, she'd been his possession. Perhaps he had been on the cusp of violence all along. Now, he was angry enough to hurt, maybe even kill her. She focused on hiding her fear, even though this was the most frightening moment of her life.

Unsure of what he was capable of next, she gathered her wits. It was time to defend herself and strike back. While he was looking the opposite direction, she stood up and grabbed a kitchen knife from the counter behind her. Out of the corner of her eye, she looked for his reaction. *He didn't notice.*

Red-faced, Parker crossed his arms and paced the floor, glaring at her silently like a lion on the prowl. He'd never been this unhinged. Blake was trembling inside, but she was doing her best to appear calm. She forced a smile.

"Hey, sweetie, we can work through this. You don't want to hurt me." She stepped back from him and tightened her grip on the knife.

He shook his head. "Why did you run away without saying goodbye? Why didn't you answer my texts? I didn't show up for dinner. So what? That's no reason to run away," he said, still clutching the blood-covered paver.

Parker's eyes narrowed, and his icy calmness returned. "You just tossed me aside. I'm not your trash." He pounded the paver on the table.

A chill went down her spine. *Don't panic; you've got this.*

His eyes snapped upward. "Let me guess. You're here with someone else. You aren't making this easy on me. You're supposed to be mine."

Blake stepped away from him, her head spinning and her knees weak. After losing so much blood, she wasn't sure she could outrun him. She smiled as naturally as possible, trying to exude calmness and a sense of amicability.

"Just sit down so we can talk through this." Blake patted the chair next to her. "I didn't get any texts. The cell reception is horrible in the mountains near Asheville. Please don't do anything you'll regret."

Parker sat down and gazed at the table again. Blake breathed a sigh of relief, but then, his black, empty eyes shifted back to the paver. He tightened his grip and tried to strike her. She swung the knife at his face, but he dodged backward. She drew a deep breath. He stepped forward, bludgeoning her over the head once again.

Coming to the second time, she couldn't move. Parker had strapped her to the living room sofa and was sitting next to her. Knife in hand, he violently removed the buttons on her shirt, cutting her at each one.

"Please don't do this!" Blake cried. She squirmed, but the rope didn't budge.

Suddenly, headlights from a car flickered on the living room windows. *Nancy! Thank God!*

"Thought you said you were here alone." Parker retreated upstairs to hide. "Get rid of whoever it is, or I'll come down and kill you both."

Through the glass in the door, Blake saw Nancy's eyes widen. Before she burst through the entrance to the living room, Nancy motioned to someone in the car to help.

"Oh, my stars! Are you okay?" she asked. Clint ran in behind her.

Still strapped down, Blake was dizzy from the blood loss but got some words out. "It's Parker, my fiancé. He's upstairs. I'm not sure what he'll do next."

Clint crouched, hiding around the corner, and motioned for Nancy to yell for Parker.

"Leave my girl alone, you bastard!" Nancy pulled her mother-of-pearl-handled pistol out of her purse. Parker slithered out of his hiding spot when he heard her voice.

"You're barking up the wrong tree." Nancy pointed the pistol in his direction.

In Parker's arrogance, he ignored Nancy's warning.

"You're not going to shoot me, you old bat." Holding his head up, he walked closer to her. "Get out of my way before something bad happens to you. I'd hate for you to break a hip."

"Hands behind your head! Isle of Palms Police Department!" Clint shouted as he burst around the corner with his badge in one hand, his other grasping a gun pointed at Parker.

"She's mine. She's no business of yours," said Parker with an eerie calmness as he hovered over Blake's body. He picked up the knife from the floor, and his eyes turned black once again. He raised the knife and aimed it over her heart. She screamed, and at that moment, Clint shot him in the leg. Parker dropped the knife and looked at him in disbelief while falling to the ground.

"Lay your weapon on the floor, and back up slowly," Clint said, still pointing the pistol at him.

"I'm going to get the old lady for that." Parker reached for his knife.

"Get down on the ground!" Clint yelled.

As Parker lunged toward Nancy, Clint pulled the trigger, resulting in a soft click instead of a deafening roar. Clint reached up and cleared the jammed gun, but it was too late. Parker had already put her into a headlock, pressing his head against hers and the knife against her neck. With a death grip on Nancy, he backed out of the front door and yelled back at Clint.

"I'm taking Grandma here with me for a little ride," Parker said. "If I see any cops on my tail, she dies. If not, I'll find *somewhere* to put her for safekeeping. Don't follow me."

"No!" Blake screamed at Parker. "Leave her alone! Your issue is with me, not her!" But it was too late. Parker had already left the house with Nancy in tow.

Clint's face was pale and pinched with fear for his grandmother. Blake frowned, her heart pounding in her throat. "What can we do? How can we help her?"

"First, calm down," Clint said. "I promise—I'm going to get this situation under control and find him. If I go after him now, he'll hurt her. And I can't...risk that." He stared off into the distance as he called for backup and an ambulance for Blake.

Within a few minutes, a sea of blue and red lights filled the Mason homestead driveway. The EMTs ran into the cottage to check on Blake, and Clint provided details surrounding his mom's kidnapping to a team of detectives and patrol officers.

The EMTs loaded Blake into the ambulance, and Clint joined her.

"Now that you have help, I'm going after Parker. Don't worry. We'll find him and make sure he serves his time. I won't let him get away with hurting you or Gram."

Blake nodded and said a silent prayer for Nancy. Her poor friend wouldn't be in danger if it weren't for her. She had to be okay, or Blake would never forgive herself.

How would her life be different if she had stayed with Clint? For one thing, she wouldn't be on her way to the hospital for treatment of injuries he had inflicted. Would they still be in love?

Moments later, the ambulance arrived at the hospital. Clint was standing in the emergency room, waiting for her. His furrowed brow concerned her, but his stance was more relaxed than it had been before he left the cottage.

"What are you doing here? Did you find Nancy?"

Clint smiled. "She's fine...thank God. One of my guys found her at a gas station in North Charleston. He's bringing her here now." He put his hand on Blake's shoulder. "I promise you, if Parker's still in the Charleston area, my team and neighboring police departments will find him. And we'll keep someone outside the cottage 24/7 until we find Parker."

The doctor came into the room and told Blake she might have a mild concussion, and he wanted to keep her overnight for observation. She sighed and dialed her mom's number to tell her what had happened. Her mom immediately said she would gather a few things and be on her way.

Half an hour later, Nancy walked into the room, disheveled and shaking.

"Oh my God, Nancy! I'm so glad you're okay!" Blake stretched out her arms. "What happened to you? How did you get away from Parker?"

"I'm happy you're doing alright, too, hon." Nancy's hands trembled. "He forced me to lie down on the back seat of his car so no one would see me while he drove. He stopped and yelled for me to get out of the car before he sped away."

"I'm grateful he didn't hurt you." Blake put her arm on Nancy's.

"Have you spoken to Susan?" Nancy stared off in the distance.

"Yep. I talked to Mom right before you got here. She's on her way."

Nancy nodded. "Good."

A lab technician came to collect Blake for a CT scan. Afterward, they returned her to her room. Several nurses came through to take her vital signs, ask her questions about her pain levels and give her some medication.

Finally, the commotion came to a stop. Blake drifted in and out of sleep, with nurses checking on her throughout the night. She woke to hear her mother's voice in hushed conversation with Nancy. Susan Nelson was standing near the window. Her dark shoulder-length hair was graying, and her worry lines were deeper than the last time Blake had seen her.

"Mom, I'm glad you're here, but you're so busy." Blake smiled. She didn't want to take Susan away from her thriving clothing boutique, but sometimes, having your mom with you made everything better.

Her mother stood up and put her hand on Blake's shoulder. "Honey, don't worry—I can leave the boutique in my staff's capable hands for a few days. I want to take care of you."

As if on cue, the doctor walked in and shook her mother's hand. "Fortunately, your daughter doesn't have a concussion. It could have been so much worse. She needs to take it easy for the next week, and if anything changes, she needs to come back to get checked out. Call me if you need anything." He handed Susan his card and the discharge paperwork. She thanked him and asked Nancy to pull her car around.

"You're not going back to the beach cottage with me?" Blake asked. Part of her wanted her mom to insist on staying for at least a week, but she was no stranger to Susan having a packed schedule.

"Of course, I am. I just need to pick up your prescriptions and some groceries. You need some things at the cottage."

Nancy drove Blake back to the Mason cottage, waving to the officer parked on the side driveway. She helped Blake get into the house, poured her a glass of ice water and helped her climb into bed. A short time later, Susan arrived at the cottage.

"I'm so sorry about everything Parker has put your through." Her voice quivered. "We almost lost you. There's no punishment harsh enough for him. I'm grateful you weren't hurt worse.

"The police will eventually find him. He won't hurt you anymore. When you're healthy enough to return home, Clint has offered to travel with us to make sure you get back safely. He'll ask the Knoxville Police Department to assign an officer to stay at my house for the next week or so."

"Mom, I'm not going back to Knoxville. I need a change of scenery and a fresh start. Isle of Palms has always been a second home to our family. Now, I'm drawn to the island more than ever."

"What about your apartment?" Susan asked. "I mean, you don't have to worry about paying the rent since Parker's family owns the building, but don't you need to pick up some of your things?"

Blake frowned. "No way! I can't go there yet. It's just stuff. When I'm able, I'll buy some clothes and other necessities. The island is my home…for now, at least."

"What about your job?"

"I refuse to work for someone who slept with my fiancé. I don't respect her, and I can't stand the thought of being near her." Blake's fingernails dug into her hands. "I have some money saved up for a rainy day. It's more than enough to cover my expenses while I look for a job in Charleston."

Blake turned away from Susan, needing a reprieve from talking about Parker. Would he return to the island? Parker had never compromised in their relationship. Why would he start now?

Chapter 4

Smiling, Susan patted the living room sofa. "Come here, honey. I have to head home today. Why don't you go with me?" She paused. Blake narrowed her eyes, but Susan didn't make eye contact with her and continued her spiel.

"We'll fix up the apartment over the garage and make it super cute. You can live there, rent-free until you get on your feet. We'll have so much fun!"

Blake crossed her arms over her chest. "I'm not going back. Don't worry about me. Clint has officers here 24/7, and Nancy is making sure I eat."

Susan frowned but embraced Blake. "I don't want to leave you here, but I know Nancy and Clint will make sure you're okay. I want you to check in with me daily via a phone call, not just a text message. I'm calling Nancy right now to make sure she can spend the day with you before I head back home."

Nancy returned to the cottage to stay with Blake. Susan hugged them and made them promise to keep her informed of Blake's progress.

"I promise, Mom," Blake said, putting her hand on her mother's shoulder. "I need a fresh start, and I think I can find it here. I'm not sure how things will pan out career-wise, but I'll start planning for my future very soon. I owe it to myself to find my self-confidence, independence and anything else Parker stripped away from me during our relationship."

"Okay, honey. I'm concerned, but I'm positive you'll find your way. For now, rest up and recover. Call me if you need anything. I love you," Susan said.

"Love you, too, Mom." Blake kissed her mom on the cheek.

Later that day, Anna, Sharon's admin, called again, saying she was patching in a call from Sharon's phone. Just as Blake moved her thumb to end the call, Sharon's frantic voice came over the line.

"Don't hang up, even though I deserve it. I deserve so much worse. I'm so sorry!" Sharon said. "

Blake fumed, listening in silence. *The nerve of this whore!*

"The police showed up looking for him the day he attacked you. They showed me the police report from the Isle of Palms Police Department. I read your statement about him attacking you after you ran away because you saw us together. I'm so sorry about everything.

"They asked me if I knew why he'd want to hurt you. I don't, but I feel responsible for this whole nightmare. If I hadn't introduced him to you and just ended our relationship, this wouldn't have happened. I hope you will come back to work for me, but I'll understand if you can't. I'm happy to give you a stellar reference to any future employer."

Blake let Sharon say her piece, but she didn't respond. She hung up the phone.

Ready to take her mind off the call and life's complexities, she told Nancy she needed some beach time. When Nancy said she was coming with her, Blake shook her head.

Nancy nodded but gave her a time limit. "Text me if you'll be more than a couple of hours." She looked at Blake over her reading glasses. "If you don't, I'll come look for you."

Blake threw a beach towel over her shoulder and walked to the nearest beach access, ready to allow the waves to carry her worries to the ocean's depths. She spread out the towel and wiggled her toes, burying them in the sand. A tall shadow appeared in her peripheral vision. *Whew!* Clint was walking toward her. She sat up and adjusted her sunglasses.

"Hey. Someone spotted Parker's car at a gas station in Hendersonville, North Carolina. Unfortunately, he sped away before officers arrived. Sounds like he's spooked. Is there anyone who might help him in that area?"

"His brother, Will, lives in a cabin in Asheville. If he finds out what Parker's up to, he'll turn him in to the police." Blake gave Clint the general location of Will's beautiful home in the Blue Ridge Mountains—the place where Parker had first professed his love to her. Just a two-hour drive from their loft apartment, the cabin had been the backdrop for many firsts with him. She shook herself back to reality.

"Good to know. I'll call the Asheville Police Department to give them a heads-up that Parker may be on his way there." Clint returned to his patrol car.

"Hey, I want to stay at the beach a little longer. Will you tell Nancy? She has me on a time limit." Blake rolled her eyes. Clint nodded and laughed.

After he left, she let herself process what Clint had said. Tears of anger stung her eyes. Why had she allowed Parker's charms to pull the wool over her eyes to who he was—a narcissist who would not only physically harm her but crush her soul?

Determined to put the pain behind her piece by piece, she focused the soothing ocean breeze until the moonlight reflected on the water.

On her walk back to the cottage, she saw Clint wave from his car. She stopped to thank him for watching out for her.

"So sorry to keep you and your team tied up with my problems this week." Blake shook her head and played with her watch.

Clint stepped out of his patrol car and sat down on the steps on the front porch of the cottage. He flashed his adorable smile. Drawn in by his dimpled cheeks, she joined him on the steps.

"It's no problem. I want to find Parker so he can't hurt you or anyone ever again." He drew a deep breath. "I don't have a childhood summer memory without you and your family in it.

Blake, South Carolina has missed you. You know Gram has, and so have I. We may have been young, but you were the love of my life. You still are."

For a moment, she couldn't speak or move. Over the years, she had thought about their teenage romance and the heartbreak she had experienced when they broke up.

At thirteen, they shared a first kiss, accompanied by the fireworks of every great cinematic love story. They were crestfallen when the time came for Blake to return to Tennessee for the school year. A series of blissful summer romances continued until the May after Blake's first year of college in California—the year Clint pushed her away. She never fully understood the reasons for their breakup, but so much living had happened since then.

"Blake?" He stared at her.

She shook herself out of her daydream, apologized, stood up quickly and said goodnight. Clint's words haunted her as she entered the house. She lay down on the living room sofa and picked up a magazine, not paying attention to the text or photos on its pages.

Then a framed picture of Papa and Granny Mason caught her eye. To Blake, they had the greatest love story of all time. They met as children and stayed together until her grandfather died. She had always loved listening to her granny describe their romance. Blake had heard the wistfulness in her voice even seven years after his death. *Would she ever find a love like theirs?*

Chapter 5

The next morning, Clint was still on Blake's mind as she cruised across the Ravenel Bridge to historic Charleston.

A cup of coffee and two ibuprofen helped dull a headache that had bothered her since she woke.

Springtime was her favorite season, not overbearingly hot but still warm enough to enjoy being outside. She couldn't think of a better place to enjoy the weather than Waterfront Park.

On her way there, someone sitting on a distant bench caught her eye. She did a double-take. Their facial features were a dead match for Parker's, but the person was wearing a baseball cap and sunglasses, so it was hard to be sure. Blake inched closer, but he got up and started moving at a fast pace while zipping through alleys and garden paths. Blake stayed on his heels for the next ten minutes, but she lost sight of him when he entered a large, overgrown cemetery.

Where did he go? Was that Parker?

Blake pulled her hair back into a ponytail and ran to a more populated street, in case he resurfaced. She started walking to the park and called Clint to tell him she may have seen Parker.

"Should I come downtown?" he asked.

She sighed. "No. I'm not sure it was Parker. Sorry I called you."

"I'm glad you did. Call anytime. Be careful, Blake," he said. She thanked him and ended the call.

Waiting at the crosswalk, Blake spotted the person she'd mistaken for Parker. They took off their hat, releasing long blond locks. The woman turned and stared at Blake. That definitely wasn't Parker. Blake's cheeks reddened. *Could I be more paranoid?* She chewed her lip and drew a renewing breath, taking in the scenery in front of her.

The expansive pier stretched out over the Cooper River, and the sun reached down to kiss the sweetgrass growing on the marshy banks. A gentle breeze grazed her skin, and she remembered the reason this riverfront park meant so much to her. Other than its undeniable beauty, she had spent many sweet summer moments with Clint rocking on the porch swings.

She walked through the oak-lined pathway toward the Battery. Near the bronze pineapple fountain at the entrance to the park, a dozen children were laughing and splashing around. She recognized the two kids who had been playing at the cottage. A cute, scruffy black and white dog chased them around the fountain and seemed to cling to their every squeal of delight. Blake smiled, turning back to the fountain. Only the pup remained.

The dog wasn't wearing a collar or tags; her rib cage protruded from her belly. Blake rubbed the pup's ears. "Hey, girl, let's go visit someone who can help us."

Blake took her to the Humane Society, where Clint's younger cousin, Kate, worked. No one had reported a missing dog fitting the pup's description. Kate checked her for a microchip but to no avail.

"She sure is sweet," Kate said as the dog nuzzled her arm. "I'll keep an eye on the local message boards to see if anyone is missing their pup."

"Thanks. If you don't find her family, I'd love to keep her." Blake petted the small Corgi mix pup. "I think Granny Mason would have approved of a dog at the cottage."

She bundled the cuddly girl into a soft jacket she found in the trunk of her car and headed to Hairy Winston, a pet boutique close to the beach. After walking into the cheerful and welcoming shop, she bought the essentials.

They returned to the cottage, and the dog walked around like she had belonged there from the very beginning.

"What should I call you, girl?" Blake called out numerous popular dog names, but nothing seemed to stick.

Looking outside, the beauty of the billowing weeping willow tree she had used as a shady reading spot as a child overwhelmed her. A name came to her. "Willow?"

The dog wagged her tail and ran over to nuzzle Blake's face.

"Willow it is," Blake cooed, laughing.

Chapter 6

Someone knocked on the front door and turned the knob. Blake's heart in her throat, she stopped in her tracks and picked up a meat cleaver, ready to attack. Willow let out a low growl.

Nancy popped her head into the living room, letting herself into the cottage. "Hi! I brought lunch for us." Holding a bag of groceries, she kicked the door closed.

"Nancy! You scared me to death!" she exclaimed.

"Sorry, hon. I just wanted to have lunch with my best girl and her new pup." Nancy bent over to scratch Willow's chin and went into the kitchen. She began frying green tomatoes and shrimp she had dredged in milk and rolled in cornmeal. A cast-iron skillet was sizzling.

Blake hopped off the couch, washed her face and hands and poured Willow a fresh bowl of water and kibble. She pulled a bottle of white wine from the fridge, along with a wine glass and a corkscrew. "Let's eat alfresco. I'll set the table on the screened-in porch."

The children were back on the tire swing, and they'd brought friends with them.

"I found your dog!" she called out to them, sure that they had missed her.

One of the older kids spoke up. “She’s not ours. We’ve seen her around, but we don’t know who owns her.”

Nancy walked over to Blake, and the two youngest children ran away.

“It’s the strangest thing. These two kids, a boy and a girl between the ages of six and nine, they play here on the tire swing. Anytime I try to say more than a few words to them, they bolt off as if I’m going to hurt them. Why would they think such a thing?” Blake asked.

“Goodness gracious. I’m sure that’s not the case. I’m positive of it, actually,” Nancy said.

Blake whipped her head around. “How do you know?”

“Remember the last words your Granny Mason said to you? Hold those close to your heart. The love behind them is stronger than any magic. You’ll understand one day.”

Before Blake could reply, they were both distracted by Clint’s patrol car crossing the street to the cottage at a fast clip. He jumped out of the car and pounded on the front door. Blake opened it. Clint stepped inside and asked her to sit down.

“I’m so sorry to have to tell you this.” Clint sighed and placed his hand on Blake’s shoulder. “Parker’s had a terrible accident. He drove his car over an embankment near Hendersonville. His family’s attorney called the station to get a copy of the report we filed when he attacked you. They wanted to prepare, in case of a lawsuit.”

Blake shook her head, and her lip quivered. She ran to the attic before the tears that stung her eyes escaped. She only stopped to get one of her grandmother’s sweaters before ascending the spiral staircase to the cottage’s rooftop balcony, where she’d spent many angst-filled moments during her teenage years.

The last bit of winter wind pierced her flesh as she put on the cardigan. She sat down on the worn decking boards on the widow’s walk. Pulling the sweater down over her knees, she allowed the waves to impart their healing magic, calming her as much as possible.

Once she had experienced all the bitter wind she could handle, Blake went back downstairs. She caught her reflection in the foyer mirror. Her eyes swollen and red, and her skin chapped from the wind. Nancy reached out to comfort Blake.

"I'm staying with you tonight. You shouldn't be alone. By the way, Clint is sleeping in his patrol car in the driveway."

"Please tell him to go home," Blake said.

Nancy walked outside for a moment. When she returned, she put her hands on her hips. "He refuses to leave you." She gave Blake a meaningful wink, but Blake was in no place to pick up on hints, regardless of their level of subtlety.

"Goodnight, Nancy. Thanks for staying with me." Blake walked upstairs to her room.

She squirmed in bed for hours. Parker had hurt her; still, his death saddened her.

After falling into a fitful sleep, her unrest turned into a series of disturbing dreams and frightening images. In a state between nightmare and wakefulness, she woke in a cold sweat, with a pounding headache. A prickly sensation tingled across her body. She turned. Parker lay behind her, smirking. Paralyzed with fear, Blake sat frozen in her bed, staring at him. His wasn't the first spirit she'd seen, not by a longshot. But seeing him, her heartrate sped up, and her breathing turned shallow.

His face illuminated by the light of the full moon, Parker smiled and traced the outline of her face with his index finger. He leaned in to kiss her, but she jumped out of bed. He began inching toward her, but Blake flipped the mattress onto the floor.

Blake turned on the lamp on her bedside table. When her eyes adjusted, Parker had disappeared. She bent over to check under her bed, jumping when she accidentally stepped on one of Willow's squeaky toys. She breathed a sigh of relief when she kicked aside the plush stuffed animal.

Someone knocked on her bedroom door. She called out, "Yes?"

"What's the matter?" Nancy asked.

Blake opened the door. Nancy rubbed her eyes. "I had a nightmare that Parker was in bed with me," Blake said. "When I woke up, he was there. It's the creepiest feeling I've ever experienced." She shivered.

Nancy gasped and placed her hands on her cheeks. "Oh, my word! Are you all right?"

"I'm frightened, but I'm okay."

Blake's chest caved inward. Over the past year, she had faced some traumatic, life-altering events. As an empath, Blake was no stranger to interacting with spirits, but Parker's was the first who had frightened her.

"Will he come back? If he does, how will we get rid of him?"

Nancy hugged her but didn't say a word, unusual for her. She had to be hiding something.

"What aren't you telling me?" Blake demanded.

Nancy put her finger to her lips. "It's a long story for another day, but you're not alone in seeing spirits. It's part of your family's past, and mine for that matter. Just trust me, it'll be okay."

Blake threw her hands into the air. "But…"

Nancy shook her head. "Shh, honey. Not right now. Please calm down. It's late. Get some rest. We'll take care of Parker all in good time."

Emotional and physical exhaustion had taken its toll on Blake. She returned to her bed but did not sleep for the rest of the night. Every time she drifted off, Parker's dead eyes stared at her, boring a hole into her soul.

Chapter 7

For the next three months, Blake was a shell of her former self. She went through the motions of everyday life but didn't leave the house except to buy groceries.

Nancy had all but moved in with her, and Clint joined them for dinner every night. God love them; they were doing their best to help her recover from the hell Parker had inflicted.

The weeks all blurred together until one day, the sun filtered through her bedroom window, coloring the entire room with its golden hue. For the first time since Parker's death, her heart didn't ache. She smiled when Willow bounced into the room. Blake leaned over, ran her hands through the sweet animal's fur. *Time to get out of the house*. She put the dog's harness and leash on her and wrote Nancy a note saying they were picking up breakfast at Acme Lowcountry Kitchen, another island favorite.

She drove to the restaurant, placed her takeout order and told the bartender she would be back to pick up the food in twenty minutes. She and Willow walked to the beach and enjoyed the salty ocean breeze. Blake laughed as the pup ran, playfully chasing seagulls. Leaving the beach, the crashing waves calmed her as she made her exit. She returned to the restaurant to pick up the food and headed to the cottage.

When Blake pulled into the driveway, she saw Clint's Jeep. She gulped and checked her makeup in the rearview mirror. The butterflies in her stomach swarmed with a vengeance. *This is ridiculous*. It was still too soon to think about anyone romantically after everything she had gone through with Parker. Not only that—she loved her career and didn't need a man to be happy or justify her existence. Nonetheless, the crazed butterflies remained.

She entered the cottage. Clint and Nancy were sitting in the kitchen, drinking sweet tea out of mason jars. Willow jumped into Clint's lap, wagging her tail and licking his face. He laughed and rubbed behind her ears. The dog let out a pleased grunt.

Blake snorted. He stared at her, and she tried to deflect his attention with a joke. "Aww... look who's become Clint's best friend."

She smiled as she spread out the goodies from Acme, including shrimp and grits, biscuits and gravy and a crab omelet, inviting everyone to dig into the impromptu buffet. When Blake and Clint reached for a biscuit at the same time, their hands brushed, and their eyes locked. A tingle went down her spine, and her cheeks flushed. Despite her hesitation to become romantically involved with anyone, there was no denying the electrifying spark between them.

Blake quickly changed the subject. During her recovery, she had asked Clint not to go into detail about how Parker had died. But now, she needed to have closure.

"My friend who works for Asheville PD said the coroner confirmed Parker's identity, but no one has figured out why he ran off the road. All they found at the wreck site was a child's doll, which was probably already there before the accident. His family searched for witnesses, but no one has come forward."

Blake sighed. "I should probably call Parker's brother and see how their family is doing. Will has texted me a couple of times, but I couldn't bear to talk to him over the phone. Despite everything, I feel like I should."

She asked Nancy and Clint to play with Willow while she went to the screened-in porch to call Will. Clint picked up the pup, and

Willow licked his face. He laughed but read the serious vibe of the room.

He placed his hand on Blake's arm. "We'll be right here if you need us."

She dialed Will's phone number, halfway hoping he wouldn't pick up the phone, but no such luck.

"Blake! I've missed talking to you. When Parker died, I lost a sister, too," Will said. "Of course, our sister, Maggie, hasn't be gone that long either. It's been a lonely life."

She drew a deep breath and reminded herself she needed to keep it together for Will's sake.

"I'm so sorry." Her voice shook as she spoke.

"Thank you…" Will paused. "I don't know how to say this, but the police told my parents that Parker had hurt you. And that's the reason he was on the run when he died. I wish you would have told me. Why did he want to harm you?"

"He'd hurt me several times. The last straw was when I caught him cheating on me. I left Knoxville and came to the island without saying goodbye." Blake's heart raced, her chest constricted. "When Parker realized I'd left Knoxville, he came here to torment and hurt me. A couple of my friends showed up. He kidnapped one of them, but thankfully, let her go before taking off to North Carolina. He wrecked while running from the police."

"Oh, Blake. I had no idea he'd ever hurt you or dream of cheating on you. He never brought her around us. As far as we knew, he was happily engaged to you. He made me promise not to tell you beforehand, but he was going to set a date for your wedding on your birthday."

Tears rolled down her face. Parker had cared about her, at least on some level. But she wouldn't have continued their relationship if he were alive.

She wiped her eyes with a tissue she'd pulled out of her pocket. "I need to be going, but thank you for taking my call."

"Please call me the next time you're driving through Asheville," Will said.

"We'll see each other soon. I'm happy to help you or your family however I can," Blake said. "Take care of yourself, Will."

She set her phone down beside her, and a few minutes later, the screen lit up again. A photo of Parker during their first trip to Asheville had popped up on her phone. She jumped, pushing it away from her.

Nancy walked into the room and stared at her.

"What's wrong?"

"A picture of Parker randomly came up on the screen. I hadn't touched my phone in a few minutes. It freaked me out a little." Blake shivered.

Nancy patted her arm. "You probably just accidentally bumped your phone."

"I'm sure you're right. I'm definitely on edge right now." She questioned if she had closed out all the applications. Technology had a mind of its own.

"Well, c'mon. I've got some delicious peach brandy to help you relax. I'm gonna go outside and hang out with Clint. He brought his guitar." Nancy winked.

Blake went to the kitchen and poured a tall glass. The twang of Clint's husky voice and guitar drifted in through the window. *God, that man can sing.* Goosebumps popped up on her arms, and she guzzled her drink a little too fast.

"Hey, you comin'?" Clint asked.

"I'll be right there. I just need to pour another drink," Blake said. *On second thought...who needs a glass.* She grabbed the bottle of brandy and took a swig before heading to the porch.

Chapter 8

Pouring a cup of coffee the next day, memories of her childhood with Clint flooded her mind.

She and her siblings had spent holidays and school breaks on the island. The Atlantic Ocean and the cottage had always held a special place in her heart.

Could she stay here indefinitely? She needed to check in with the rest of the family. Now that Blake's generation of the Mason family had grown up, no one in the family used the cottage except for a week or two during the summer. She would play hostess when family members wanted to visit. There were four bedrooms in the main house and two in the detached carriage house, plenty of room for anyone who wanted a week at the beach.

Her permanent presence would allow the family to stop paying a groundskeeper. It seemed like a win for the entire family. Blake had an idea for starting a business in the house, but she'd have to convince her mom, the legal owner. And Susan would need to talk it over with her siblings to make sure they were on board with her running a business out of the cottage.

Before she could give this more thought, Willow began barking. The usually calm dog ran onto the screened-in porch with Clint behind her.

"Willow is going nuts. I'll take her outside." Clint led the dog to the fenced-in portion of the yard.

Willow ran over to the tire swing, which was gently moving in the breeze. She stared at the swing as if she were looking at a long-lost friend.

"She's creeping me out," Blake said. "No one is standing there."

Clint scanned the room and shrugged. "Is Parker back? Is it another spirit?" he asked.

"Great. Just what I need—more ghosts. Now I'm going to have a *really* easy time falling asleep tonight." Blake shivered, Parker's appearance in her bedroom still fresh on her mind.

Nancy walked outside. "What are you two talking about?"

"Something's got Willow spooked," Clint said.

Nancy frowned. "Blake, you should take a nap in the hammock. We'll make sure Willow gets enough water and goes back inside after a while."

"Thanks, guys. After the night I had, I could use some sleep."

Blake chugged a glass of tea and went to the hammock, hoping to drop off right away. She needed a reprieve from some of the emotions that were weighing her down.

She stirred. Her life had undergone dramatic changes in the blink of an eye. Who was she now? She'd been proud of her accomplishments in digital marketing. Why had she jeopardized that by dating Parker, a client?

She napped until something tickled her nose. The children were back, the boy swinging and the girl standing only a few feet away from her blowing dandelion seeds in her face, giggling.

Willow began whining to come outside. Blake went to get her from the screened-in porch, and Willow frolicked into the yard and greeted the children.

"Is this your dog?" Blake asked.

The little girl smiled, wrinkled her nose and shook her head.

Relieved not to have to give up her newfound canine friend, Blake sat down on the steps to the porch. Willow ran circles around the children. She laughed, her heart lighter than it had been in months.

Someone was watching her. She turned her head. *Whew!* Clint walked toward her. She breathed a sigh of relief. "You scared the crap out of me!"

"I'm sorry! I poured you a glass of wine," he whispered.

"Thank you." Blake stared at him. He wanted more to their relationship than she could give right now.

His hand swept her face. Her heart ached. Old memories of their relationship rose to the surface, but she needed to give herself some time to recover.

"Clint..." she pleaded. "I'm not ready yet."

He pulled her close so that her head rested on his shoulder. "Right now, I'm happy to be your friend. That's all I need."

She smiled and went to check on Willow and the children. Willow lay in the grass asleep, but the children had left. Where did they go? Who were their parents?

"Did you recognize those kids?"

"Sorry, I wasn't paying attention. What do they look like?" he asked.

She described them and how Willow loved playing with them. "I wish I knew their parents so I could let them know they've been playing here. I'd hate for someone to be missing their kids."

"I don't recall having seen kids meeting that description, but they might be tourists or even just seasonal residents," Clint said.

She nodded, allowing herself to become lost in his eyes. She shook herself out of the trance. Even though she wasn't ready for a relationship, he was cute and funny. His presence warmed her heart.

Chapter 9

Clint stopped by with dinner for Blake. She smoothed her hair and bit her lip. Was this more than a friendly gesture?

She scrunched up her face. "What's this?"

Clint laughed. "You've been through a lot. Can't a friend bring you dinner? I came by to ask you something. I have a week of vacation coming up next week, and I'd like to hang out with you."

She locked eyes with him and drew a deep breath before answering. "I'd like that."

Nancy entered the room, smiling, her eyes twinkling. Blake sighed, running her fingers through her hair. If she and Clint belonged together, it would happen in time.

Starting Saturday morning, Clint picked up Blake at the cottage every day that week. Nancy took care of Willow, allowing the two to spend a full day away from the cottage.

That week, they explored the island, Clint taking her to all her favorite spots along the beach, restaurants and shops. They visited the cobblestone streets of downtown Charleston, enjoying the architecture and immersing themselves in the history of the people who had lived and worked in the buildings that surrounded them.

On their way back to the cottage one evening, Blake brought up a topic she'd avoided for far too long, not wanting to risk bringing old wounds to the surface. “I have an awkward question. Why did you break up with me when we were younger? I’ve always wondered.”

Clint’s knuckles turned white as he gripped the steering wheel. “I don’t want to talk about this while I’m driving. Let’s stop for some grub and a beer.” He signaled, exited the main road and pulled into a shopping center. He was quiet as they walked into the restaurant. Blake shuddered, regretting her question. *Here goes nothing.*

She sat down at a booth across from Clint, and he grabbed her hand.

“I was just a stupid kid. I loved you so much, but I felt like you were slipping away. You moved across the country and didn’t come here to visit for an entire year. I felt like I couldn’t give you the life you wanted or deserved. I just wanted you to be happy.”

Blake jumped in her seat. “Why didn’t you tell me that back then?”

Clint looked down at their clasped hands. “I regret it every day, but I stopped talking to you because I knew you would have argued with me or felt guilty about leaving me behind. You had a full ride to your dream school. You couldn’t pass that up. I wish I’d kept in touch and tried to make it work. When I came to my senses, word got back to me that you were dating someone else…some guy in California.”

Blake sighed. “I wish you’d reached out; obviously, I didn’t end up with him.”

“I didn’t want to interfere. By the time I heard that you guys had broken up, too much time had passed. Besides, we wanted different things out of life. I wish I’d gotten over myself and called you anyway, but I made a lot of stupid decisions back then.” He sipped his beer. “While we’re talking about guys you dated, I want to ask you something. Why did you start dating Parker?”

“I’m not sure anymore. He was charming and handsome. He just had this way about him.”

“And I guess having that lawyer money didn’t hurt either, right?” Clint asked.

"No. I thought I loved Parker. Part of me loved him."

"And the thought of being financially secure?" Clint asked.

"Seriously, let's change the subject." Blake walked away from the table, but Clint grabbed her hand.

"I really want to know, though," Clint said.

"You're stressing me out. Please take me home," Blake said.

"But…"

"I said, take me home!"

"Okay, okay. No problem. Let's go."

They walked back to the car and rode back to the cottage in silence.

"Blake, I'm sorry..."

Before he could finish apologizing, she jumped out of the car and slammed the door shut and ran to the front door, closing it behind her. She screamed and held her hands up in the air.

She looked at Nancy and shook her head. "Your son is infuriating!"

"Lord, have mercy…" Nancy said. "I'll be back in a bit."

Blake didn't care if Nancy went to confront Clint. She wasn't ready to discuss her relationship with Parker with him.

Tired, she went to her bedroom and plopped onto the mattress. Willow joined her and began snoring after only a few moments.

Blake woke up the next morning to rustling in the backyard. She peeked out the kitchen window. Clint had set up breakfast in the garden and made her a homemade card. She had to give him credit for putting forth effort. She stepped outside, and he took her hand.

"I'm so sorry. I didn't mean to hurt your feelings. I'll understand if you don't want to, but I hope we can continue our fun week. You don't have to talk to me ever again. It's your call."

"That promise might be hard to keep on such a small island," Blake said. "How do I know you'll keep your word?" She fought a smile.

"Scout's honor," Clint said.

Her smile broke free. "You weren't a Boy Scout."

"Shoot. I was hoping you wouldn't remember that."

Blake laughed. His grin warmed her heart.

"Can I pick you up tomorrow? We could check out the aquarium. Then, you could go with me to the Windjammer for my show. What do you think?" Clint asked.

"That sounds great. See you in the morning."

After he left, she couldn't get Clint out of her head. They were different, but he made her laugh. The electricity between them was undeniable. Falling asleep wasn't easy. When she finally did, she dreamed that Clint had proposed.

The next morning, she sighed. *Too bad, it was just a dream.*

As she pulled on a sundress and sandals, the doorbell rang. "Be right there!" She glanced in the mirror, smudging some pale gloss on her lips and running her fingers through her hair. What a change from her intense morning routine from before she had moved to the island!

Blake ran down the steps and opened the front door to see Clint balancing two cups of coffee. Handing her one, he smiled. "Here you go, I already added some cream and sweetener to yours, just how you like it. Mine's decaf. Doc told me I have to lay off the caffeine."

"That's no fun," Blake said as she took a sip. She raised the cup to him. "Thanks for the coffee. I'll be ready after I grab my purse."

Climbing into the Jeep brought back memories. Clint had always driven Jeep Wranglers. The vehicle fit his personality—rugged but made a good impression in most situations.

They pulled into a parking lot near the aquarium and walked inside. Approaching the otter exhibit, Clint walked over to the waterfall. "Hey, let's take a picture together." He stood close to Blake, and her heart raced. She pulled her lips into a smile, trying not to let them quiver.

After taking in all the colorful fish and reef exhibits, they walked around downtown Charleston, looking for a place to have a late lunch. The scent of fried fish filled the air outside of a waterfront café.

"Whatever they're cooking smells delicious," Blake said.

Clint patted his stomach. "It's making me hungry. C'mon."

Blake's eyes widened when their server brought out an overflowing fried seafood platter for two. "I'm pretty sure we won't be able to finish all of that."

Clint snorted. "Sounds like a challenge to me."

In between bites, Blake caught Clint staring at her. "Do I have something on my face?" Her cheeks reddened.

He shook his head. "Nope. I'm just excited to hang out with you this week."

She smiled, but her cheeks burned again. Clint wasn't making it easy to stay just friends.

He paid the bill, and they left for the island.

"Do you mind if we walk over to the beach before your show?" Blake asked.

"No problem." Clint parked at the police station, and they walked over to the beach access. The sun warmed Blake's shoulders, and a soft breeze blew her hair.

"You've never been more beautiful," Clint whispered as he walked ahead to the shoreline.

Blake gulped. Would she be able to control herself if he tried to kiss her?

Their beach excursion flew by, and it was time to walk to the Windjammer. They walked into the dimly lit bar. Clint's deputies, Roger and Shane, were setting up instruments and sound equipment on the stage.

"It's about time you got here. You gonna leave the heavy lifting to us?" Roger asked, slapping Clint on the back.

Clint scowled. "I've been busy today. Blake and I've been hanging out."

Roger's jaw dropped. "I'm so sorry. I didn't see you there, Blake. Clint didn't tell me you guys were hanging out again." Roger's voice boomed. He fist-bumped Clint.

Blake turned and looked at her feet.

"Don't pay him any attention," Shane said. "We're glad you're here. Whatcha want to drink? You guys are on my tab tonight. Ladies first."

"Get me a shot of moonshine," Blake said.

"Dayum, Brother, this one's a keeper." Shane walked off to the bar to order their drinks.

While the guys did their soundcheck, Blake texted Nancy.

Blake: *Hey, is Willow doing okay?*

Nancy: *Yup. She just gobbled up her dinner, and we're watching a movie.*

Blake: *Thanks for watching her this week.*

Nancy: *Anytime, especially if you're spending time with Clint.*

Geez, way to be subtle, Nancy.

The stage lights flashed, and the spotlight paused on Clint.

"Hey, y'all. I'm Clint Parsons. We've got Roger on the bass and Shane on the drums. We're Marshal Law."

Blake almost choked on her drink, trying not to giggle. *What a corny Southern rock band name for a group of police officers!* But when Clint started singing, she couldn't take her eyes off him. She studied the way he moved with the music and strummed his guitar. His gaze caught her attention. She shifted in her chair, and a warmth overtook her body.

Still staring at her, Clint flashed a dimpled grin. "It's great seeing everybody out there tonight. This next song is for someone special who's come back to the island. A lot of you probably remember her from the summers she spent here. Give Blake Nelson a big South Carolina welcome."

As the bar erupted in applause and whistling, the spotlight hurt her eyes, and her cheeks flushed. Not one for being the center of attention, this was her nightmare. Still, she didn't want to embarrass Clint. She waved and forced a smile.

Finally, the spotlight drifted back to the stage. Clint's original lyrics pulled her heartstrings. "I've waited for you for a long time. Now that you're here, I'm whole."

Gulp—he's putting it all out in the open for the entire island. Blake's glass slipped out of her clammy hands, but she caught it before it hit the floor.

When the show ended, Clint drove her home. "I had another awesome day with you. Thanks for going to my show." He leaned toward Blake, kissing her forehead. "Goodnight."

Walking into the house, Blake couldn't make herself stop smiling.

Nancy walked into the living room with Willow behind her. "You look happy, hon. Anything you want to tell me?" Blake shook her head. Nancy patted her on the back. "Sleep well. See you tomorrow."

Over the next couple of days, Blake and Clint made it a point to enjoy things they had never done together, like visiting the Charlestown Landing historical site and the Angel Oak Tree. They laughed, reconnected and found common ground to help cement their rediscovered friendship.

Later that week, Blake asked Clint to take her to the section of Folly Beach near the decommissioned but still magnificent Morris Island Lighthouse. Wild groves of tangled trees shot out of the ground. Waves broke against the shoreline and foamed onto the sand.

As they walked, the view transported Blake to the first time she and Clint had visited this secluded piece of the beach together. They'd kissed, sitting on a tree branch that the wind and sea had bent to form an almost perfect bench. Clint had taken her hand and gazed into her eyes. At eighteen, she'd given in to her desires and made love to her best friend, changing her life forever.

She snapped out of her flashback trance when Clint kissed her hand. "This place has held a special place in my heart for all these years."

He traced a heart on her palm. *Oh, my God!* Her chest tingled. Taking a deep breath, she allowed herself to relax.

All the old feelings for Clint flooded her body. She let go of everything that had been holding her back as she kicked off her sandals, slipped off her sundress, revealing her bikini, and jumped into the water, splashing Clint. His jaw gaped, but he joined her in the water. “I’m coming in before you change your mind!”

Clint splashed her. The frigid water chilled her to the core, but the dimples in his smile warmed her. When they got out of the water, he spread a beach blanket and pulled out a picnic dinner, two glasses and a bottle of wine.

They talked about moments they had held onto for all these years. It was like no time had passed at all. Talking to Clint was easy, and he made her laugh.

After dinner, they walked the beach again, but this time, he pulled her in for a kiss. She kissed him back, and they returned to the blanket. Clint locked eyes with her, and she let go of her inhibitions.

Just as he had more than a dozen years ago, he asked her, “Are you sure you’re ready for this?”

She nodded, massaging the lump in her throat. The butterflies in her stomach had transformed into a herd of stampeding elephants. She was unsure of what sound her vocal cords would make. At this very moment, she was confident in one thing—Clint made her happy.

Blake took off her dress again, this time also slipping off the bikini she was wearing underneath. She lay down on the beach blanket. For a moment, he stood staring at her. Then, he quickly joined her on the blanket, kissed her cheek and neck, and finally rekindled their love, with the waves lapping a mere twenty feet away.

They stayed cuddled on the beach blanket for two hours. At midnight, Blake pulled on her clothes. “We’ve gotta go back to the cottage. Your mom’s still there with Willow.”

Clint pulled her close to his body. “Okay, but just one more kiss.”

She pressed her lips to his. *Perfection.* During the car ride home, she smiled and held onto her mouth as if it held a delicious secret.

When they returned, they found a note from Nancy: *Hope you have had a fun evening. I took Willow home with me tonight.*

Clint scooped her up into his arms and carried her to the bedroom. She squealed with delight, and he laughed. They made enough memories that night to last a lifetime. Clint and Blake dared not speak about the future. It was too fresh, too new. They would see where things went.

The next morning, Nancy snuck into the cottage with Willow. They hadn't planned on telling her about the previous evening's events.

Nancy's eyes sparkled. "I'll be happy to watch Willow for you today."

Clint blushed. "Thanks, but all of us should spend the day together. What do you ladies think?"

Nancy smiled. "Now that Blake is okay, I need to get back to the restaurant."

She said no more, but winked and handed Willow's leash over to Blake.

They spent the remainder of the week taking advantage of the perfect spring weather and the peacefulness of the island before tourists flooded every nook and cranny.

On the last day of Clint's vacation, they walked on the beach and played with Willow, who enjoyed the sand and attention she received from other beachgoers more than the actual surf itself.

Clint stared off in the distance but pulled Blake in close. "Thank you for the best week of my life so far." She smiled and kissed his cheek, warmth radiating throughout her body.

Later that evening, they dined under the stars in Granny Mason's garden—the fireflies dancing, serving as a spotlight for their romance.

Chapter 10

Throughout the next week, Blake caught several glimpses of the children playing on the beach, in the backyard of the cottage and various places around the island.

One afternoon, Willow attempted to wander off to join them. Blake jumped in front of the dog. "Hey, girl, I don't want you to leave the garden. Stay here with Momma."

The children's home and family were still a mystery; one Blake needed to unravel. Since Clint had returned to work, Blake had time on her hands. She devoted herself to searching local news websites and school social media pages, hoping to find a photo of one or both children. Her searches did not prove fruitful. *Oh, Nancy, what are you hiding?*

Blake hadn't spoken to her mom on the phone in a week, just texted back and forth a few times. She dialed Susan's number and propped the phone on her shoulder.

"Hi, honey. Is everything okay?" Susan asked.

"Yes. I'm more than okay," Blake said, smiling and twirling her hair. "I need to tell you something. Clint and I are dating again. I didn't plan on starting a new relationship, but it just happened. He is kind, supportive, and makes it clear I'm his priority. I'm falling for him."

Susan cleared her throat. “I’m glad you’re happy if you’re sure you haven’t rushed into anything. I love you, Blake. Make sure you’re taking the right steps to get your life back on track.”

Fidgeting with her hands, she put Susan on speakerphone. “Mom, I want to stay on the island to see where everything goes with Clint, but also because I’ve rediscovered my love for Granny Mason’s cottage and the ocean.” She paused. “I have a business proposition. The cottage is more space than one person and a dog need. No one from the family makes time to visit the cottage anymore except for holidays and the occasional beachside week. Have you ever considered converting part of the house into a bed and breakfast? I could start by renting out the carriage house first. If it works out, I can always flip flop, move out to the carriage house and rent out the main house.” Blake held her breath, anticipating her mother’s answer.

“Blake…” Susan started.

“Mom, I’m not finished. I’ve done the math.” Blake tapped her fingers against the kitchen counter. “We’re paying the groundskeeper $2,000 a month to keep up the house and grounds. We could cut our contract down to the basics, which would cost $500 a month. If we’re fortunate enough to rent the carriage house out half of the nights in every month during the prime tourist season, we’ll net $4,500—that’s if we try to keep our prices middle-of-the-road.

“I’ve got this one hundred percent. Don’t forget, marketing is what I do. I work well on a tight budget. We’ll be the hottest Lowcountry B&B before the end of the year!”

Susan laughed. “I’m glad you’ve found something to pique your interest. Start doing some research on how to open a bed and breakfast on the island. I’ll check in with your aunts and uncles.”

Blake went to the police department to ask Clint to walk her through starting a new business. After just a few phone calls, he had set up meetings with all the necessary municipal employees, an insurance agent and the director of the chamber of commerce. Later that evening, she started to call her mom, but she had missed text from her.

"Everyone said, 'Go for it!' Good luck. Call me later. Love you!"

Just before city hall closed, she raced to turn in her paperwork to become the owner and general manager of a bed and breakfast. Blake hugged herself. She could picture it now. The carriage house would make a great bed and breakfast, with two bedrooms, two bathrooms, a shared kitchen, living room and dining room.

Blake clapped her hands and left to shop for home decor items to help fix up the space. She danced in her car before going into her favorite shop.

Walking to her car, someone called her name. She turned, but no one was behind her. *How weird.* She opened the trunk, and it slammed shut, barely missing her hand.

Jumping back, she yelled, "Damn it!"

Blake clicked the trunk button on her car remote again and quickly put her shopping bags inside. Her heart was still pounding. She climbed into the driver's side of the vehicle. Her text notification sounded, and she jumped again. A message from Clint popped up on the screen.

> **Clint:** *How did everything go? Do you own a business?*
>
> **Blake:** *I'm so close. I'm waiting for some zoning paperwork to be approved. The health inspector will make an appointment to check out the kitchen.*
>
> **Clint**: *I'm so happy for you! Come home, and we'll celebrate!*

Chapter 11

When she returned home, Clint covered her eyes and led her to the kitchen. "No peeking!"

The aroma of fresh seafood sizzling teased her senses. Clint uncovered her eyes, and Nancy yelled, "Surprise!"

As Clint handed her a bouquet of fresh yellow roses, Nancy poured her a glass of sparkling wine.

"Aww! Y'all know how to spoil a girl," Blake said, inhaling the roses' divine scent.

"You're more than worth it." Clint kissed her on the cheek, and Blake blushed.

"We're so proud of your accomplishments!" Nancy said. "I'm sure your Granny Mason is watching over you today. She'd be so proud!" She looked outside with a wistful expression. Blake turned to see what had captured Nancy's attention. The two children had returned to play on the tire swing.

She started to walk outside to talk to the children, but Nancy handed her a plate of homemade crab cakes and succotash. "Eat up, so we can enjoy dessert!"

After savoring Nancy's blue-ribbon-winning pecan pie à la mode, everyone changed their clothes so they could take Willow for a walk on the beach.

While they were waiting for Nancy to finish getting ready, Blake told Clint how the trunk lid on her car had almost smashed her hand.

"I'll go check the struts to make sure they're in good shape. I don't want you to get hurt," Clint said. Blake grabbed her car keys, and they walked outside.

Clint examined lift supports in the trunk and shook his head.

"Everything's fine. Keep an eye on it. I can have one of my mechanic buddies check it out."

Blake thanked him, and when Nancy came out with Willow, they began making their way to the beach. As they walked, Blake asked Nancy if she would be interested in picking up some orders as bed and breakfast customers requested on-site catering.

"I can handle making biscuits and gravy or French toast for breakfast, but my culinary skills are not even remotely close to yours. If we end up with a wedding or family reunion, I'll need your help."

"Not a prob, hon. With all the excitement here lately, I've decided to back off my hours at the Sea Biscuit. They don't need me now. I'd rather spend time with you three!" Nancy said. "Plus, pretty soon, the rest of the family will be here to visit."

"When will they be here, Nancy?"

Clint's four brothers and their wives lived in towns throughout Georgia and the Carolinas. Clint's commitment to staying on the island had mystified them.

"They should be in over the weekend. Say, would you want to practice your bed and breakfast hosting skills?"

"That's an outstanding idea, and at least they're family, so they'll forgive me if I fall flat on my face." Blake laughed.

"You'll do great. We'll be here to help, and I can still whup all of those boys if they give you any grief," Clint said, punching the air.

Blake carried a bag of trash outside. The gate to the garden swayed back and forth on its own. At first, she'd dismissed the incident altogether, blaming it on the wind. The sun beat down on her shoulders, no breeze blowing. Pressure built up in her head and ears. She massaged her head and struggled to keep her balance.

Clint ran outside. "What's wrong?"

"My head's hurting, and I'm lightheaded."

He put his hand under her chin and frowned. "How long has this been going on?"

Blake closed her eyes. "Ever since…"

"I see." Clint grimaced. "Are you sure you are up to hosting my family?"

She nodded.

"You need to go to the doctor. I'll go with you." Clint pulled her into an embrace.

"I'll make an appointment tomorrow," Blake said. A large, blurred black object floated in her peripheral vision. Clint didn't mention seeing it. She didn't want to worry him, so she didn't bring up the visual disturbance. Maybe she'd seen Parker. Perhaps it was the long-term effects of having a head injury. She shivered.

Chapter 12

Two days before their guests arrived, Clint took Blake to her doctor's appointment.

Her hands shook as she filled out the required paperwork. Clint grabbed her hands and kissed them. "It will be okay. I'm here for you, no matter what."

Blake smiled weakly and nodded. She zoned out while the doctor ran a gamut of tests, including an MRI, to rule out any serious medical conditions.

Afterward, the doctor met her in the examination room. "Ms. Nelson, thankfully, the test results came back clear. The bad news is you have unexplained migraines. Most people respond well to a combination of medication, diet changes and supplements. The symptoms could lessen or even disappear in a matter of months." He handed her a few prescriptions and told her to check in if she wasn't doing better in a month.

Returning to Clint's Jeep, Blake frowned and stared off in the distance.

He rubbed her forehead. "Migraines are horrible, and it upsets me to see you in pain. But I have to tell you, I'm relieved it didn't turn out to be anything life threatening."

"Same. Hopefully, they'll go away soon." Blake rubbed her temples.

He drove them home, and they shared the news with Nancy. She fussed over Blake, doing everything she could to make her comfortable. And leading up to their company's arrival, they encouraged Blake to rest as much as possible. She curled up in her bed with Willow and watched reruns of her favorite '90s sitcoms. Clint and Nancy served her meals in bed and walked the dog so she wouldn't need to leave the room.

When the Parsons brothers and their families flooded the Mason homestead, Willow immediately fell in love with the children, following them around wherever their daily adventures took them, from the garden to the beach.

After work each day, Clint served as the entertainment director. Blake loved how Clint enjoyed spending time with his nieces and nephews, planning sandcastle building competitions, outings to the nearest playground and the South Carolina Aquarium. Being their uncle, he stopped for ice cream or shaved ice as much as he could without receiving a lecture from their parents.

"I'm so thrilled to have all of my sweet great-grandbabies with us!" Nancy said, squeezing Clint's hands. "I'll babysit if y'all want to go out on the town this week."

Clint's eyes lit up. "That sounds great! Thanks, Gram!"

"Do you want me to stay to help?" Blake asked.

"Shoot, no. Hon, I've been watching young'uns since I was one myself. Anyway, we've got plenty of family and close friends in the area if I need to call in reinforcements."

Each evening, they stopped by local bars for happy hour and dancing. And the adults seemed at home and eager to relax. Clint's youngest brother, Landon, congratulated Blake on her new business.

"This is so cool. Thanks for hosting us this week. We're proud of you, and most of all, we're glad to see you and Clint together again. He's so happy. You guys are meant to be together."

Clint caught the tail end of their conversation and spun Blake around the foyer. "You got that right, brother." He lowered Blake into a dip. His brothers began whooping and clapping. Blake's cheeks reddened as she giggled.

After dinner the last evening of the mini family reunion, Clint and Blake set up a makeshift outdoor movie theater, hanging a white sheet on the backside of the house and bringing out a collection of recent movies, a laptop and a projector. Nancy popped popcorn and built a fire in the fire pit for two purposes—for warmth and, most importantly, to make s'mores.

"Thanks for a night none of us will forget," Landon said. "It will stick with the children because they love sweets. The adults will always remember it as the night all the children consumed too much to sugar to fall asleep." Teasing Blake had been an enjoyable pastime for these brothers when they were children, and it seemed they hadn't outgrown it.

The week had gone by without a hitch. Blake had learned several lessons from her trial run—not to underestimate how much food children could consume, or the number of bath towels guests might need. She had enjoyed Nancy and Clint's family being around, and she suspected she would see more of them soon.

Before they packed up their cars, Clint's brothers stopped to thank Blake, Clint and Nancy for everything and wished them luck on a successful new business.

As soon as they finished cleaning, Nancy excused herself. "I'm glad everything went so smoothly. It was great spending time with all my sweet babies, but now, I need to go home and sleep for three days." She blew them a kiss and left the cottage.

Clint made a fist and pulled it toward his waist.

"Yes! They're gone! I love them, but I'm glad everyone went home so we can have some time alone now." Clint poured each of them a glass of wine and led her to the backyard, where the fireflies sparkled brighter than any night she could recall.

"Dance with me." He held out his hand and queued a soft, romantic music station to stream on his phone. They began slow dancing, and he pulled Blake closer to him, running his hands through her long dark curls.

His hands melted the stress she had been carrying. She let her shoulders drop and sighed. Clint had a way of putting her at ease, something she desperately needed. He led her to the hammock where they stayed overnight. She rubbed her eyes and woke when the sun rose over the canopy of oaks and greeted the arrival of a new day.

Chapter 13

Still curled up with Clint in the hammock, Blake thought about their teenage relationship again.

He shifted and nuzzled her cheek. "What's on your mind, babe?"

She smiled and rubbed his arm. "Just remembering the bonfire parties we used to go to during my winter breaks from school. The chilly winter breeze gave us an excuse to cuddle under a cozy blanket. Do you remember that?"

"Mmhmm. Just thinking about it makes cuddling even cozier." Clint snuggled in closer and pretended to snore. Blake laughed but continued her walk down memory lane. During the last bonfire of their senior year of high school, Clint had given Blake his class ring and letterman jacket. Living two states apart during the school year, they'd helped her feel closer to him. When they'd broken up, she left them behind at the cottage. She hadn't thought about the mementos in almost 15 years.

The clanging of the screen door caught her attention. Clint had gone into the house to get Willow some kibble and water. Maybe the ring was still in her dresser. She went into her bedroom. Migraine medications be damned, the vice grip on her skull tightened. She drew a deep breath. Blake closed the door behind her, and a vase flew across the room. It hadn't suddenly grown wings.

She jumped to grab the vase, but she couldn't reach it. "Parker, put that down!"

The vase crashed into the wall with supernatural force, throwing sharp shards across the room. Blake shrieked, and suddenly her arm began throbbing. Blood pulsated out of two deep gashes.

She screamed again, more out of shock than pain, and Clint came running from downstairs.

"Are you okay? What happened?" he asked, poking his head through the door.

She caught her breath and pulled a clean towel out of her laundry basket, applying pressure to the wound. "I may need stitches," Blake said, resisting the urge to scream.

"Be careful when you come in here. There's glass everywhere."

Clint grabbed the first aid kit out of his Jeep and helped her slow down the bleeding. Then, he took Blake to an urgent care clinic, where the doctor had patched her up in no time.

"Well, that was pretty much painless. Hopefully, I won't end up with some ugly scars." Blake smoothed the bandages on her arm.

"Scars add character. Don't worry."

When they returned to the cottage, Clint helped her out of the car. He placed his hand on her chin and gave her a gentle kiss. "Why did the vase fall?" he asked, opening the front door.

Blake stepped into the living room and sighed. "It was Parker. I was trying to find your class ring in my jewelry box, but the vase flew through the air and crashed against the wall."

Clint walked into the house and punched the wall. "What? Why is he messing with you again?"

"I don't know." Blake clenched her fists.

"We'll get rid of him, but for now, you need to rest," Clint said. "I'll sweep up the broken glass."

While he cleaned, Blake went to the kitchen to begin dinner.

"These are incredible," Clint said, biting into a blackened shrimp fajita. "I was hoping you'd get some rest while I cleaned, though."

"I'm fine. And I needed to cook that shrimp today." She put her arms around his neck.

His lips gently brushed her cheek, and he asked her to sit down with him in the living room.

"Is everything okay?" Blake asked, her eyes narrowing.

"Yeah. I just want to talk to you," Clint said, patting the couch cushion next to him. "When Gram said you were back in town, my heart broke into a million pieces. I'd heard you were engaged, and I assumed you were here with your fiancé.

"I was terrified of running into you. Then Gram convinced me to join you guys for dinner. When I saw him at the cottage that night, I wanted to hunt him down and make him regret his actions."

Clint's face reddened. "I'm not the type to wish death on anyone, but Parker deserved what he got."

Blake sat silently, allowing him to continue.

Clint drew a deep breath and exhaled. "With all the negativity out of my system, I want to focus on positive things like spending time with you."

"So much has happened. Reconnecting with you has been the best part." She rested her head on his shoulder and allowed herself to bask in her happiness for a few moments before she sat up.

"Did you find my class ring?"

She handed it to him, and he slipped it onto her finger. "It's killing me, but I'm trying to take things slowly. I understand you've been through a lot. I'm committed to you one hundred percent."

Blake's eyes misted over. "I don't want to be with anyone else."

Clint played with her hair. "I'm not ready for the weekend to be over. I love my job, but I'd rather be with you. Several new officers are starting tomorrow. I should be at my desk most of the week since I'll be helping train them."

"I'll be fine. Nancy has all but quit her job at the Sea Biscuit to help me run the bed and breakfast and take care of Willow," Blake said. "I'm planning to have a low-key week, adding pictures from your family's visit to the website and social media pages. And I might invite my family down to help me finish getting things together for the grand opening."

"If they're free, they should visit around your birthday," Clint said, his eyes sparkling.

"Oh, I love that idea! That would be fun," Blake said.

Over the next couple of weeks, Blake committed herself to promoting the B&B. She was proud of her newly launched website and excited to build a following on social media pages. She attended a handful of local networking meetings, where she passed out brochures. Meeting people who shared her passion for the island had scratched her itch to return to a marketing career.

While answering emails from her bedroom, a loud noise came from downstairs. A sharp pain crept up the back of her skull and radiated to her temples. She massaged her head and focused on breathing.

"Clint? Nancy? Who's there?" Blake called out, but no one answered.

She got up from her desk, and Willow followed her down the steps. She checked each of the downstairs rooms. Not a soul in sight, but then, the door to her bedroom slammed—a sound she remembered from her teenage years.

Willow growled, and Blake had to admit she was nervous herself. She grabbed a cast-iron fireplace shovel from the living room and tiptoed up the steps. Her head throbbed. *He's definitely in there* She flung her door open. Parker's apparition faded, but the imprint of his body remained on her bed.

Blake slammed the door shut and ran downstairs in a panic. She stopped only long enough to collect her purse before going outside. She began dialing Clint's phone number just as Nancy pulled into the driveway.

Wincing, Nancy stepped out of her car and walked over to Blake's. "What's wrong?"

"Parker's in our house!"

Nancy raised her eyebrows. "What? Where did you see him?"

"In my bedroom. He led me on a wild goose chase, and eventually, I ended up finding him in there," she said.

Blake's jaw dropped as Nancy entered the cottage with her hands on her hips. She couldn't let her older, though sassy friend take on evil Parker by herself. She found Nancy sitting on her bed.

"There wasn't anyone up here." Nancy smoothed Blake's quilt.

"He must have left. I'm sure I saw him." Blake frowned. She checked the entire top floor of the house, but there was no sign of Parker.

"I believe you. I'm so sorry he scared you," Nancy said, putting her arm around Blake to console her.

"I don't understand why he's showing up. It's nerve-wracking, wondering when he will pop up out of the blue. I've seen my share of ghosts, but I'm afraid of him," Blake said.

"We've got your back, dear."

"But this is frightening. How can I, or any of us, prevent Parker from appearing? Can he hurt us? What are we going to do?"

"Try to stay calm. We'll figure this out one step at a time," Nancy said.

"How do you know we'll get rid of him?"

"I just do. Trust me; we can't do anything yet."

"But when?" Blake asked.

"I swore to your grandmother—I would wait until the right time." Nancy hesitated. "Well, I guess this is it." She sighed. "Let's go talk."

They took a seat on the living room couch.

Nancy lay her shaking hands on her lap. "When she was dying, she made me promise I would watch over you. She suspected you had inherited her keen sensibilities, which would open you up to the spiritual world."

"Right. I've seen several ghosts since Granny died. Unfortunately, I was out cold the only time I've seen her." Blake frowned.

"Yes—the women in your family can sense and, sometimes, see spirits. What you probably suspect is a traumatic event activates your ability to communicate with ghosts. Yours began when your granny died. But what you hadn't faced until Parker is a spirit blaming you for their death. That's when seeing ghosts goes from being creepy to life-threatening. Thankfully, you should get some sort of warning when he enters the room."

Blake's jaw dropped. She rubbed her head. "Oh, my God! My headaches! The visual disturbances and sounds! That explains a lot. This is so weird."

"I'm sure it sounds ridiculous, and it doesn't end there. You have yet another gift; you can send spirits on to their next destination. It's complicated. You have to do a special cleansing ceremony that coincides with a major life event like a graduation, wedding, baby being born or buying a new home. The event has to align with a lunar eclipse, making it even more difficult to manage."

"Whoa, how do you accomplish that?" Blake sighed. "How did Granny Mason figure out she had these gifts?"

"When your grandmother was nineteen years old, she was engaged to your papa. Their fathers had feuded with each other for decades. Your grandfather's dad had a heart attack and died when he heard the news. That night, his spirit came to your grandmother's bed with a knife and threatened her life if she followed through with marrying your grandfather. Julia Caroline lived with her grandmother, Clara Reid, at that time. Since the gift skips a generation, Clara helped your granny figure out how to protect herself.

"Naturally, the experience frightened Julia Caroline on many levels. Throughout your grandparents' engagement, several similar events occurred, but they eventually ceased on the night they got married. She figured out that the wedding ceremony put an end to the haunting. I've never mentioned my first husband, a physically abusive man I was lucky enough to escape. When he died, his spirit tried to kill me. He was a real doozie to get rid of because his twin brother, who'd died when they were teenagers, teamed up with him. Your Granny helped me send their spirits on to their final resting place."

Blake put her hands out in front of her. "Hold up, Nancy, why didn't you tell me about your ex-husband?"

"I try not to relive that whole mess," Nancy said, shaking her head as if to clear her thoughts. "I've seen spirits since I was a child.

Don't worry about that, though. This should be your takeaway—your granny put an end to unwanted hauntings. You have the power to do the same. Julia Caroline even wrote a book about sending spirits to their next destination."

Blake gasped. "Why didn't she tell me any of this herself? I didn't know she wrote a book! Where can I find a copy?"

"Your grandmother hoped you would never need to use these gifts. She wished for a safe and happy life for all her children and grandchildren. I don't know how to find the book. The pastor at your grandparents' church demanded that the community destroy all the books. Your grandfather was afraid people would shun grandmother. He refused to let her keep even one copy."

"Wow. I bet that pissed her off," Blake said.

"Oh, yeah, your granny had a fiery temper, but your papa asked her not to make a fuss. He was concerned someone might lash out at her. She listened to him, even though she was infuriated."

Blake laughed at the thought of her grandmother pouting and giving her grandfather the silent treatment. Her papa hadn't ever denied Julia Caroline anything her heart desired. It must have crushed his soul to ask her to surrender her books.

"There is someone who might help us. Growing up, your grandmother and I had a friend named Paulene. She is gifted, too. I haven't spoken to her for a long time, but she loved your granny. She volunteers at the library. We should stop by tomorrow and invite her to lunch."

"It's definitely worth asking," Blake said.

Chapter 14

As planned, Nancy and Blake went to the Mount Pleasant Library to invite Paulene to lunch.

When they walked inside, Nancy stared at a slender woman with salt and pepper hair and black cat-eye glasses. The woman ran toward them, waving both of her ring-covered hands.

"Why, Nancy Parsons, it's been ages! I've been hoping to bump into you."

Nancy extended her arm to shake Paulene's hand, and Blake had to stifle a giggle. Nancy wasn't the handshaking type. She hugged everyone, friend or stranger.

"And who do you have here?" Paulene asked.

"Hi, I'm Blake Nelson, Julia Caroline Mason's granddaughter. We wanted to ask if we can take you out for lunch or a cup of coffee."

Paulene paused. "I had wondered if you or one of your sisters would end up finding me one day. The spiritual blessing usually skips a generation."

Blake's mouth gaped. "That explains why Mom hasn't had supernatural experiences."

"That's right. I'll get my purse, and we can go wherever you want. I'd love to hear more about what you're experiencing."

Nancy and Blake followed her to her desk, and as they walked out of the library to Nancy's car, Blake explained how Parker had been tormenting her.

"That's awful. We'll find a solution. I thought the world of your grandmother. Tell me what you know about Julia Caroline's powers."

"My grandmother had a blessing or a gift for communicating with spirits, but I don't fully understand how she figured out how to send them on to their next destination."

"Your grandfather's father died of a heart attack after he overheard her, telling me she and your grandfather had planned to elope."

Paulene turned to Nancy from the passenger seat and patted her shoulder.

"I don't want to make this awkward, but that's when Nancy stopped trusting me."

Nancy's face crumpled, and she bit her lip as Paulene continued.

"It was all a big misunderstanding. Nancy thought I'd told your great-grandfather about the elopement. Your grandparents were young, and their families had feuded. When he died, he haunted your grandmother. She figured out steps to get him to leave his earthly home and go to his final resting place. She helped dozens of other people get rid of unsettled spirits."

"Wow," Blake said.

"She was truly remarkable. Now how can I help you?" Paulene asked.

"Could you try to help me find a copy of the book?"

Paulene grimaced. "I've been trying to find the book ever since it was banned, and I'll never stop. The pastor knew I had several copies, and he forced me to allow deacons from the church to search my house from floor to ceiling. They took every last book."

Nancy, who had been silent, sighed. "Things were so different then. The men folk just didn't get that it wasn't about using magic or working with the devil. It was about using the blessings God gave us to destroy evil. Paulene, can we agree to let bygones be bygones? Can we be friends again?"

Paulene nodded. “I’d love nothing more.”

After lunch, they dropped Paulene off at the library and returned to the cottage.

Blake sat down on the oversized gray slip-covered sofa in the living room. She had a lot of information to unpack and a book to find. But her family was coming to visit in a few days, and she needed to prepare.

Nancy examined Blake’s to-do list and gasped. “Oh, my…I guess we’d better get started.”

Over the next couple of days, Nancy helped her shop for groceries and prepared the sleeping spaces for guests.

Time flew by, leading up to her family’s visit. Her parents, sisters and a few of her cousins stopped by to help spruce up the cottage and carriage house. They tended to the colorful flower beds in the garden and hung some striking, high-contrast black-and-white photos in the carriage house.

When the rest of the family went to the beach, Blake asked her sisters to stay behind so they could catch up on girl talk.

“You guys should be proud of everything you have done to the cottage. Granny Mason would be beside herself if she were here to see your handiwork.” Elaina kneeled to pet Willow. “By the way, I love your new pup!”

“Me too!” Brittany signed. The youngest of the three sisters, took her turn petting Willow. The dog’s tail wagged. “So, where’s this thing with Clint going?” she asked, playfully batting her eyes and hugging herself, signing the word “love.”

“Stop it. Just stop it.” Blake groaned and threw a couch pillow at Brittany. “It’s going at the perfect pace. We couldn’t be happier.”

Elaina sighed, running the front of her hand across her forehead and pretending to faint. Brittany giggled.

“You’re both just too much. Way too much. Why don’t we join the others at the beach?” Blake laughed.

They ran to the beach and dug their toes into the sand, soaking up the sun for hours.

Their dad, Jeremy, walked up to them. “Come on, you guys. Dinner’s ready. I’ve made margaritas, too!” This reminded Blake of all the summer days she and her family had spent on the island. Of course, libations hadn't been part of her childhood summers, but as an adult, she'd be happy to drink a couple.

Everyone started running to the cottage where they ate and enjoyed cocktails and played several rounds of Trivial Pursuit until 1:30 a.m.

"I'm too old for this. I'm going to crash," Susan said, and the rest of the family went to bed, too.

On Blake's birthday, Nancy made a delicious breakfast for everyone. Blake smiled at her family.

"Okay, I can't stand it. We have a surprise for you!" Elaina said.

"What are you talking about?" Blake asked wide-eyed.

"You know those beach books you're obsessed with?" her sister asked.

"You mean Liza Montgomery's Lowcountry books?" Blake asked.

"Those are the ones! We're taking you to meet Liza today!" Elaina exclaimed.

Speechless, Blake sat down again. "I can't believe it! When I read her books, it's like I'm on the island with my toes in the sand."

Clint walked into the kitchen, wearing his uniform. "Happy Birthday, babe! I'm sorry I can't go with you guys today, but I have meetings at the station. I'll be home by the time y'all get back."

"Oh, I wish you could come with us!" Blake frowned. "But, I understand."

Nancy piled into the car with the Nelsons, and they made their way to Charleston's historic district. The tires on their vehicle rumbled over the cobblestone streets, and the towering single houses cast shadows onto them as they searched for a parking space.

"We have time to walk for a little bit before the book signing." Susan smiled. "Where would you like to go?"

Blake's eyes lit up, and her focus turned to the open-air Charleston Market. "I would love to get some new artwork for my bedroom," she said. "Let's go check out the artisan stalls."

Blake went from booth to booth, flipping through the treasure trove of paintings and photographs featuring Charleston and island themes. She found one of the Morris Island Lighthouse, which had represented many things at various points in her life.

As a child, its magnificence had impressed her. Although the lighthouse wasn't in use, she'd dreamed of climbing the interior stairs and looking down at the Lowcountry sprawled out before her. In adulthood, it had taken on more personal meaning after the beautiful moments of love and connection on the nearby shore. Although the light no longer glowed to provide a safe harbor, its former presence served as a beacon into the depths of Blake's soul, revealing what she needed most.

"I'll take this one," Blake said to the artist, handing her the large black-and-white photographic print of the majestic lighthouse. She planned to hang it over her dresser. When she woke up, the picture would be the first thing she saw. Considering the role the lighthouse had played in her and Clint's relationship, it seemed only fitting.

After taking the picture back to her parents' car, she met up with her family in a small bookstore near the market. A line formed in front of a folding table filled with Liza's books.

Moments later, a petite, dark-headed woman in her sixties sat down at the table. A long seashell necklace and matching earrings complemented her turquoise linen dress. *That must be Liza.*

Sure enough, the woman began talking to the customers standing in line. One by one, they handed her their books. She smiled and spoke to them for a few moments before signing the title page of her latest bestseller, *Magnolia Sun.*

Blake stepped up to Liza and thanked her for providing a mental and emotional getaway for her readers. "Your work has always inspired me. Someday, I hope I write a book that moves others the way yours has influenced my life," she said.

"I have a feeling you will. Being passionate is the first step," Liza said.

"Thank you so much," Blake said, holding the book to her chest as she walked back to her family. "Best. Birthday. Ever."

"Now that you're on cloud nine, we'd like to take you out to lunch," her dad said. "You name the place."

"Does the Fancy Flounder sound good to everyone?" Blake asked. Its quirky name wasn't the only thing driving its popularity. The restaurant served fresh seafood prepared with a gourmet Southern flair.

"Yum. I could go for Fancy's pecan-crusted fish," Elaina said.

They walked into the restaurant and ordered cocktails and their entrees, but what made lunch special for Blake was all the great conversation and laughter they shared. Her mom asked her what she wanted to do next.

"Hmm…let me think. I'll be right back."

Blake walked down the long hallway and through two sets of doors to the ladies' room. While washing her hands, a cool breeze grazed her shoulders. The hair on her arms stood up on end, and her head began pulsating.

She continued washing her hands, but her curiosity got the best of her. From the mirror, Paker's green eyes bore holes into her.

"You shouldn't be here! Go away!" Blake cried. She'd never been so glad for a restroom to be far removed from a restaurant dining room. Anyone who couldn't see spirits would think she was crazy. *They might not be wrong.*

"Happy Birthday, beautiful. What—you thought I'd forgotten? No way. I have to celebrate with you. Did I see your family out there? I sure have missed them. Wouldn't it be nice if I came out to say hello?"

"No! Leave them alone. It's bad enough that you're tormenting me. They don't deserve to be tortured. Seriously, please go somewhere, anywhere else."

He stood behind her and put his arm around her waist. "I've missed you, Blake." His icy breath frosted the mirror, and her chest compressed. She inhaled and pried his icy fingers off her abdomen, and he laughed. How would she be able to get rid of him now that he was strong enough to materialize and touch her?

"Why do you insist on wrecking my life every chance you get?" Blake asked.

"Isn't it obvious? You ruined mine. I'm dead." He chuckled.

"That's your own doing. Now go to hell where you belong!" Blake opened the bathroom door and slammed it behind her.

Parker just had to show up today of all days. Blake clutched her purse to her chest, took a deep breath and gathered her wits. She wanted to make a run for it and try to hide from him, but she couldn't.

As she returned to her family's table, they were talking, oblivious to the nerve-wracking scene that had just taken place in the bathroom.

Smile and breathe. You don't want to worry them.

Susan grinned. "Glad you're back. What do you want to do?"

Trying to hold herself together, Blake bit her lip. She'd completely forgotten to plan their next activity. She smiled weakly and came up with an excuse to go home.

"Thanks for everything today, but we probably need to get back to Willow," Blake said. "Can we take her to the beach?"

Nancy nodded and winked at Susan.

"What's going on?" Blake asked Elaina, who shrugged. They were up to something. Blake didn't bother asking her parents or Nancy what they were hiding. Her family took keeping birthday secrets seriously.

Chapter 15

On their way back to the island, Nancy asked to stop at the grocery store. Blake and the rest of the family waited in the car and sang along with an '80s flashback radio station.

Just as they started singing the fourth song, Nancy left the store and began loading the trunk. Getting back into the car, she made it a point to wink at Susan yet again. Blake raised her eyebrows at Nancy, who smiled and patted her shoulder.

When they arrived back at the cottage, Nancy asked Blake and Elaina if they could take some groceries over to the carriage house. Blake played along with the weird game Nancy and her mom were playing. She welcomed the distraction from Parker's terrifying impromptu appearances.

The sisters loaded the cold items in the freezer and refrigerator and crossed the yard to the main house. Blake opened the door. Their family and friends had gathered in the living room.

"Surprise!" they yelled in unison.

"Oh, my goodness! I'm shocked, y'all," Blake said, hugging everyone within reach.

Each party guest took a moment to tell Blake why she was special to them. Nancy started the conversation. "When you were a child, I could see your spark, and I knew you would grow into an incredible young woman. And you have done just that. I'm proud of you, and there is no one I would rather have in my grandson's life. Just because lightning doesn't strike in the same place twice, doesn't mean love can't. You guys have proven that."

Blake's eyes misted over, and she smiled as the rest of her family and friends said the kindest, most thoughtful words she could have imagined. Finally, Clint took his turn.

"You're the most incredible person I've ever met. Thank you for loving me."

Blake gushed and jumped into his arms. Everyone applauded.

"Before everyone gets too carried away, I have a birthday surprise for Blake. Jeremy, is everything ready?" Clint asked her dad, who nodded and gave him a thumbs-up.

"Oh, good. I'll finally find out why everyone is making strange faces and gestures today. Y'all are being so weird," Blake said, following her family to the driveway.

She froze in her tracks, and her eyes widened at the sight—Granny Mason's mint-green vintage Thunderbird convertible. The last time Blake had seen the car, rust had eaten away part of the side panels; springs had poked through the seats; and it had needed a complete overhaul. She'd never questioned where the car had gone after her grandmother died, assuming it had gone to its great reward along with Granny Mason herself. But there she sat in the driveway, restored to her original glory. Blake's reflection danced across the body of the car.

"Where did you find her?" she shrieked, examining each inch of the car's beauty.

"When your grandmother passed away, she left the car to Gram. They had some fun times driving up and down the coast in this car. She knew Gram loved it as much as she did," Clint said. "But now Gram wants you to have it. A few years ago, she asked me to restore it for you. It helped me work through the pain from our past and focus on the future. I can't wait to take our first road trip together!"

"I loved riding in this car with her when I visited." Stunned, Blake ran her hand over the leather driver's seat and hopped into the car. "Nancy, it means the world to me that you want me to have the car. Clint, thanks for making it as good as new for me. You two never cease to amaze me. Thank you." Blake walked around to appreciate the car's beauty fully.

The rest of the party guests joined them in the driveway.

"It's just like I remember," Susan said. "If Mom were here now, she would be so happy to know that you have her prized car, and you're launching a new business in her home. She would be proud of you, Blake."

"Thanks, Mom. I love you." Blake grinned.

"I love you, too, honey," Susan said.

"Now, you need to plan a trip down the coast," her dad said. "That's a nice car."

Blake smiled and turned back around to see Nancy holding a sculpted cake decorated to look like the Thunderbird, complete with a figure of a woman modeled after her likeness in the driver's seat, and in the passenger's seat, a police officer resembling Clint holding a corgi.

Elaina lit the candles, and everyone began singing, "Happy Birthday."

Blake drew a deep breath and smiled. She preferred not to be the center of attention, but she owed gratitude to her friends and family. Clint and Nancy had given her the gift of their time. How had they had found a surplus of even a few minutes, let alone the numerous hours the car restoration and party planning had taken?

Blake spent the evening enjoying the company of her friends and family, grateful for their love and support. All the same, she couldn't help but be on edge. Something told her she hadn't seen the last of Parker. He'd always gotten his way in life. Most likely, he hadn't lost this drive.

Chapter 16

Three days after her birthday, Blake's family left. The carriage house bookings started coming in, and a couple booked their wedding in the garden. Blake called Nancy to share the news.

"How exciting! How many people are we expecting for the reception?" Nancy asked.

"About twenty. The bride said she would get back to me with a final count next week. She wants us to book some local vendors. Do you have any suggestions?" Blake asked, jotting notes as Nancy made recommendations.

Blake busied herself, calling the vendors and getting estimates for their services. After talking to them and answering dozens of questions, she had an idea; she needed to host an open house to invite the community to enjoy the Mason Bed & Breakfast in person.

On the morning of the event, she put the last batch of miniature biscuits for the refreshment table into the oven, set the timer and went to the bathroom to freshen up her makeup. She jumped at the sight of a pale creature staring back at her in the mirror. As Blake chuckled to herself, she bent down to wash flour off her face. When she stood upright again, a second face had joined hers. His evil grin widened in the mirror. She gasped and froze in place.

Goosebumps raced up her arms, and a numb sensation tingled across her forehead. Blake gathered her wits, turned around and pushed against him, using all her body weight. Parker only laughed and winked as he faded into a cold mist. Blake leaned back on the sink, her heart racing. She rubbed the back of her head and fanned her face with her other hand.

The timer for the biscuits went off, startling her. She sighed and ran into the kitchen, grabbing a potholder and pulling the oven door handle. To her dismay, the door wouldn't budge. As she struggled to open the door, smoke seeped around the edges and filled the room.

She couldn't find anything jamming the door. With eerie speed, flames began shooting up from the biscuits. *What on earth?*

A loud bang echoed throughout the kitchen. *Where did that noise come from?* She turned back to the stove. The flames had consumed the inside of the oven completely. Panicked, she pulled a fire extinguisher from a nearby wall and, using its base, attempted to break the glass oven door. After a few tries, she succeeded. Flames erupted into the room, but she sprang into action, extinguishing the fire. Taking a deep breath, she assessed the damage. The countertop and tile flooring closest to the oven had some singed marks. It could have been worse.

Tears welled up in her eyes as she sat down at the table. Clint and Nancy ran into the house from the garden.

"What's wrong?" Clint asked, bending down to console her.

Blake explained her struggle to put out the flames. "What if I hadn't been able to? I can't imagine life without Granny Mason's cottage." She wiped her eyes with a napkin.

"We've got to get this devil under control," Nancy said, squeezing Blake's arm. "Why don't you let us clean up this mess? You can shower and change. I'm sure you'll feel better."

She thanked Nancy and went to get ready. With the water raining down her body in the shower, she sobbed in frustration and banged her fists on the frosted plexiglass wall. She sat on the built-in bench, trying to calm herself. Parker had mistreated her in life, and now, he was continuing to cause her grief and pain after death.

Did Nancy have another long-lost secret? Regardless, she needed a solution to get rid of Parker now. If Nancy couldn't tell her, Blake would have to find out on her own.

After showering, Blake lay down on her bed, doing her best to relax and let go of the negativity Parker had inflicted that day. While lying there, she searched the Internet for ways to rid a home of evil spirits. She found numerous articles recommending burning sage throughout the house while praying for God to cleanse the home.

Easy enough and certainly worth trying. Clint texted her to say he and Nancy were picking up lunch. This was the best time to perform the ritual undisturbed. She slipped on some yoga pants and a t-shirt and went to Granny Mason's herb garden and pulled a bundle of sage from an overflowing bush. Some online articles recommended drying it first, but she couldn't wait.

Blake went back inside and wrapped the fresh leaves in a piece of burlap, tying several strands of jute around the fabric. She placed the fragrant cachet inside one of her grandmother's many hurricane lamps. Hopeful she had discovered a solution, she struck a match and dropped it into the glass lamp. The cachet began smoldering, and Blake started praying.

"God, please cleanse our home of evil spirits and send them to their next destination. We trust in you to provide safety and shelter in every storm. Amen."

With the burning sage in hand, Blake moved from room to room, repeating the prayer. Once the aromatic essence filled the cottage, a sense of peace came over her. She closed her eyes for a few seconds and focused on something positive—meeting new people during the open house. Channeling as many cheerful vibes as she could muster, she put on a yellow summer dress, a pair of rose gold hoops and white sandals. She pulled her dark curls back into a simple updo to help avoid frizz in the humid South Carolina air.

An hour later, Charleston area event vendors gushed over the B&B. Each guest complimented the Mason Bed & Breakfast, commenting on its charm, location and amenities. Some asked for detailed information on hosting events and snapped photos of the garden and other gathering spaces.

Chapter 17

When the event ended, Clint tallied the number of guests on the sign-in sheet.

"Wow! We ended up with 133 people attending. Who would have thought? Did you get any bookings?"

"Between events and overnight stays, the carriage house is booked for almost the entire month of June and for a couple of weekends in July, August and September," Blake said. "If we get much busier, I'll need to move the guests and events to the main house and start hiring some staff members. Not that I'm complaining!"

"I'm as pleased as punch," Nancy said.

"It's great to see my two favorite ladies so happy." Clint handed Blake the sign-in sheet.

Blake smiled, reading the names of some new friends she had made that day. But when she flipped to the last page, a familiar signature almost caused her eyes to pop out of their sockets…P.A. Sutton.

As in Parker Andrew Sutton? No. Not possible.

She reread the name. Not only did the signature match but also the color of ink stood out among the other signatures. It had a faint tinge of green. Parker had always signed his name with a fountain pen filled with deep green, almost black, ink.

"Did either of you see the person who signed this name?" She waved the list in front of them.

They both shook their heads.

Blake clutched the clipboard so tightly that her knuckles turned white. The comment to the side confirmed her suspicions.

"I love what you've done with the place. I enjoyed the room fragrance...was it sage? See you soon."

She hurled the clipboard, and it clanged against the wall.

"I know what you're thinking," Clint said, pulling her close. "But I'm sure there is a logical explanation. Someone else probably has the same initials and last name. Please don't worry."

No question the signature belonged to Parker. She didn't want Clint or Nancy to worry, so she forced a smile and nodded.

The sage hadn't done the trick, or at least not to the extent she had hoped. When Parker wanted to make his presence known, he didn't hold back. She balled her fists, angry with him for causing her pain both in life and after his death. He had made it clear he wasn't giving up. She would have to step up her game to fight back.

Blake needed to clear her head, so she excused herself and took Willow for a walk on the beach. The boardwalk glowed in the fading light, and the beach had begun emptying as weekend visitors handed the island back over to the locals.

Inhaling the salt air restored her soul. Shoes in hand, she walked in the lapping waves. As she trudged through the sand, someone said, "I hope you drown."

Parker sat in the lifeguard stand and staring at her with a stone-cold expression.

Blake jumped back, almost losing her balance. Willow growled and snapped in his direction. "Willow, calm down!" When Blake looked back up, Parker had vanished. A familiar-looking woman sat in his place. "Uh, do you need something?" She glared at Blake through her mirrored aviators.

"This may be a weird question, but how long have you been sitting there?"

The woman stared cooly, "Three hours. It's almost time for me to leave, though." Studying her face and long blond hair, Blake remembered she'd mistaken the same woman for Parker during her trip downtown. *Uncanny*—she looked a lot like Parker. That must be why she kept mistaking the woman for him—*just a coincidence. Get a grip, Blake.*

Blake's cheeks reddened, and she walked to the water again, the sea-foam tickling her toes. She made herself clear her head, focusing on the waves crashing before her.

Over the past several months, she had been through countless harrowing experiences. Blake hadn't done as much paranormal-related research as she wanted. No time like the present.

She sat down at the kitchen table with her phone. A loud noise interrupted her search, and she turned to see what had happened. A kitchen drawer had fallen out of the cabinetry, crashing to the floor and sending utensils in every direction. Willow stared at the base of the table where a large knife had landed. A low-pitched growl escaped her jowls.

Blake gulped. "Parker? Are you there?"

Willow, ordinarily calm, barked furiously.

A chill trickled down Blake's neck, and the hairs on her arms stood on end. The two mystery children were playing in the backyard. Why did the children appear when things went wrong?

Shaken, she cleaned up and prepared to drive to Nancy's house. But she received a call from her first guests and wedding clients. The couple had booked the property for a long weekend, starting the following day. The mother of the bride insisted the wedding party arrive a day early. Their timing couldn't be worse, but she owned a business. Scared or not, she had to take care of her customers.

Blake called Nancy and Clint, filled them in on the unsettling incident and begged them to come over to help set up for the last-minute guests. Moments later, the wedding party arrived in several large SUVs, loaded down with luggage, garment bags and clothing steamers.

Not living near the coast, the soon-to-be-married couple, Emily and Cooper, wanted to capitalize on as much beach time as they could. Blake and Nancy provided everything they needed for a fun day, including a picnic lunch and an umbrella and chairs.

After they sent their guests on their way, Clint made lunch for the ladies, and they took it outside to enjoy in the garden. Pink roses climbed the trellis beside the white iron benches where they were sitting. Willow frolicked around the yard, wagging her tail as she chased butterflies.

The serenity of the moment helped Blake calm herself. She breathed in the salty ocean air and sat down on the hammock, letting the sunshine wash over her skin. Thanks to Clint and Nancy, in their unique ways, her heart had mended. If these strange occurrences with Parker could stop, her life would be back on track, finally.

Clint came over to sit on the hammock with her, and she massaged his hand, surprisingly smooth considering the conditions he worked under as a police officer.

He grinned. “I’ve had the best day, all because it’s been with you.”

She agreed and cozied up to him, the last bit of tension in her shoulders melting away.

“I’m gonna take Willow for a walk and give you two some privacy.” Nancy winked at them as she led the dog out of the yard.

They ran into the cottage and up the stairs to her room. Clint grinned. “We’re finally together! It’s incredible.”

“We missed out on so much by being apart all those years,” Blake said.

“Oh, don’t worry. We’ll make up for lost time.” Clint kissed her sweetly and then, again, more passionately.

“I like the sound of that.” Her heart overflowed with emotion, but she didn’t want to reveal her innermost thoughts just yet.

Chapter 18

Distracted the evening of Emily and Cooper's wedding rehearsal, Blake had spent the entire day reading articles about getting rid of unwanted spirits.

Most of them centered around burning other herbs like a combination of lavender, frankincense and myrrh or asking the ghost to leave. She added them to the list of things to try after the guests left.

When everyone arrived in the garden, the officiant started the rehearsal. Cooper and Emily's exchanges were sweet and straightforward. She smiled, glad for the distraction.

After the rehearsal ended, Clint walked over to Blake and wrapped his arms around her.

"So, when are you two getting married?" Cooper winked.

"Good question." Clint gave Blake a meaningful glance. She giggled, but she could tell he was serious.

They served dinner, dessert and champagne to the wedding party and sent them on their way for a night on the town. When Nancy went to bed, Clint asked Blake to take a walk on the beach. The gentle breeze kissed her shoulders.

"The weather is perfect," Blake said.

"I couldn't agree more." Clint tilted his head toward her. The moon reflected in his eyes, and the warmth of his hand on her shoulder helped her relax.

"Blake, I missed you all the years we were apart, and I feel complete now that we're back together." Clint gazed into her eyes.

"I love you." Blake kissed him, her long, flowing hair moving with the wind. "Being with you is what I want."

"I want to be with you, too. So much that I can't imagine losing you again," Clint said. "I need to ask you an important question, even though this may not be the ideal time. I want to spend the rest of my life with you."

Clint kneeled in front of Blake, holding a beautiful but unusual ring, a princess cut diamond, flanked with a sapphire and diamond marquise stones on either side. "Will you marry me?"

Blake pursed her lips. She loved Clint and couldn't imagine living her life with anyone else. Her last engagement hadn't ended with a fairytale wedding. *Was she ready to take the plunge?*

"Clint, I…" Blake started, trembling.

"Don't feel pressured to answer me now." He put the ring box in her hand. "Keep it. We'll talk more after the wedding guests leave tomorrow."

Chapter 19

Excited to host their first wedding, Nancy and Blake set out a brunch buffet so the bridal party could eat as they had time.

The vendors began arriving and setting up. A couple of hours later, they had transformed the garden into an enchanting wedding setting.

"It's breathtaking!" Blake said, stepping into the garden as she made her way to the room where the bride and bridesmaids were getting ready.

When the photographer arrived, Blake took her to Emily.

"You are such a beautiful bride!" Blake said, picturing herself in a white dress and her grandmother's pearls.

Emily smiled. "You will be, too."

The wedding was a blur for Blake. As the ceremony played out in front of her eyes, she imagined marrying Clint. The couple had faced hardships, but they always found their way back to each other. That had to mean something.

"You may now kiss the bride," the officiant announced, bringing Blake back to reality. She scurried to make sure the caterers had set up the reception buffet in the garden.

After dinner, the bride and groom cut an elegant two-tier cake, delicately feeding each other a bite.

Not interested in a lot of dancing, Emily had opted for an alternative to the traditional reception—a private moonlit tour of the Charleston Harbor aboard a yacht.

She invited Clint, Blake and Nancy to join the wedding party for the tour. Nancy stayed home but told them to have fun. When they arrived downtown, Blake gasped at the sight of the church steeples spanning the skyline of the Holy City, named for its sheer number of churches.

"It's beautiful." Emily grinned.

"Not as beautiful as my girl." Clint stood behind Blake, wrapped his hands around her waist and kissed her cheek.

Emily gave them a knowing smile.

As they stepped onto the boat, the steward handed each of them a glass of champagne. Everyone took a seat on the deck, except for Cooper, who climbed onto a railing and began making a toast.

"Thanks to all of our friends and family who made our wedding day so incredible. Tomorrow, we leave for our honeymoon, and everyone knows what that means…"

"Okay, bud, come on down." Clint offered his hand and helped him down just as the yacht motor began purring, keeping him from falling on his face and possibly overboard.

Emily's cheeks flushed, and she took Cooper to the seat next to hers.

Clint took over the toast. "To Cooper and Emily! Thanks for trusting us with the most important day of your lives. Here's to many happy years together." Clint raised his glass, and everyone else followed.

Emily mouthed the words "thank you" and took a deep breath.

Underneath the blanket of stars, the tour guide delivered a dramatic monologue about Charleston's cobblestone streets, unique architecture and storied past.

"The beautiful oleander flower is quite poisonous and had no scent or taste. It was undetectable by medical examiners in the 1800s. The running joke was to be careful who you accepted a cup of tea from back in those days, or it might be your last."

Clint seemed to eat up this account of his hometown's history. Blake had to stifle her laughter when his amused grin faded, and he placed his finger and thumb on his chin.

After the tour guide finished his spiel, Cooper's parents asked everyone to join them inside for a surprise. Blake told Clint to go ahead. She needed to use the ladies' room on the other side of the deck.

Leaving the restroom, she began making her way across the series of wooden deck planks. The gaps between the boards started blurring. She pressed her head between her hands to right her vision and alleviate a splitting headache.

With the swell of the waves, the boat shifted onto its side. And Blake fell over the railing. Her foot became trapped underneath a trim board—the only thing standing between her and the gray, choppy water. Taking deep breaths, she told herself a powerful gust of wind had sent her tumbling, not Parker's vengeful spirit. Regardless, the more she struggled, the looser the grip of the board.

She began screaming for help; her body dangled mere feet from the swelling waves.

The door to the cabin opened. "Don't move, we're coming to help you!" Clint yelled as he and Cooper ran to her, freeing her foot and pulling her back over the railing.

Blake sat on a bench, shaking and her chest heaving.

"Are you alright? What happened?" Cooper asked. Blake stared at her feet in silence.

Clint patted Cooper on the back. "Thanks so much for helping, man. I've got it from here." Cooper frowned but nodded and walked away.

Wincing, Clint asked Blake what had happened. Tears began streaming down her cheeks before she could open her mouth to speak. He held her close and consoled her.

When the boat finally returned to the marina, Blake silently vowed not to travel by sea for a while. Her body trembled. What if Clint had not been there? Would Parker have succeeded in drowning her?

Clint drove them back to the cottage. She climbed out of the Jeep, tempted to kiss the ground. Parker had been a creep in life, but his spirit could show up in the most random places and do things Parker could not have done in his human form.

Walking into the kitchen, Blake put on a pot of decaf coffee. The crisp night air and Parker's icy grip had chilled her to the bone. She poured a cup for each of them and grabbed a handful of fresh-baked chocolate and toffee cookies.

Clint leaned over the table to kiss her on the forehead. "Are you okay? Really?"

"Yeah—It was just a shock. I guess I'd better get used to it until we figure out how to get rid of Parker."

"I'll do whatever it takes to keep you safe. I love you," Clint said. "If I didn't tell you already, you look gorgeous tonight."

"I'm glad I don't look the way I feel…exhausted," Blake said with a half-smile.

"You're the most beautiful person I've seen on the island, in South Carolina, and throughout the world." He always said the right thing, but that didn't mean she couldn't tease him.

"So now you're a world traveler."

"I could be anything as long as I'm with you." *Damn!* He led her to the bedroom, where he kissed each of her fingers delicately. The couple became intertwined, connecting on a spiritual level. Their love was more than a fleeting romance. They were more complete, more themselves together. Who could ask for more?

Chapter 20

They lay in bed together, talking, holding onto the moment as if it were the most delicate china.

"I love you," Blake said. "I want to marry you. I want to have a life together. I've never had someone support me the way you do. You have stood back and allowed me to find myself again, but you have been loving and supportive, too. I'll always be there for you."

A tear rolled down Clint's left cheek. "I'm so grateful. I love you, and I can't wait to be your husband."

Excited, he quickly jumped out of bed to retrieve the ring from Blake's vanity. Before she could scream to warn him, the solid cherry vanity mirror crashed down, striking a lamp and shattering it.

"What the…!" Clint yelled as a large shard of glass launched itself at his face, cutting his chin.

"Are you okay?" Blake asked, quickly applying pressure to the wound with a clean washcloth.

"I think so."

Once the bleeding stopped, Blake examined Clint's chin to make sure there weren't any chunks of glass inside the skin. Of course, Parker had attempted to interfere with their engagement, but she didn't want to give him the satisfaction of mentioning his name.

Nancy, who had stayed overnight to help send off their early departing guests, came and knocked on the door. "Is everything all right?"

"Yes. Sorry for the commotion," Clint said. "Everything's fine, give us a sec to clean up some broken glass. Meet us in the kitchen for tea. We'll be down in a few." His eyes met Blake's, and a smile passed between them. "We have something to tell you."

After cleaning up the glass, Clint slipped the ring onto her finger. "I have déjà vu about broken glass in this room and one of us getting injured. I would freak out, but I'm too excited."

Blake's heart danced as she held her hand out to admire the ring. "It's gorgeous. I love it." She kissed him. "Now, let's go tell Nancy!" The couple walked downstairs.

When they entered the kitchen, Nancy handed each of them a cup of tea. "So, what happened, and what's your big news?"

They told her about their engagement and how Clint had wanted to make it official by putting the ring on Blake's finger, but the freak accident with the mirror caused a little chaos.

"Well, Hell's bells, I'm sure your chin will be fine," Nancy said, beaming. "Most importantly, so will your heart. Forget the tea! This celebration calls for champagne." She retrieved a bottle of Blake's favorite bubbly from the fridge and poured each of them a glass. "To a happy future. I love you both!"

For the next hour, they discussed the future. Blake's cheeks hurt from smiling. After everything Parker had put her through, she hadn't been sure she would find love again. Clint made her happy. Nancy would always be more than an in-law. She was her second grandmother. After the excitement wore off a little, they each took turns yawning. *Time to return to bed.*

At two a.m., Emily and Cooper's parents returned to the cottage. Clint stirred when they came inside. Blake cuddled in closer, nuzzling his shoulder.

A text notification came through, but she ignored it. Soon another message came in, followed by a couple dozen more. Concerned her family might have an emergency, Blake picked up her phone off the nightstand. She had missed thirty text messages, all from Parker.

Blake gasped, and the phone slipped out of her hands, crashing onto the hardwood floors. Sweat beaded up along her brow, and she began hyperventilating.

Clint, awakened by the crash, jumped out of bed. "Blake? Blake, what's wrong?"

She reached over to pick up the phone, but it jerked back and forth, almost slipping out of her hands. Finally, she got a grip on the phone and handed it to Clint. "He's never going to leave us alone."

His skin went pale. "How could you receive one text, let alone thirty, from his phone now?"

"I have no idea," Blake whispered, pulling her knees to her chest, and her breathing turning even more shallow. "He defied the rules in life. I guess it makes sense that he will in death."

"Don't worry. I'll look into this first thing in the morning." He pulled her close to him. They lay back down in the bed but did not sleep. Clint made her promise not to read the messages until the morning, and Blake agreed they needed to maintain their composure through breakfast with their departing guests. Nauseous, she wanted to scream. Why did this have to happen? She wanted to bask in the glow of her engagement and business success, but Parker kept coming to mind.

In the morning, she threw the comforter aside and stomped across the bedroom to get dressed before walking downstairs. Blake was thankful for the flurry of activity with the wedding party packing up their belongings and preparing to leave. Once everyone had left, Clint told Nancy what had happened.

"That makes no sense at all." She held the phone out at waist length as if it had sprouted horns.

The three of them sat down at the kitchen table to flip through the messages, which were time-stamped and dated, starting with the night Blake had caught Parker with Sharon and continuing through the night he died. He must have attempted sending the first message when he arrived at their Knoxville loft after Blake had left.

Where are you? I just got home from work. I'm guessing you went out with your friends. Come home as soon as you get this.

The next day, the messages started sounding concerned. *Did you go to your parents' house? That's the only acceptable place for you to be right now. I'm not kidding. Come home now!*

Clint's jaw dropped. Tears welled up in Blake's eyes.

"No one should talk that way, especially to a woman," Clint said. "I'm not saying I'm surprised he was abusive. He tried to kill you. But I'm pissed. It doesn't do any good being angry with a ghost, but damn it, Parker! Death was too effin' good for him!"

Blake clenched her jaw as she read the remaining texts through her tear-filled eyes. The day he came to the island to find her, emotions in the texts became increasingly more intense—*Have you left me?*; *Why did you leave?*; and *Damn it! Who are you with?*

His final message: *Since you're starting a new life without me, I'll show you. Just wait.*

Blake shuddered. Parker *had* tried to reach her. *Why were the texts just now coming through to her phone? Could a ghost text*?

Clint had called in some favors with a friend who worked for the cell phone company.

"While you drove through the mountains on your way to Charleston, you lost phone signal repeatedly," Clint said, staring at his feet. "When your phone picked up a signal again, the towers redirected it to a different tower and somehow missed all the messages."

"But thirty messages?" Blake examined her phone, unsure of what she was hoping to find.

"Damn technology," Clint said, shaking his head. "Damn, Parker."

Chapter 21

After a week of Blake not talking much, Clint convinced her she needed to get away from the cottage for a few days.

"We could all use a change of scenery. Let's go to Savannah. What do you think?"

"That might help. I haven't felt like myself. I'll pack a bag. Would you mind gathering some of Willow's food and toys?" Blake asked.

"I'll take care of it right now. I love you."

Clint put the luggage into the trunk, helped Willow get settled, and put the top down on the Thunderbird. As he started driving toward 17 South, the fresh spring air helped rejuvenate Blake's soul. After the quick drive down the coast, they wandered through the town's lovely squares with Willow, taking in the flowers in bloom and the historic homes. Afterward, they enjoyed a leisurely lunch alfresco on the patio at a quaint Italian restaurant near the City Market. Their waitress brought Willow a bowl of water, and she wagged her tail in excitement.

Following lunch, the couple checked into the Marshall House, a charming boutique hotel. Clint gathered their bags while Blake took Willow for a quick walk.

They went up a flight of stairs to their room, and they opened the door to find a bottle of champagne in an ice bucket and a dozen white roses.

"What a nice surprise!" Blake kissed Clint. She forced herself to focus on the romantic scene instead of Parker.

"They must be from the hotel. I didn't order them. That is nice of them!" He popped the cork on the champagne bottle, pouring a glass for each of them. Blake opened the door to the balcony in their room so they could enjoy the sunset. He put his arm around her and kissed her forehead and lips, and Blake melted into him.

She needed to escape the anguish Parker had put her through. Sweet and loving Clint could not be more different from Parker. Clint put her needs first.

Parker had charmed her, but being with him had been like an unhealthy addiction. Everyone had loved him. Being his girlfriend had made her feel special. Living in their downtown loft, they had gone to all the best parties and events in Knoxville. Their friends had considered them a power couple, but no one had known how he treated her when they were alone.

Life with Clint would be simple and relaxing. She didn't need designer shoes or handbags to be happy any longer. She had something worth so much more.

Clint pulled her closer and embraced her. Their lips met, and he kissed her from head to toe. They made love, not thinking about anyone or anything else for hours.

After the perfect night together, they walked to the Marshall House garden piazza for a delicious breakfast. They planned to spend the day on Tybee Island. While Blake went back to their room to get Willow, Clint waited in the lobby.

When she opened the door, someone was talking to Willow. She couldn't quite make out the words. She flung the door open the rest of the way. Willow sat alone, growling, barking and staring at the sliding glass door to their balcony.

"Parker, are you out there?" No one was on the balcony. Blake checked under the bed and ran into the bathroom. He'd vanished yet again.

She grabbed hold of Willow to break her concentration on whatever had captured her attention. Once again, cold chills crept down her spine, and she began crying.

Clint came back into the room. He ran to her and wrapped his arms around her. "Blake? What is wrong?" He wiped the teardrops from her face.

"Parker was in here talking to Willow," Blake said in between sobs. "Everything I've tried to get rid of him hasn't worked. There has to be an answer." She lay back on the bed, and Willow laid next to her, with a concerned expression on her adorable, furry face.

Clint sat down at the writing desk next to the bed and picked up a white piece of paper underneath the coffee table where the roses were sitting. A card fell out of a tiny envelope.

My beautiful Blake. I knew there was someone else, but I still love you.—Parker

Chapter 22

Blake rubbed her eyes. "Let's pack up and leave. I won't be able to relax, so it defeats the purpose of this trip."

Clint nodded and pulled the car around so they could load their luggage.

During their drive back to South Carolina, Clint smacked the steering wheel. "Parker has found you wherever you've been, but let's try my place."

"It's worth a shot." Blake sighed.

Clint punched in the gate code for his neighborhood. "You're a strong woman, but Parker's spirit is trying to wreak havoc on our lives. We have to take every precaution we can. I'll have an officer watch the house."

Blake nodded, even though the officer and the gated community wouldn't provide any more protection than the cottage.

Women's voices and laughter boomed, coming from outside. *What on earth?* Blake opened the door. Nancy and Paulene were walking around the house, sprinkling a white powder, occasionally throwing some at each other.

"Hey—what are y'all doing? Is that salt?" Blake asked.

"We're forming a circle of protection. Paulene thinks it will keep the spirits away in the short-term while we find a more permanent solution." Nancy crossed her fingers.

After Paulene left, Clint and Nancy insisted Blake take some time away from running the bed and breakfast. Biting her lip, she checked their reservation calendar. They didn't have any guests arriving for a week and a half. She agreed she would not take any new reservations for that time frame, but she wanted to keep an eye on her business email for messages from guests with existing bookings.

For the next week, Blake tried to stay distracted. Clint didn't want her leaving his house without him, so she asked him to buy supplies for her to make some improvements. After their wedding, they planned to sell his home, move into the carriage house and turn the main building into a full-fledged bed and breakfast.

At the end of the week, Blake showed Clint everything she had accomplished. She had painted every room a light gray except for the kitchen, which she had painted sea-foam green to match the tile backsplash over the stove. In the bathrooms, oiled bronze fixtures replaced the shiny brass ones, and driftwood gray laminate covered the floors. She printed black-and-white copies of photos she had taken around Charleston, framing them in simple black metal frames.

"You did an incredible job. We need to stay here more often."

Blake laughed, rolling her eyes.

"It's so great hearing your laugh!" He grabbed her hand and spun her around the kitchen floor. Willow wagged her tail and smiled with her tongue hanging out of her mouth. Blake kneeled to cuddle Willow, and the dog licked her face.

They invited Nancy over for dinner. Afterward, she patted Blake's hand. "Hon, are you sure you'll be up to returning to work in time for the arrival of our guests?"

"I'll be fine," Blake said. "After the next guests leave, I have almost a week before the Nichols wedding. I need to go back to Knoxville, clean out our loft apartment and spend time with family."

"Let me go to Knoxville with you," Clint said.

"This is something I've got to do alone. Besides, I need you to take care of Willow and the B&B."

"But Parker's spirit is stalking you. I don't think you should go alone."

"Seriously, I'll be fine. I promise to check in with you and stay around my family as much as possible."

Clint shook his head. "You can be so stubborn, but I still love you."

The next day, they returned to Mason B&B to prepare the carriage house for their guests, who were arriving in two days. Nancy did the grocery shopping, and they scrubbed the cottage, floor to ceiling, and touched up landscaping here and there.

At dinnertime, Nancy insisted Clint and Blake go out to dinner without her. "You two need a romantic dinner alone before the guests arrive. Now go on, I'll take care of Willow and put fresh linens in the cottage," she said, picking up a laundry basket full of towels and shooing them out the door.

As Blake walked to Clint's car, children's laughter came from the garden. Why did they randomly appear when terrible things happened? Should they be playing at her house in the dark? She expected Parker to pop up at any moment.

Clint stared at Blake. "I love you. We'll figure out a way to send Parker packin'. I want you to be happy. That's all that matters to me."

"I love you and want you to be happy, too." Blake tried to smile. She wanted to enjoy life with Clint, but images of Parker flashed through her mind. When would this nightmare end?

Chapter 23

The afternoon sun sparkled as Blake and Nancy walked to the beach with Willow.

Blake set down her tote and slathered on some sunblock. "I want to go for a swim. Do you mind watching her?" Blake asked, handing Willow's leash to Nancy.

"No problem, hon. I brought a book, so I'll sit here and read. Have fun!"

Splashing in the saltwater revived her spirits. No matter how hard she'd tried, she had never recaptured this peaceful feeling anywhere else.

The odd sensation that someone was watching her swim overcame her, and suddenly something grazed her shoulder. A massive wave crashed over her head, pulling her underwater. Resurfacing, an enormous piece of driftwood floated beside her. *Oh, thank God!*

"On that note, it's time to get out of the water," Blake said aloud. She swam as fast as she could toward the shore, but she got pulled underwater again. This time, someone held her head underwater, not allowing her to surface. She tried not to panic, struggling to break free for what seemed like an eternity.

Finally, Blake fought her way out of her captor's hold. Her legs were tired, but she swam for her life. *Giving up is not an option! Keep going!*

As she surged her way toward the beach, Parker cackled. "Where do you think you're going? I just wanted to play. Don't worry; I won't kill you yet. You haven't suffered enough."

Terrified but determined to survive, Blake continued swimming. Reaching the shallows, she stood up and began walking. Something hit her from behind, knocking her down face-first into the sand. The ordeal had exhausted her. She sat on her knees, sank into the sand and began sobbing.

Nancy ran over to her. "What is wrong? Are you hurt?"

Blake described the struggle with Parker, and tears streamed down Nancy's face. "I'm so glad you're okay," she whispered. "You need to rest. Good gravy, what's on your hip?"

"What do you mean?" Blake struggled to look at her hip.

Nancy took a picture with her cell phone to show Blake the unusual mark. The letters "P-A-R-K-E-R" had been traced onto her back before her sunscreen had set, causing a sunburn featuring her notoriously horrible, dead fiancé's name.

"Nancy, it's pretty clear that wasn't an accident. Did you see anything strange before I got into the water?"

Her eyes widened, and she shook her head. "If Parker ever shows his face again, I'll put him in his place. I don't mean a stern talking-to. I'll put him where he belongs."

They sighed in unison, walked over to their beach chairs and sat down with Willow.

Parker's hauntings were becoming more frequent and intense, and they didn't have an answer for how to get rid of him.

Frustrated, she turned to Nancy. "How am I going to find this book? I can't keep this up."

"Hon, you've been through some traumatic events. I would put an end to Parker's miserable existence if I could, but I'm afraid we'll have to wait. We can't do anything right now. We need the book, a lunar eclipse and...your wedding."

Blake nodded, shivering. "He keeps getting stronger and more terrifying. I need Granny's book, stat!" She had searched all the bookstores in the Lowcountry and scoured the depths of the Internet, trying to find a copy of her grandmother's book, with no success. She refused to give up.

The women walked back to the cottage to clean up and start cooking. When Clint came home, they devoured dinner like they hadn't eaten all day. Willow begged for some, but Blake didn't allow her to eat table scraps, so Clint filled her food bowl with kibble, gave her fresh water and petted the sweet dog's head.

"What did you guys do today?" he asked.

"We went to the beach," Blake said, forcing a smile.

"I'm jealous. I'll change out of my uniform; then, we can walk back down there." He pulled Blake in for a kiss.

She and Nancy exchanged a knowing glance.

"What's wrong? Am I missing something?" Clint asked.

He clenched his fists in anger when Blake described the terrors she had faced on the beach.

She held him close and rubbed his shoulders. "I'm scared, but I'm okay. Try not to worry."

"That's not possible. I'm already worried. If Parker were alive, I'd arrest him. I'd feel like I had control over our safety."

"She's right, son." Nancy patted his back. "You can't control this situation. We're trying to send Parker to the Other Side. Let us do our thing."

Clint nodded and stormed out of the kitchen.

Blake grabbed a hard cider from the refrigerator and a book off the shelf in the living room. She relaxed on a plush-cushioned lounge chair and lost herself in a chapter. Out of the corner of her eye, she saw a tall shadow slinking through the garden.

She jumped up, ready to attack. She threw the door open and yelled.

"Who's out there?" Blake demanded. "What do you want?"

Clint ran outside with Willow, who began growling. He pointed his flashlight across the yard. "Blake, I don't see anything. What was it?"

"Just a shadow."

"Why don't we go inside? I'll ask an officer to hang out in the driveway overnight." While Clint texted one of his officers, he paced across the kitchen floor.

They went to bed, but Blake tossed and turned. Whose shadow had been lurking around their yard? When Clint dozed off, giggling and chatter caught Blake's attention. The mystery children were outside.

Why were their parents okay with them being out at this hour? She'd ask Clint to find their parents to ensure their wellbeing. Her staring caught the girl's eye. She curtsied, waved and ran away.

Blake's restlessness did not improve. She wrestled with a million questions. Parker didn't hesitate to show himself. And the shadow was too tall to belong to the children. Who else would wander around their yard in the dark? Why would they bother? Would he harm the children?

When she drifted off, Parker haunted her dreams. He held her like he did before their world had turned upside down, stroked her hair and held a paver up over her head. Only this time, the two children stopped him before he could harm her. They wrapped their arms around her, creating a force field. Parker collapsed and disintegrated. The wind carried off the pile of ashes.

She sat up straight in the bed, drenched in sweat. Clint stirred. She didn't want to worry him further, so she lay back down gently. The glow of the alarm clock caught her eye—only one a.m. She tossed and turned, making herself more miserable.

At six a.m., Blake showered, put Willow's leash on, wrote a note to Nancy and Clint saying she needed some air. She walked down to the beach to let go of the darkness that had consumed her, but she was too distraught to even notice the picturesque view.

After an hour, she walked back to the cottage and zoned out at the kitchen table. Clint tried to console her.

"I'm sorry, but I can't miss work today. I'm speaking at several training sessions for officers who have traveled here from across the country."

Blake overhead him talking to Nancy before he left. "Please don't leave her side today. I can tell she is having a hard time," he said.

"Sure, son. We were planning to spend the day together anyway," Nancy said.

"Thanks. If I can, I'll stop by on my lunch break, but I'll be home by 4:30 to help check in the Jacobs family."

After Clint left, Nancy patted Blake's hand and encouraged her to take a nap, reminding her they were ready for their guests, even if they arrived early. "Rest up, dear. Don't worry about anything."

"I could use some extra sleep," Blake said, walking to her bedroom.

Willow followed Blake to bed and curled up with her. At noon, they woke up refreshed. Blake showered, put on makeup and a new outfit she had picked up from a boutique in Mount Pleasant.

Clint came home at lunchtime to bring the ladies some fried chicken, okra and macaroni and cheese. "They catered the last training session, and we had tons of leftovers. I wanted to make sure you had a tasty lunch." He left and promised to return in a few hours. When he did, he brought a few colorful wildflower bouquets—one for each Blake and Nancy, and one for the kitchen table in the carriage house.

"You're too good to us." Blake grinned. Nancy agreed, patting him on the shoulder.

The Jacobs family arrived promptly at five p.m. in their minivan. Blake and Clint greeted them and helped bring their luggage.

"Text me if there's anything you need tonight. Otherwise, we'll see you at breakfast tomorrow at 8:30," Blake said.

Nancy said she needed to go home to check on her house. She hugged them and left for the evening.

Blake and Clint returned to the main house.

She poured a glass of wine and massaged her shoulders. "I'm going to take a bath."

"Enjoy a nice long soak. I might join you." Clint winked.

"Sounds nice," she said, looking him up and down before walking upstairs. She added some aromatherapy oils to her bathwater and sank into the tub, allowing every muscle in her body to relax. The tension melted away as she closed her eyes and enjoyed the lavender-scented bath oils.

She was in a Zen-like state and finding it challenging to stay awake. The Top 40 playlist on her iPod energized her, but she was so comfortable she didn't want to open her eyes.

Someone was standing over her. Her body tensed up but relaxed when Clint's lips brushed hers. She cupped his chin with her hands. The kisses became more heated and passionate. Suddenly, he bit her, and blood dribbled down her chin. She pushed him away from her and screamed, "Ow! What the…?"

Blake opened her eyes. Parker shot her a menacing smile. "No!" she cried. Her stomach churned, and a chill went through her body. She began dry heaving, positive she would throw up.

She clutched her stomach. *This can't be happening!*

Blake attempted to get out of the tub, but he knocked her down and pushed her underwater. After struggling for a few seconds, she broke loose and stood up, locking eyes with him.

"Get out of my house! Get out of my life! Go on to where you belong!" Blake picked up her glass of wine. She threw in his direction, but it went right through him, shattering against the bathroom wall.

Parker stood in front of her, sneering. "You haven't seen the last of me," he said, disappearing into thin air, but his devious laugh echoed throughout the second floor of the cottage.

Clint ran into the room and found Blake sitting on the bathroom floor, hugging her knees, crying uncontrollably. He kneeled in front of her and wrapped his arms around her.

"What's wrong? What happened? I was outside with Willow and started running as soon as I heard you scream. Please tell me you're okay," he said.

Through her sobs, she shared what had happened. Clint listened with a disturbed expression on his face but continued to hold on to her.

"No effin' way! I don't pretend to understand everything that is happening, but we'll take him down. You're strong, but all the same, I promise to do everything I can to protect you. I love you, and I hate seeing you in pain." He gently brushed her face with his hand.

He cleaned up the bite marks on her mouth, helped her slip on her robe, and she pulled her hair back into a messy bun. He led her out of the bathroom to the oversized chaise lounge on the opposite side of her bedroom. She lay down; he cuddled behind her, and they snuggled to the sound of raindrops pitter-pattering on the roof.

After she calmed down some, a suggestion she had read online for removing evil spirits from your home popped into her head.

"Do you know any preachers or priests who would bless and cleanse the cottage?" Blake asked.

Clint's eyes widened, and he shook his head.

"I'll ask our chaplain at the station. If he can't do it, he may have a friend who can. I'll talk to him tomorrow. Please try to rest. I hate seeing you this way."

He stroked her hair, and she lay silently, hoping for a miracle.

Chapter 24

After work the next day, Clint told Blake the chaplain had recommended a local preacher who had experience in ridding homes of unwanted spirits.

"I've already called him. He'll come over after the Jacobs family checks out."

Embracing Clint from behind, Blake rested her head on his back. "Thank God!" She was hopeful for the first time in weeks. "Paulene may have some ideas for ways to help. I'll chat with her later."

Nancy entered the house, her eyes glowing. "You two look cozy, and I couldn't be happier." She started making coffee and grabbed a pitcher of orange juice.

Blake smiled. "Clint found a preacher who will bless the house."

"Oh, I'm so glad to hear that. I hope he can help." Nancy pushed the cart into the garden.

The Jacobs family came outside. Seven-year-old Sarah folded her arms across her chest and stuck out her pouty lower lip.

"What's the matter, sweetie?" Nancy asked, stifling a laugh.

"I wanted my new friend to spend the night with me!" Sarah said in a shrill voice.

"Did you meet your friend at the beach?" Blake smiled.

"No. In the garden. My friend was swinging over there," Sarah said, pointing at the tire swing.

Melissa Jacobs kneeled to talk to her daughter. "I don't know her parents, honey, and I didn't want anyone to worry about her." Turning toward Blake, Melissa asked, "Is the girl a relative or friend of yours?"

"No. She and some other neighborhood kids come to play on the tire swing. Nancy? Do you know the girl's parents?" Blake put her hands on her hips and cocked her head.

Nancy wrung her hands nervously, appearing to want to dodge the question. "Oh dear, I forgot I put a batch of biscuits in the oven. I need to run in and grab them. Be right back."

Clint prepared to leave for work, said goodbye to everyone and kissed Blake on the forehead. The Jacobses asked for information on some local attractions and restaurants. Blake recommended visiting Charlestown Landing Historical Site, thinking the children would enjoy walking through the nature preserve and zoo, and the adults would like the history exhibits.

After the Jacobs family set out for their day, Blake and Nancy went to Sullivan's Island with Willow for lunch. Luckily, they had gotten their pet license for Sullivan's earlier that year, which allowed the pup to be on the island. They walked onto the beach near the lighthouse and snapped a few photos of her frolicking through the sand. Blake waded into the ocean, ankle-deep, laughing and smiling.

Nancy smiled back at her, patting Willow on the head. Blake walked back, and they headed to Poe's Tavern for burgers. They sat down at a picnic table, and a server brought them menus and a water bowl for Willow.

"The burgers smell incredible," Blake said, her stomach rumbling. "It has been years since I've been here."

"I've already said it, but I'll repeat it—I'm so glad you're back with us," Nancy said, holding Blake's hands in hers.

"I'm glad to be with you and Clint again, too. My life is back on track. All that's left is to get rid of Parker. Hopefully, one of Granny's books will turn up soon." Blake said.

After paying for their lunch, they went shopping. Blake had not regretted leaving the corporate world one bit. The career and lifestyle change meant she needed to revamp her wardrobe. She'd spend one day of her Knoxville trip cleaning out the closets at the loft apartment and donating most of her and Parker's clothing to Knox Area Rescue Ministries, a charity in Knoxville. His father served on the board and would approve of her sending his son's belongings there.

The women took turns trying on outfits and sitting with Willow. Hours later, they filled the trunk and backseat of Nancy's car with shopping bags.

"I'm glad we didn't bring my car." Blake laughed, imagining the bags toppling out of the back of the convertible on the drive home. Nancy chuckled too.

When they returned home, Clint handed each of them a frozen margarita. They took their drinks to the screened-in porch and followed them up with three rounds of Scrabble. The Jacobs family was returning home from their fun-filled day and asked if they could join.

"Sure. Make yourselves comfortable. I'll get some chairs," Clint said. When he returned, the game started up again, and they tried to best each other for the next couple of hours.

"*Perp* isn't an actual word, Clint!" Blake laughed.

"Well, I let you get away with *selfie*."

Everyone laughed and teased each other. At the end of the evening, the Jacobs family thanked them and returned to the carriage house.

Blake and Clint cleaned up the screened-in porch while Nancy made some chamomile tea.

They sat down in the kitchen to relax and catch up on each other's news. After talking about everything from friends' babies being born to new officers joining Clint's team, they began talking about the minister blessing the cottage.

"Prayer is always worth trying. I'm a believer, but it may take something more aggressive to get rid of this spirit," Nancy said.

"What do you suggest?" Blake asked.

"Let's see what happens after the minister leaves. We'll hope and pray he can solve all of our problems."

Blake told Clint to go to bed without her. He had to work the next day, and she didn't want to keep him awake. She paced the kitchen floor. Where else could she search for the book? Antique stores—why hadn't she thought of that yet? They were a dime a dozen in Charleston. The book's contents must be powerful. After all, she had gone her entire life oblivious to them.

Blake cozied up in the living room with Willow, and for the next three hours, searched furiously for stores that carried used books. She bookmarked some pages to check into the next day and researched ways to get rid of Parker. Ads for holy water, rosaries and cross pendants popped up on her phone. She giggled but considered their potential usefulness. It wouldn't hurt to prepare.

Later that afternoon, she left for a networking event for small business owners at Patriots Point Park. When Blake took a few photos for her social media feeds, orbs floated in the background. She shook it off as dust on the camera or lens flare.

Before leaving the event, she said goodbye to her newfound friends and invited them to stop by the cottage for coffee sometime. She walked back to her car, grateful for the beautiful star-filled sky overhead and the opportunity to drive with the convertible top down on her way home.

She took the scenic route back to Isle of Palms and followed Coleman Boulevard toward the ocean. Traffic was light. Just before the bridge, crossing over to Sullivan's Island, a stray raindrop pelted her forehead. A lightning bolt struck a few miles away. She pulled over to pull up the top on the Thunderbird.

Just as she climbed back into the car, the sky opened up, and rain began pouring down onto the concrete.

Headlights of an approaching car made it almost impossible to see through the windshield. Blake squinted, unable to see the lines. The other vehicle was less than a car length away, heading straight for the Thunderbird.

"What in the hell?" Her head throbbed, and blood pulsated through her veins. She swerved onto the embankment, and the other driver veered in the same direction.

Blake held her breath, waiting for impact. When nothing happened, she opened her eyes. The car had disappeared. Her jaw dropped, and she slammed her hands into the steering wheel, screaming, "Damn you, Parker!"

She growled and gripped the steering wheel, swerving onto the shoulder to collect herself. After making sure nothing was coming, she pulled back onto the road.

The rain let up, helping make the rest of her drive home more pleasant. But she fumed. Parker had a knack for causing disasters. She wanted to move on to her new life and couldn't wait to leave her old one behind.

Something drew her attention to the rearview mirror as she pulled into the driveway. *Well, shit.* Moving on wouldn't happen tonight. A message—*Don't worry. I'm still here*—appeared in the condensation on her rear windshield.

Blake grabbed her purse and ran inside. Clint and Nancy were waiting for her in the kitchen.

"What happened? Are you upset?" Clint reached out for her.

"Parker strikes again." Blake filled them in on the details and crossed her arms, trying to comfort herself.

"I haven't figured out how yet, but we'll get rid of him once and for all," Clint said. "It pisses me off how he hurts and frustrates you."

Blake's jaw dropped. As the police chief, Clint hadn't threatened to harm a living criminal, at least not around her. This case was personal, and Clint would stand by his word to do whatever it took. She rubbed her head and popped one of her abortive migraine pills into her mouth.

Suddenly, Parker appeared in the kitchen.

"Challenge accepted." He laughed.

"Leave him alone! Your beef is with me, Parker!" Blake stared at him. He pushed her, and she fell onto the floor.

Clint's veins in his forehead pulsated. He balled his fists.

"Never push a lady!" Clint said through clenched teeth and helped Blake to her feet. "You won't hurt her ever again. Got it? You had your chance to be with her, but you failed. You broke her heart and ran her off from your home. Thank God you're dead; you have a second chance to stop disappointing her. She's here with me now."

Parker stood quietly for a few moments.

"You can see me?"

Clint nodded, balling his fists. "I sure can. Her love for me gave me the gift to see you, so we can have each other's backs. Now, how about you disappear?"

"She was mine first," Parker spat.

Clint put his hand out to silence him.

"That's where you're wrong. I've loved Blake as long as I can remember. You can't come between us."

"And that's where you're mistaken. Blake left you fifteen years ago." Parker flashed a devilish sneer. "I gave her a life you can't. With me, she had everything—designer shoes, a fancy loft apartment and a social life that a Kardashian would kill for. She wouldn't have left except she got jealous of Sharon, who meant nothing to me."

Clint jumped toward Parker but grunted when he fell through the apparition, and Parker laughed.

"You're not funny!" Blake yelled.

Determined to get Parker out of their hair, she opened the Bible app on her phone and began reading.

"The light shines in the darkness, and the darkness has not overcome it." John 1-5.

He faded slightly, but before disappearing completely, he brushed her cheek with his hand.

Clint rushed to her side. "Are you okay?"

Blake nodded and breathed a sigh of relief.

"The nerve of that asshole!" Clint stomped off to the kitchen and stood in front of the open refrigerator for a few moments before grabbing a beer.

"How do you deal with his B.S. all the time?"

"I guess I'm getting used to it, as much as a person can." Blake sighed. "I've been doing a bunch of research trying to figure out a way to get rid of him. Reading the Bible alone isn't enough to get rid of an evil presence, but hopefully, the preachers will have an idea for a more permanent fix."

Clint pulled her into his arms and held her tight to his chest. "They've been dealing with paranormal stuff for a long time. But if they're not able to help us, we'll figure something out. There has to be something we haven't uncovered yet. Keep researching. Stay aware and strong. Don't let Parker wear you down."

"I wouldn't give him the satisfaction." Blake gritted her teeth. Parker thought he had the upper hand, but she would show him. It might take a few tries, but eventually, he would regret the day he crossed her.

Chapter 25

The rest of the week disappeared. After breakfast each day, the Jacobs family had entertained themselves, sometimes asking for dining recommendations but not much more.

On the last night of their trip, Blake invited them for a Lowcountry boil in the garden, followed by a couple of rounds of board games. They happily accepted the invitation.

"That sounds like fun! I've been looking for something to do with the kids tonight. Both of them got sunburns today. We reapplied sunscreen once an hour, but they were in and out of the water so much," Melissa said.

"Poor kiddos. That's rough," Blake said. "If you haven't already found it, there is some aloe in the bathroom cabinets. Please help yourselves. We'll have dinner ready around 6:30, and we can play a few rounds of games."

They had another fun, laughter-filled evening with the Jacobses. The children fell asleep during the last round of Clue.

Melissa groaned. "It's probably time for us to turn in since we're hitting the road early tomorrow.

"What time do you guys want breakfast?" Blake helped her gather up the kids' toys.

"If you have a snack we can eat in the car and want to bring it over tonight, that will be fine. We're leaving around five a.m., and I don't want to ask you to get up that early."

Blake put some homemade muffins and fruit into a tote bag and took it over to the carriage house patio, where Melissa was standing.

"I didn't want to say anything because I completely dismissed it until last night. All week, Nate kept describing a tall shadow walking around outside his window," Melissa said. "I thought he was making up a story, but I dozed off in his bed while reading him a book last night. When I woke up, I saw a shadow. It would disappear and come back as if someone were walking circles around the carriage house."

Blake sat down on the steps to the carriage house and put her head into her hands.

"I'm sorry. I didn't mean to frighten you, but you may want to keep an eye out for anyone who is lurking around your property at night."

Blake forced a smile and thanked her. "I'll have Clint post an officer outside the carriage house tonight. I don't like the idea of anyone being on the property or around our guests."

Roger, an Isle of Palms deputy, arrived and set up on the screened-in porch at the main house, saying it would be more inconspicuous than having an officer standing in front of the carriage house. Blake thanked him and gave him a key in case he needed to come into the house for anything.

She walked upstairs to go to bed. Nancy and Clint were already asleep. Blake shivered, thinking about the intruder lurking in the garden.

Once again, she tossed and turned. Sighing, she pulled herself out of bed and looked out the window. The moon perched just above the canopy of oaks. The beautiful view soothed her, and she returned to bed. Cuddling with Clint, she snuggled closer, grateful for the second chance to spend her life with him. She put her arms around his waist, and he held her hand the entire night.

The following morning, she woke up after Clint had already left for work. The chaplain and minister would meet Clint at the police station at lunchtime and ride to the cottage with him. Nancy drank coffee while watching television in the kitchen. Blake poured a mug of coffee and grabbed a muffin to take to Roger.

"Thanks. Unfortunately, I didn't see anything. I expected to find a teenager trying to break into the shed to smoke a joint, but I didn't even see a squirrel." Roger took his hat off and scratched his head.

"Thank you so much for staying. If you want more muffins or coffee, you're welcome to come inside the house," Blake said, gesturing toward the kitchen.

"I appreciate it, but I need to go back to the station before I go home."

She and Nancy busied themselves with picking up the cottage, and just as they finished, the doorbell rang. They welcomed Paulene, whose eyes darted around the living room.

"Could I talk to you before the preachers get here?" Paulene asked.

"Sure. Let's go sit down in the kitchen and drink a glass of sweet tea," Blake said.

As she filled three glasses, Nancy pushed a crystal platter of her decadent chocolate chip cookies in front of Paulene. "What's on your mind?"

"You know how some religious people don't take stock in seeing or talking to spirits?"

Blake and Nancy nodded.

"Well, I won't mention hauntings or being gifted while the preachers are here. I want to respect their beliefs, but I'll pay attention to the strength of the spirit's presence. I'll weigh in after they leave."

Blake heard the front door open, and Nancy and Paulene followed her to the living room, where Clint stood with two men, one in his early 60s with gray hair and the other in his late 40s with dark but thinning hair. Both were wearing suits and carrying Bibles. Clint introduced everyone, and Chaplain McGreary, the elder of the two, explained his friend's expertise.

"Rev. Phillips has been blessing homes in the Lowcountry since he was old enough to read a Bible. His father was a pastor, too."

"Can you tell me why this spirit's hanging around?" the reverend asked.

"He's my former fiancé. He tormented me while he was living. I guess that's his unfinished business. He wants to stay here and drive me crazy," Blake said.

He gave a slight nod, adjusted his glasses, flipped through his Bible for a few moments and began reading.

"*Even though I walk through the valley of the shadow of death, I'll fear no evil, for you're with me; your rod and your staff, they comfort me.*" Psalms 23:4.

"Heavenly Father, bless this home and family. Give the unsettled spirit the peace he needs to move on from his earthly home to his final destination, in Jesus name we pray, amen."

Everyone looked around the room as if they expected a sign it had worked.

Blake exhaled and broke the silence. "How will we know he's gone?"

"Every spirit's different, but in my experience, if a cleansing hasn't taken hold, it will be clear within a few days," the reverend said.

"Is there anything else we should do?" Blake asked.

"No, I'm afraid we'll have to wait and see what happens. Try to stay positive and put this in God's hands. Should you need protection from him again, try reading from the Bible, any verse that brings peace to your mind and heart will do."

Blake nodded and thanked him for coming to the cottage. Clint handed the chaplain his Jeep key and told him to start the car; he needed to talk to Blake for a moment.

"It may be too soon to predict how things will play out, but how are you feeling?"

"The reverend has a lot of experience getting rid of ghosts, so I'm optimistic," Blake said. "Paulene, do you think we were successful today?"

Paulene closed her eyes and lifted her hands into the air. She held her hand to her heart and stood still. Upon opening her eyes, she shook her head.

"He isn't here now. I'll pray he doesn't return."

"Thank you for supporting us today. It means a lot. I hope you'll come back and hang out with us again soon," Blake said.

After Paulene left, Blake pulled a blue quilted overnight bag out of the living room coat closet.

"Now that the preacher has blessed the house, I need to get ready to leave for Knoxville. I'll pack today and leave tomorrow."

Clint said goodbye and returned to work.

Nancy handed her a glass of iced tea. "Do you need help packing?"

"No, thanks. I'm not taking much with me. I'll only be away for a couple of days," Blake said. "I do have a question, though. Do you mind taking care of Willow while I'm gone?"

"Sure, hon. Willow is no problem at all. I'll take her to my house while you're away. Clint will be around, so I can always bring her over here. Don't worry about a thing."

"Thanks so much!" Blake threw a few outfits and some sandals into her overnight bag.

That evening Clint, Blake and Nancy played cornhole in the backyard and teased each other.

"You shuck at cornhole," Clint said.

"Tell me what I'm doing wrong. I'm all ears," Blake bantered back.

Nancy giggled. "You two are so corny! What a fun night! We should do this more."

They both agreed, and Clint asked them if they were up for having a drink at one of the local beach bars.

"You two go ahead. I'm too tired. I'm gonna go crash," Nancy said.

They said goodnight and hopped into Clint's Jeep to drive into downtown Isle of Palms. The warm but breezy evening refreshed her soul. When Clint parked the car, she leaned over to kiss him, and she relaxed. They jumped out of the Jeep and walked up a flight of stairs that led to an oceanfront bar and restaurant.

A server took them to a table, and they ordered drinks.

"Have you ever been paddleboarding? I've always wanted to try it, but I'm pretty clumsy." Blake laughed.

"Yeah, one of my buddies took me one time. I was terrible at it. I kept falling off." Clint grinned.

"Oh, good. We should try it together sometime. There's no way I can be as bad as you," Blake said in a devious tone.

"I thought Southern girls were sweet." Clint tickled her side, and they laughed.

"Oh, we are, but we can be a little salty, too."

The server arrived with their drink order and with a sour expression on her face. When she turned away, the couple started laughing even harder.

After they finished their drinks, they went for a walk on the beach and embraced by the shoreline. While kissing, desire overcame Blake. She caught her breath. Clint stared at her and ran his hand from her waist to her thigh, causing her to moan. He grabbed her hand, and they ran back to the Jeep. He sped to the cottage, where he picked her up, carried her to their room and fulfilled her every need.

She lay in bed, holding her sweet fiancé, not wanting to leave him.

The next morning, Blake embraced Nancy and kneeled to love on Willow one last time before she left. Clint had already left for work, so she called him to ask if he had time to meet at a new cafe that had recently popped up on the island. She ordered each of them a cup of coffee and a croissant breakfast sandwich and sat down at one of the wooden picnic tables outside the restaurant.

Clint joined her a few minutes later.

"I'm so glad you could meet me before I got on the road," Blake said, reaching for his hand.

"I wouldn't have missed it. Call me anytime if you feel like your safety is in jeopardy."

"I'll be fine. Don't worry." She kissed him.

"I love you. I haven't left yet, but I can't wait to be back already." She climbed into her car and waved.

Chapter 26

The playlist Clint had created for Blake's road trip helped her get through the journey without making one stop.

She sang along to hits from the '80s and tried to ignore the lump in her throat as she drove past the interstate exit she usually took to go to her and Parker's loft apartment and went straight to her parents' house in West Knoxville.

"Blake! I'm so excited you're here!" her mom hugged her.

"Glad to see you, too! Where's Dad?" Blake asked.

"He's working, but he'll be around for the rest of your visit. Now, come on, I want to hear how things are going with Clint and your business."

Blake told her about the wedding and the guests they had hosted so far at the B&B, sharing how helpful Nancy and Clint were day-in and day-out.

"I can't imagine running the business without them. I love them both dearly," Blake said.

"Clint, especially?" her mom asked, jokingly.

Blake rolled her eyes. "I should've been with him all along. I couldn't be happier."

Her mom grabbed her hand to inspect the engagement ring. “It’s striking, but not cookie-cutter. When are we going wedding dress shopping?”

“We haven’t set a date yet, but when we do, we can start planning and shopping,” Blake said, playing with her ring.

“Sounds great.” Her mother smiled.

Blake and her mom began cooking dinner so it would be ready by the time her father got home from work. He came into the house carrying a strawberry pie from the Buttermilk Pie shop, Blake’s favorite Knoxville dessert.

“Thanks, Dad.” She wrapped her arms around him. “I can’t wait to dig into that pie. I’ve missed you!”

He smiled and helped Susan dish out spaghetti and meatballs for the three of them. During dessert, Blake caught her dad up on a lot of the same things she had discussed with her mom. She’d missed them since moving to the island, but she didn’t regret her decision.

The next day, Brittany, her youngest sister, returned home from college for the weekend.

Walking into the house, Brittany dropped her tote bag in the foyer and ran to her sister. “Oh my God, Blake! You’re here!” she signed, embracing Blake and jumping up and down.

Brittany, the youngest, was excelling in her senior level interior design classes and had a job offer at a design firm in Atlanta for when she graduated the following May. She and Ryan, her high school boyfriend, were engaged, but they hadn’t set a date, just in case she went to grad school instead of taking a job right away.

“Let’s have a double wedding,” Blake teased her sister, who had always demanded to have her own place in life, not to live in anyone’s shadow.

“As if.” Brittany rolled her eyes and laughed.

The sisters climbed into Blake’s car, and she drove them to the loft apartment. She shivered, unsure of how to react to being back inside the apartment where she and Parker had lived. No one had moved her belongings since she’d left. A wave of nausea threatened to take hold, but she didn’t want to worry Brittany.

The sisters went through her closet, saving two suits and a handful of business and cocktail dresses, which would be more than enough to get her through the formal events she would attend in a year in South Carolina. They piled the rest of the business and dressy items into a donation pile. Next, she went through her casual wardrobe, realizing even those items were too formal for her life on the island. She kept some swimsuits, a few pairs of jeans and T-shirts. The rest needed to go.

Then came the dreaded task of going through Parker's things. *Ugh!* She didn't want to touch his belongings, but she wanted this process to end as soon as possible. She called his father and asked if he would have time to go through the items before she donated anything to make sure she hadn't missed something sentimental. He said he was out of town but gave her permission to donate his clothing and drop off valuable and sentimental items with Will on her way home. She told him she would take care of everything.

Brittany wanted her furniture, linens and kitchen goods, so they hired movers to take it to their parents' house for storage until she bought a house. The movers offered to drop the clothing and other items they were donating to the rescue ministry. Blake agreed, tipped them and sent them on their way. Brittany rode with the movers in case their parents weren't home.

After her sister left, Blake's hands trembled. She quickly packed up Parker's remaining belongings into a small box. A pang of sadness pulled at her heart. Did a person's life only amount to a Kindle, a laptop, four concert T-shirts and some family photos?

She stumbled across a photo of the two of them hiking in the Blue Ridge Mountains. Tears welled up inside, but she pushed them back down. Blake's stomach rumbled again, and she ran to the bathroom to throw up. Dizzy and her head pulsating, she walked back to the living room. Even though no open windows were open, a cool breeze swept through the room.

"Welcome home. I always loved that picture." Parker appeared next to the fireplace. "I died close to that trail. I go there all the time. Why don't we go for a hike together, now? You could die there, too, and we could be together forever!"

He moved closer to her and put his hand under her chin. She jumped backward.

"I'm not going anywhere with you, my greatest mistake," she hissed. "I'm reclaiming my life, my independence. You can't control me anymore! I'm getting rid of your crap, and I'm getting rid of you!"

"Oh, you'll never get rid of me." Parker laughed. "I'll kill everyone you love. Then, you'll want to die, too. I'll be seeing you real soon."

Blake screamed in frustration as he disappeared. Maybe the reverend's blessing only covered the cottage, or worse, it didn't work at all. Determined to leave the apartment, she grabbed the box of his belongings. Locking the door, she breathed a sigh of relief, glad never to return.

She loaded her car and laid her head on the steering wheel. Shaking, she drove back to her parents' house to find her family waiting for her at the dinner table. Not wanting to worry them, she swallowed her emotions and forced a smile. How would they react if they learned the extent of Parker's haunting? Her Sociology 101 professor hadn't covered this; she wasn't sure of the etiquette.

Relax. Blake had so little time with her family since moving to the island. Despite being stressed when she arrived, as the evening went on, she found herself laughing while playing cards, watching old family movies and making homemade ice cream. Spending time with her family warmed her heart and comforted her. She would deal with Parker soon enough.

Chapter 27

The next day, Blake loaded up her car and said goodbye to her parents and Brittany.

"I'll miss you guys, but I'm so happy on the island. Come see me soon."

"We're so proud of you, and we love you. Be careful," Jeremy said. "Call us when you make it back home."

"Thanks, Dad. Love you." Blake climbed into her car, setting course for Will's cabin in Asheville.

The box with Parker's belongings lay beside her on the passenger seat. She shivered, texting Will—*I'm on my way*. How did Will turn out to be such a nice guy? His brother had been abusive in life and after death. *Once an asshole, always an asshole*.

A rainstorm started thirty miles away from the Tennessee-North Carolina state line. She stopped in Newport to put the top up on the Thunderbird, fuel up her car. While pumping gas, she saw her reflection in a shiny silver SUV parked at the pump next to hers, and she almost screamed. She smoothed her windblown ringlets and pulled them into a bun on top of her head.

The driver of the SUV appeared out of nowhere. Blake jumped and laughed at herself for being so easily startled. The driver of the SUV probably laughed at her expense. Their Smoky Mountain

College vanity plate reminded her of the many weekends she had spent visiting friends at the small liberal arts school.

After running into the convenience store to buy refreshments, she was on her way again. Driving through the steep mountainous, winding road, she caught glimpses of the SUV in her rearview mirror.

She queued up her college favs playlist and began singing along with hits by Katy Perry and Rihanna. After taking the I-26 East split, she veered right and took the Blue Ridge Parkway exit and followed the narrow, curvy road to Will's cabin. Wildflowers dotted the edge of the road, painting the way with their colorful hues.

When she arrived, Will handed her a glass of sweet tea. "I'm so grateful that you're happy and healthy after everything Parker put you through." He paused. "I probably shouldn't say this now that he's gone, but I've always wondered how he swooped you up in the first place."

"He had a way about him," Blake said.

Will nodded. "Indeed, he did."

They chatted for an hour. When Blake checked the time, she got up out of her chair.

"I'm sorry, but I have to leave. We have guests arriving at the B&B tomorrow."

He gave her a thermos filled with the remaining tea and some sandwiches he had made for her drive home. "Please say you'll come back. I'd looked forward to having you as a sister, and I hope you don't mind me considering you as one," Will said, putting his arm around her.

"Of course not! You're family. Come to the island to visit us sometime. Take care of yourself."

She drove back down the winding mountain road to get back on I-26. A few minutes into her drive, the silver SUV with the Smoky Mountain College license plate appeared in the rearview mirror.

What are the odds of running into them again?

She pulled on some wayfarer sunglasses, adjusting the rearview mirror. The driver began following a bit too closely, giving the Thunderbird not-so-gentle taps. Blake sped up, and the other driver matched her speed. She tried to identify them, but they were wearing a black hoodie and sunglasses. She couldn't make out the details of their appearance.

Taking her eyes off the road for a moment too long, Blake swerved to miss a deer crossing the street. Her heart palpitated as the animal ran to safety. She checked her rearview mirror. The other driver had swerved onto the shoulder. *This is my chance to get away*. She drove as fast as she could without wrecking. The Thunderbird hugged the curves tightly. Just when Blake thought she had escaped, the silver SUV crested the top of a hill.

"Oh, no!" she cried.

The road straightened as she approached the interstate on-ramp. With no other cars in sight, she ran a stoplight and sped up onto the interstate. She checked her mirrors. The driver of the SUV hadn't caught up yet. Not wanting to take a chance, she held steady at seventy-five miles an hour, the old V-8 engine roaring in protest. Her hands were shaking, gripping the steering wheel as she used her hands-free calling phone app to call Clint.

"This driver in a silver SUV with a Smoky Mountain College vanity plate has been chasing me through the mountains in Asheville. I'm on I-26 now. I'm driving to the Asheville Police Department. If they catch up with me again, I'm sure they won't want to stop there," Blake said.

"You're doing the right thing. Just be careful. I wish I were with you. I'll stay on the phone with you until you get there."

Suddenly, the SUV slammed into the Thunderbird's bumper. She screamed.

"What happened? Are you okay?" Clint asked nervously.

Blake eyed her rearview mirror. "I'm okay. The driver of the silver SUV just rammed my car. I'm so pissed off!" she exclaimed.

Soon, the SUV slammed into her car again. Thankfully, her vintage vehicle weighed more than the newer model SUV. The driver's last attempt to run her off the road resulted in the opposite of the desired effect. Instead of Blake wrecking her car, the silver SUV flipped onto its top.

"Clint, I have to go. The other driver flipped their vehicle," she said in a panic.

"Be careful! I love you."

"I love you," Blake said, hanging up with Clint and calling 9-1-1 to report the incident.

"Usually, we ask all parties to remain onsite until emergency crews arrive. However, you should get away from the other driver as soon as possible." The emergency dispatcher explained how to get to the nearest police department. "Please drive there right away."

Despite the driver's attempts to run her off the road, she couldn't leave someone to die. Against her better judgment, she pulled over to the side of the road and walked back to the SUV. As she got closer, she scanned the scene. The driver was unconscious, but she grabbed her can of mace just in case that changed.

Blae paused for a moment. She should follow her impulse to return to her car and drive away, but she would regret not taking this opportunity to save someone's life.

"Well, here goes," Blake said.

Balling her fists, she walked toward the SUV, noticing the window glass had busted out. Blake reached into the car and pulled the sunglasses off the driver's face, revealing their identity.

"Sharon!"

Soon, Sharon's eyes opened and widened. Sirens drowned out Blake's scream of surprise, and Sharon fell unconscious once again.

Chapter 28

When the EMTs arrived, they insisted Blake go to the hospital. She agreed after protesting for a few minutes.

At the hospital, the paramedics wheeled her into an examination room. An officer paced the floor, waiting to talk to her. She groaned silently.

"Miss, please describe the accident from your point of view." Officer James Branson asked.

"Sure. It was more than just an accident—Sharon followed me for an hour today." Blake's hands and voice shook as she filled him in on the details.

"Why would Ms. Johnson want to follow you? What is your relationship?" he asked.

"She was my boss. I worked for her for six years. Almost a year ago, I discovered she was having an affair with my fiancé, Parker Sutton. Two weeks afterward, he died in a wreck just a few miles away from here. I hadn't seen her since I left Knoxville."

"Do you know why she attempted running you off the road?"

Blake took a deep breath. "Since Parker died, someone has been sending me texts, flowers and champagne. I can only guess it was her, but I'm unsure why she would bother now that he is dead."

Officer Branson thanked her, gave her his card and asked her to follow up with him if she thought of anything else relevant.

Blake had forgotten to call Clint back. She picked up her phone—nine texts and five calls from Nancy and Clint. At that moment, her phone rang.

"Where are you? Are you okay?" Clint's voice shook.

Still shaking, she rattled through the details of the wreck and asked him to call Nancy and her mom.

"Are you sure you're okay? Do you want me to drive there?"

"No, that's okay. My nerves are a little shot, but I'll be alright. The doctor should release me within the next couple of hours. The police have asked me to stay in town until tomorrow just in case they have additional questions. Would it bother you if I called Will and asked to stay with him?"

"Go wherever you feel the safest, and don't worry about the guests arriving tomorrow. Mom and I've got it covered," Clint said. "I'll ask her to get some of her friends to come help, just in case we need them. Please text me when you get back to Will's place."

After being examined by the doctor and receiving a clean bill of health, she called Will, who welcomed her to come back to stay.

She ended their call and breathed a sigh of relief, happy to stay with a friend. Blake was ready to leave the hospital. But the police officer who had been sitting outside of Sharon's room got up and walked into the nearby restroom. Adrenaline racing through her veins, she opened the door. Sharon was lying on the bed. Blake closed the door behind her, and Sharon's eyes opened wide.

Blake took a step backward, hitting her hip on the doorknob.

"Did you come to finish me off?" Sharon asked through clenched teeth.

"You're the one who tried to run me off the road. Your plan just backfired, right?" Blake's voice grew louder, and she placed her hands on her hips.

"You think you're so perfect, Blake. Your curls and syrupy sweet smile are enough to make me want to barf."

"Why did you try to make me wreck?"

"Because it's your turn to die!" Sharon screamed. "I'm waiting for you. We can be together again, my Blake. I want our souls to be together."

Sharon's pinched face transformed into a familiar wicked smile. She had cheated with Parker, but she wasn't intentionally cruel. Blake's pulse sped up. An ice pick headache drilled through her skull, and her heart raced. She tried to calm her nerves by taking soothing breaths.

No question about it, she wasn't talking to Sharon; she was looking into Parker's eyes.

She took a calculated step backward. "We wouldn't be together, Parker! I know where I'll go when I die, and I certainly wouldn't expect to find you there. You've made your bed. Now you will have to lie in it, alone."

"That's where you're wrong, Blake! I'll find a way for us to be together forever."

With Sharon's lips curled devilishly, she pointed at Blake and began hissing. She rose to her knees and held her arms over her head. Suddenly, her body started shaking violently and went limp and lifeless, collapsing onto the mattress. The rhythmic beeping of the heart monitor stopped. Blake gasped and screamed, "Parker, you allow Sharon to come back into her body right now!" No response. "Damn you, Parker!"

Trembling and numb, Blake ran through the door to the nurse's station to tell them Sharon had died. She stood in the hallway as the nurses attempted to revive Sharon. Blake stared into space, saying a silent prayer for Sharon. The officer returned with a cup of coffee in hand.

A nurse asked, "Did anything happen before she died?"

"No. I was talking to Sharon, and then she was gone," Blake lied. No one would believe her if she shared the truth.

The officer locked eyes with her as he assessed her statement. He seemed to accept it but asked her to stop by the station the following day for an official statement. He offered to take her back to the police station to get her car. Blake nodded and thanked him. On the way there, she wept. Parker had used Sharon, draining the last bit of life she had left. How many people's lives would Parker ruin?

On the way to Will's house, Blake called Clint to describe the evening's bizarre, frightening events, Blake sighed.

"So, what can we do next?" Clint asked. "I'll call the reverend and see if he has any advice."

"That's a good idea. Nancy knows more than she has let on. Try prying more information out of her."

"Easier said than done. Nancy Parsons is one stubborn lady when she sets her mind to it," he said. "Hey, be careful on your way home tomorrow."

By the time Blake got to Will's house, he had baked a homemade pizza for her and laid out some clean towels in the guest bedroom. "If you want to get cleaned up, I'll finish up your dinner and find some wine to go with the pizza."

"You're an amazing friend. Thanks for everything," Blake said.

"It's nothing. I'm happy to help."

As she ate dinner, Will asked her about her life with Clint.

"We've had a rough start, but he has been beyond supportive," Blake said.

"I've been worried since everything that happened with Parker. I'm glad you have found someone who makes you happy. You deserve the best."

Blake thanked him for dinner and allowing her to stay with him and said goodnight. She climbed into the bed in the guest bedroom and slept peacefully.

The next morning, Will cooked breakfast for them, setting out juice, biscuits, homemade strawberry preserves and thick-cut bacon. Resting and eating made all the difference in regaining her strength.

"Do you want me to go to the police department with you?" Will offered.

"It's sweet of you to offer, but I need to do this on my own. Plus, I'm hoping I can head back to South Carolina after I talk to the officers this morning," Blake said.

"I completely understand. Call me if you end up needing to stay here again tonight. I'm just glad you didn't get hurt in the accident."

Pulling out of the driveway, she thought about Parker's most recent intimidation attempt. She would never forget the sound of Sharon's SUV flipping onto its top or the moment she pulled off Sharon's sunglasses to reveal her identity.

Blake pulled up to the police department. Officer Branson met her in the lobby and said he had some things he wanted to run by her. "Ms. Johnson confessed to stalking you. Parker Sutton told her he still loved you, and she was furious. That's why she tried to run you off the road yesterday. I just wanted to tell you in case you needed closure."

The events from the previous day flashed through Blake's mind, and beads of sweat formed on her forehead. Her head spun in circles, and her legs were weak. She had to sit down for a minute to collect herself again.

"You've been through a rough time. Are you sure you should drive back to South Carolina by yourself?" Officer Branson asked.

"Now that you mention it, I have a friend who lives in the area. I'll ask him if he can pick me up and take me to lunch. Hopefully, I'll be less shaky if I eat something. It was a lot to take in at one time."

Blake called Will, giving him an update and asking if she could spend a few more hours with him before she hit the road. "No problem. I'll be right there."

Will took Blake to Tupelo Honey Café before they went back to his house. She sent a group text to Clint, Nancy and her parents to tell them she was safe and spending a couple more hours in Asheville to collect her bearings.

She took a brief nap in the guest bedroom and drank some lemonade. Ready to try again, she went to find Will.

"Let's try this for the third time." Blake smiled.

"You're in better spirits," Will said.

"I'm doing much better now. I appreciate all of your support and hospitality." she said before climbing into the Thunderbird.

Once she got onto the interstate, she texted Clint, saying she had left Will's house. The four-hour drive to the island drug by as slow as molasses. She had missed Clint, Nancy and Willow.

Chapter 29

Coming to the end of the Isle of Palms Connector, Blake began swaying along with the '80s music blaring from the stereo speakers in the Thunderbird. *Almost home*.

She had never been so happy to pull onto Palm Court in her life. As she walked to the back door, a conversation in the garden caught her attention. Her parents were sitting on one of Granny Mason's beautiful wrought iron benches. Willow ran to Blake and happily climbed into her arms, licking Blake's face.

"Mom? Dad? What are you guys doing here?" she asked.

Her mother burst into tears. "We're so relieved you're in one piece."

Her dad walked over and embraced her. After he let go, he reeled her back in for another hug. Nancy's eyes were teary. Blake held her emotions together until Clint walked up to her. His eyes were bloodshot and puffy. She wept, collapsing into his arms.

"I thought I was going to lose you again!" Clint said, holding onto her for dear life. "We have so much left to do together. Our life together is just beginning."

Their emotional welcome made Blake's tears turn into sobs. She had always tried not to dwell on the unfortunate events in her life, but Parker's torment had taken its toll. Seeing her family upset was the last straw.

Her parents said they had driven in the previous day and would stay through the weekend to help guests check-in and get settled so that Blake could rest. For once, she didn't fight them or refuse their offer to help.

Blake thanked them. Struggling to keep her eyes open, she said, "I need to go lie down. Please wake me up at dinnertime. I want to take you out to dinner while you're here."

Her parents agreed, but Blake didn't wake until six a.m. the following day. Yawning, she apologized.

"I'm sure your body needed the rest, sweetie," Susan said, resting her hand on Blake's shoulder. "Besides, we can go out to dinner tonight if you're up to it. Your B&B guests are leaving after lunch today. Dad and I will help Clint grill lobster for them. Why don't you take Willow for a walk on the beach, to help you relax?"

Blake packed her tote bag and grabbed Willow's leash. They walked for half an hour before settling into the perfect spot. Temperature-wise, September on the beach was much more comfortable than the summer months. It had the added benefit of being less crowded. She lost herself in her book and didn't see Clint walking up behind her. He put his hands on her shoulders, and she screamed, ready to jump out of her skin.

"I'm so sorry! I didn't mean to scare you," Clint said, rubbing her shoulders. "You were all tensed up, and I wanted to help you relax. We worried the entire time. I can't imagine what would have happened if Sharon had managed—well, I can't even..." He stared off in the distance.

Blake shivered, and an unexpected tear rolled down her cheek. Clint took off his jacket, put it around her shoulders. "Weren't you supposed to grill lunch for the guests?"

"Our parents said they had it under control and asked me to check on you. They've seen me struggling to hold it together the past few days. I should have just driven to Asheville. These guests have made themselves scarce, visiting every plantation between

Charleston and Georgetown. The good news is we'll have the weekend to ourselves to rest up before the next guests arrive."

"And the bad news?" Blake asked.

Clint winced. "They're a group of fifteen, so it's going to be a lot of work when they get here. If you're not up to it, we could hire some of Gram's friends temporarily."

"I'll be fine, but that *is* a huge group. Let's hire a caterer and a housekeeper," Blake said. "Plus, we need to spend some time planning our next move to send Parker away. Did the reverend or Nancy have any tips for us?"

Clint shook his head.

"He's traveling across Europe with his wife for the next month. Gram talked to Paulene. We need the book. She hasn't seen a spirit this powerful since your grandmother was alive. And because Julia Caroline wrote the book, she didn't need it to follow the instructions."

Blake pinched her lips together, but she couldn't blame Clint for not wanting to press Nancy for details. Blake would have to wait until her parents left to ask Nancy for more information. Susan had always expressed a distaste for anything paranormal. Blake wanted to avoid dragging her parents into the mess Parker had created.

That evening, she took her parents to dinner in downtown Charleston. Clint and Nancy stayed behind to give them some alone time and take care of Willow.

Following dinner, they walked along the Battery. They stopped to admire sailboats in the harbor, and in the distance, Ft. Sumter and the *U.S.S. Yorktown*.

"Thanks for suggesting we come here for dinner instead of just grabbing something on the island." Susan's head dipped down. She fidgeted with her hands before making eye contact with Blake again. "Not to change the subject, but are you positive you're up for running a business right now? You've made enough money to hire someone to take care of the guests who have already booked stays."

"Mom, I'll be okay. I promise. I just needed to chill this week. I've got all the help I need—Clint and Nancy and her friends."

"We're so proud of you regardless of what you need to do to take care of yourself," Susan said. A moment later, her eyes lit up. "Now, let's stop to pick up a key lime pie to share with Nancy and Clint."

"Sounds delicious," Blake said. The three of them piled into her parents' Audi station wagon, drove to the island and stopped by the grocery store.

When they returned to the B&B, Nancy put on a pot of coffee while Susan plated the pie. Blake grabbed forks for everyone, joining the others on the screened-in porch.

"So, let's talk about what's on everyone's minds," Jeremy said.

"What's that, Dad?" Blake asked, looking around the table.

"Your wedding, of course! When and where are you getting married?"

"We haven't set a date, but you guys will be the first to know."

"We'll figure it out soon so we can begin making plans," Clint said, pulling Blake onto his lap.

"Y'all are too cute!" Susan said. "We're excited. Tell us how we can help. I guess we need to turn in for the night. We have a six-hour drive ahead of us tomorrow." She stretched and yawned. "Goodnight, everyone."

Everyone followed suit, heading to their respective rooms, except Nancy. "I'm going to my house for the evening. Goodnight, everyone!"

Blake told Clint she needed to take a quick shower to help relax her muscles before bedtime.

A few moments later, he joined her in the shower. "I'll help you relax your muscles," Clint said, kissing her shoulder and lips. Blake yawned.

"That wasn't the reaction I was hoping for." Clint laughed.

"Sorry. I'm tired, but please continue." Tired or not, she had longed for him. He made her feel valued, special and loved beyond belief. She was engaged to one of the few existing good men.

After a bliss-filled evening, they lay in bed together, holding onto each other. "I missed you more than I've ever missed anyone," Blake said. "I love you."

"I missed you terribly. I can't thank God enough that you made it through that crazy situation. I love you." Clint wiped a tear from his eye and pulled her closer.

She leaned into him. "I love you more than I thought it was possible to love another person. Thanks for loving and supporting me."

For the next hour, the lovers held each other. Blake's heart was full, even though Parker wouldn't make living happily ever after with Clint an easy feat.

Chapter 30

"I'll miss having you and Dad here with us." Blake pouted to her mom as she pulled five coffee mugs out of a cabinet the next day.

"We'll miss you too, but the holidays will be here soon," Susan said. "It's hard to predict how many customers you'll have in November and December. If you would like, we can plan to have Thanksgiving and Christmas here this year."

"That would be great! And I can put the entire family to work. Seriously, though, I would love to host everyone. Plus, we could take a day while you're here to shop for wedding dresses. Clint and I have talked. We're planning to get married next fall. That will give us a year to plan, and it will be so much cooler."

"Fall sounds beautiful for a wedding. Are you planning to get married here?"

"Yeah—I want Granny Mason's presence to be strong that day. After the wedding, I want to do a photoshoot in downtown Charleston and on the beach. That way, if the dress gets ruined, it won't matter at that point."

Blake hugged her mother, who wiped a tear from her eye. They started laughing. "Sorry for the waterworks," Susan said. "I'm feeling so many emotions. I'm grateful you're alive. I'm so relieved you got back together with Clint. Not only does he come from a wonderful family, but he loves you deeply and always puts your needs ahead of his own. I couldn't imagine a better life partner for my daughter."

Blake's eyes misted over. Her dad and Clint walked into the kitchen and stared at them.

"What's the matter?" Blake's dad asked, handing each of them a tissue.

"We're talking about wedding plans." Blake laughed. "I told Mom—Clint and I are planning to get married next fall. We wanted plenty of time to plan, not only the actual wedding but to get the business and our lives in order. Clint needs to sell his house, and we're considering adding another bedroom and bathroom to the carriage house."

"We want to go on our honeymoon and come home without a lot of loose ends," Clint said. "Blake made a lot of improvements to my house right after our Savannah trip so we could sell it tomorrow, and I would just go ahead and officially move in here."

"It sounds like you two have everything figured out," Jeremy said. "Make sure you want to get married. It's not required anymore. You can live a wonderful life together as a couple without all the wedding nonsense."

"Dad!" Blake lightly slapped her dad's shoulder. "We want to get married. It's important to us."

He laughed. "I figured that wouldn't be a popular idea, but I at least had to tease you a little."

Blake just shook her head and laughed, grabbed a slice French toast and poured a cup of coffee. "This is so delicious. I love that you used the pecan bread, Mom."

She soaked up the last few minutes with her parents, talking about her mom's successful boutique and her dad's new sailing hobby. He would talk about his lessons with anyone who would listen for a few minutes. After breakfast, she helped her parents pack their car and said goodbye.

"Be careful! Text me when you get home."

"Who sounds like the parent now?" Susan smiled.

Blake rolled her eyes, waving goodbye.

As her dad pulled out of the driveway, their car come to a sudden stop, and her mother began sobbing. Her dad parked the car and jumped out a little too quickly as if he had just been stung by a bee.

"What's wrong, Dad?"

Tears in his eyes, he cleared his throat. "Brittany's professor just texted your mom. She's gone missing. She stopped showing up for her classes and the part-time job she had picked up in a local cafe. None of her friends have heard from her in three days," Jeremy said. "This is not like her at all. We're so worried." He walked over to the passenger side of the vehicle to help Susan get out and to comfort her.

Blake gasped. "Oh, my God! That is horrible. I hope she is okay."

Blake's parents called the police to file a missing person report and discussed hiring a private detective to find Brittany. Blake shivered. Where was her sister? She and her parents texted friends and family members who Brittany might contact. At two a.m., they had made no progress in finding her, and they kept drifting off at the kitchen table.

"It's time for bed, ladies. We'll be better at helping find Brittany after at least a few hours of rest." Jeremy put his arm around Susan, who had cried most of the evening.

Blake wanted to help ease her parents' minds, but what else could she do? She climbed the steps, crashed into bed and said a prayer for Brittany.

Chapter 31

Checking her messages, Blake read one from Brittany's best friend saying she had seen her two days ago. Someone had been stalking her, and she needed to get away from them.

Blake shot out of bed. Her parents were in the kitchen, cooking breakfast and drinking coffee. She handed her phone to her mom so she could read the message for herself.

"Thank God. At least someone has seen her more recently than her professors and friends. That gives me hope," Susan said, rubbing her arms.

The screen door from the backyard to the screened-in porch clanked. Brittany entered the kitchen, red-faced and covered in sweat.

Susan stared at Brittany and ran to her. "I'm so grateful! You're okay!" she signed, crying. "What's going on? Why are you here, and why didn't you tell anyone you were leaving school?"

Brittany stood there, hanging her head. Her hands trembled as she signed, "My stalker threatened me, saying they would kill me if I didn't come here. I didn't know who I could trust, so I didn't tell anyone in the program what was happening."

Jeremy wiped tears from his cheek and kissed Brittany on the forehead. "You gave us quite the scare, kiddo."

Blake threw her arms around her sister and squeezed her.

Brittany gasped for air. “Hey—not so tight,” she said vocally. Blake let go of her and took a deep breath. Her sister was safe. *Thank God!*

Clint walked into the kitchen and put an arm around Brittany. Then, he pulled back so she could read his lips. “Hey! I’m so glad you’re okay! I overheard what you were saying. How did you receive the death threats?”

“It started with some texts from a blocked number. I completely ignored them for a few days, thinking someone from school was messing with me. The other day, when I got out of the shower, someone had written a threatening message in the fogged-up mirror over the sink in the communal bathroom. The worst was when I returned to my dorm. There was a message on my wall, written in blood.”

“What did the messages say?” Clint asked, going into full-on police mode.

“The texts were pretty tame—*Go to your grandmother’s house in South Carolina, or I’ll kill you*. The one in the mirror was a little more direct: *I guess you weren’t listening, or you just want to die*. And the message on my wall said, *Go to your grandmother’s house, or your whole family dies. They’re waiting for you, and so am I.*” Brittany cried.

Clint called in a report to his team. He called his contacts at the Asheville and Knoxville police departments just in case someone, other than Parker, was trying to intimidate the Nelson family.

Blake stayed close to her sister, studying her body language and facial expressions. Only one thing could help under these circumstances.

“Want to go to the beach?” Blake asked. Clint had patrol cars circling the area just in case anyone tried to harass the family any further.

“Sure. I’m sorry that I haven’t been around while you’ve been going through these scary incidents. Being away from the family has been hard,” Brittany said as they walked to the beach.

Blake hugged her sister. "We're glad to have you back here with us. We were so worried, not knowing why you hadn't shown up for your classes or to hang out with your friends. Why would anyone from Parker or Sharon's families want to pull you into this mess? You were in a different state, minding your own business."

"I may have an idea, but I don't want to put you or the rest of the family at risk yet. I'm here, and I'm hoping that's enough for whoever thought it was worth bothering us again. When things calm down again, I'll tell you more."

"I love you, little sister. Please don't hold onto things that are bothering you. We'll get through this together." Blake squeezed her hand, and they sat together on the beach, letting the tide pull their worries away.

That evening, her family went to visit friends, and Clint had band practice. Nancy asked Blake if she wanted to catch up on some of their favorite shows in the second-floor den. With Brittany sharing her bone-chilling story, Blake didn't want to be alone.

"Want some popcorn?" Nancy asked.

"What do you think?" Blake giggled. "Please."

While Nancy walked downstairs, Blake gathered her favorite throw pillows and made herself comfortable. Someone walked up the steps and entered the room. Not looking before she spoke, Blake said, "I hope you made that popcorn extra buttery. I'm not counting calories tonight."

"You probably should. You're getting a little chunky. Keep it up, and you won't be able to run away from me anymore. On second thought, I'll tell Nancy you want extra butter."

A stabbing pain jolted through the center of her skull. She did a double-take but then jumped to her feet. "You're dead! Why do you keep showing up?" she screamed. "What's it gonna take for you leave for good?"

Parker chuckled cruelly. "Listen darlin', when I'm ready to leave you alone, I will, but not a moment before. Who are you to tell me what to do?"

"I'm the person who's tired of dealing with your crap. You made me miserable while you were alive, and it sure isn't getting any better now that you're dead," Blake said through her teeth.

"Whatever you say. Being dead is underrated. I'm having a glorious time. You should join me. From my perspective, if I killed you, I'd be doing you a favor. By the way, that's why I brought your sister here. Say your goodbyes."

"Go straight to hell, Parker!" Blake screamed and threw the remote control at him. He vanished, and it landed right in front of Nancy's feet as she entered the room.

"Gee. I guess you want me to pick the first TV show?" Nancy laughed, focusing on not spilling the overflowing bowl of popcorn in her hands. When she set the bowl down, she ran over to Blake, who was crying with a crumpled expression. "Oh no, what happened?"

Blake's hands shook. "Parker snuck up on me. I thought it was you walking up the steps." She wiped her tears, smudging her mascara. "He threatened to kill Brittany."

"He didn't! I'm so sorry he upset you. Tell me everything."

Through her tears, Blake described the horrific scene, and Nancy consoled her. After a half-hour, Blake relaxed slightly.

"Do you want me to throw out the popcorn?" Nancy asked.

"Are you for real? I'm never too upset to eat popcorn."

The women laughed and watched three of hours of late-night television to take their minds off the incident. However, once the first show began, Blake couldn't pay attention to the TV screen. Parker had become a regular nuisance, like the blood-sucking mosquitoes that plagued the island. Every Southerner knew there was only one way to get rid of a mosquito—to squash it.

Chapter 32

The next morning, Blake and Brittany spent a relaxing hour talking on the beach.

When they returned to the cottage, an ambulance was in the driveway with its lights flashing. EMTs were pulling Nancy out of the house on a stretcher. Clint stood by her, quietly answering their questions.

"Oh, my God! What happened?" Blake screamed at the sight of Nancy's bruised, unconscious body.

"A bookcase fell on her," Clint whispered, wiping tears out of his bloodshot and puffy eyes.

"What? How? Where?" Blake asked.

"Calm down. We'll talk later. All that matters right now is that Mom gets help right away." Clint bent down to kiss Nancy's forehead.

"Which hospital are they taking her to?"

"East Cooper Medical Center…"

"Okay, I'll be right there. I'm going inside to grab a few things." Tears stung Blake's eyes as she ran into the cottage and threw Nancy's robe, slippers, driver's license and insurance card into a backpack.

"Please keep us posted once a doctor has seen Nancy," Susan said in a shaky voice.

"Oh, Mom, I'm so scared, but I had better go now."

She drove straight to the hospital ER parking lot. She parked the car and ran inside. Blake couldn't find Clint in the ER waiting room, so she asked the information booth worker if Nancy had been admitted. But she wouldn't provide any details due to privacy restrictions.

Blake was on the verge of becoming hysterical when Clint walked into the waiting area. She ran to him and threw her arms around him.

"How is she?" Blake teared up, and her voice cracked.

"She broke both of her wrists, right hip and right leg. She is still unconscious, but her heart rate and blood pressure are all good. I've hated seeing her like this. She has always been strong."

He put his head in his hands. Blake sat close to him with her arm around him as they waited for the doctor to come out to give them a status update. She prayed silently for this woman who she loved deeply.

Please, God, don't take her home.

Three hours later, Dr. Bryan Remington came out to tell them Nancy had opened her eyes momentarily and responded to his attempts to get a reaction from her. She had closed her eyes again.

"Her body has been through a great shock. She isn't out of the woods yet," Dr. Remington said.

After the doctor left the waiting area, Blake texted an update to her parents. Then, she took Clint aside to learn what she could about the bookcase incident. "Please tell me what happened. I'm so worried."

He pulled his head up out of his hands. "After you and Brittany left the cottage to go to the beach, Gram walked upstairs with a basket full of Brit's clean laundry. The load she was drying had just finished. She was planning to set it on her bed so she could dry some linens for the carriage house since we have guests checking in tonight.

"She walked upstairs. I heard her open the door to Brittany's room, and the next thing I know, Gram screamed, and there was a loud crash. Your dad and I ran up the steps to check on her. She was lying on the floor with the solid mahogany bookcase from Brittany's room on top of her. We yelled for your Mom to call 9-1-1 and pulled the bookcase and several books off her. She was unconscious when we uncovered her."

"Oh my God, Clint," Blake whispered.

They prayed for a positive outcome. Nancy had impacted the lives of everyone she had met. Blake fell asleep on Clint's shoulder, waiting for more news. At one a.m., a nurse came to get them, saying Nancy had a private room.

When they got to her room, Nancy looked small and frail, lying in her hospital bed. *Had this observation crossed Nancy's mind when Blake had been the one in the hospital?*

The moment Clint sat down in the recliner in Nancy's room, he fell asleep. Blake covered him with a blanket and stayed awake in case Nancy's condition changed. She read every magazine in the room and scrolled through all the social platforms on her phone, grateful she always kept a phone charger in her purse.

Something bothered Blake about the way Clint had talked about Nancy's accident. He had left out some details surrounding the incident, but why? She'd wait for the right time and ask again. Surely, after everything she had been through, he knew she could handle anything.

Chapter 33

Blake woke up in the hospital, gasping as Nancy stirred. She loved this woman who had been like a grandmother to her as a child. As an adult, she had become a confidante, a friend. Soon, their relationship would change again, with Nancy becoming her grandmother-in-law.

Dr. Remington came into the room, and Blake shook Clint to wake him up.

"Mr. Parsons, your grandmother's vitals are still strong. We didn't find any internal bleeding or any permanently debilitating injuries. Once she is fully responsive, we'll keep her here for a few days while we find a suitable rehabilitation center where she will receive the care and the physical therapy she needs to build strength in her arms and legs again. She has a long road ahead of her, but I can tell she has support from her family."

The doctor left the room. Clint grimaced and rubbed his temples.

Blake hugged him. "We'll all feel better when she is fully conscious, but it sounds like she will eventually be okay again."

Tears filled his eyes, breaking Blake's heart. "It's just hard to see her like that…helpless. She's always been there for my brothers and me. Plus, the way she got hurt, it was horrible. Something's off about the way it all happened. I didn't want to say anything until I mulled it over, but there was no humanly way possible that bookcase hurled itself across the room when Gram opened the door to Brittany's bedroom."

"Did the house settle? Maybe the bookcase toppled over because it was top-heavy."

"No. I helped Brittany get her luggage into her bedroom when she got home. The bookcase was across the room from the door. It's almost as if someone or something moved it across the room and waited to crush the next person who opened the door."

Blake needed fresh air. She kissed Clint and stepped outside to call her mother. "Hi, Mom. Are the guests doing okay?" Blake asked.

"Everything is fine. Brittany made breakfast and even made them a picnic lunch to take to the beach."

"How is Brit?" Blake asked. "Clint thinks someone tried to rig the bookcase so it would fall on her when she opened her bedroom door. Please tell her to be extra cautious. Someone may be trying to hurt her."

Blake walked back into the hospital, stopping by the cafeteria to pick up breakfast.

Returning to the room, Nancy was conscious. A tear of relief rolled down Blake's face. "Oh, my goodness, Nancy, I'm so happy you're awake!"

Nancy smiled and whispered, "I love you."

"She is coming back around, but we just need to be patient with her," Clint said, winking at Nancy. "Why don't you go back home to give your parents a break? I'm going to wait for the doctor to come back and talk to me. I'll get a ride home to shower, change clothes and eat lunch."

"Okay. I love you both." Blake kissed Nancy on the cheek.

Walking into the cottage, she let out a sigh of relief. She had never been a fan of hospitals, even less so since she had been a patient herself recently.

Her parents and Brittany were in the kitchen folding towels. She shared the good news with them. "Thank God!" Susan said.

"I've been so worried," Blake said. "Hey, Brit, please come upstairs with me for a minute."

She followed her. "What do you need, sis?"

"Can we check out your bookcase? I'm trying to figure out how it fell over on Nancy," Blake said.

"Sure. It was across the room when it fell and somehow made its way to the door."

Blake nodded, inspecting the bookcase, which Clint and their dad had pulled back into the room after they pulled Nancy from the wreckage.

"Oh, my God!" Blake screamed a blood-curdling scream, grasping a scrap piece of paper, which she found taped to the back of the bookcase.

> *"Sorry, Blake—I didn't mean to hurt the old lady...yet. I was aiming for your sister; like I said the other night, you need to tell her goodbye. I guess it doesn't matter, though. I want to take away everyone you love until there isn't anyone left.*

Brittany grabbed the note and shrieked, "What?" She jumped to her feet. "Who is responsible for all of this?"

Blake shook her head. She didn't want to drag her sister deeper into Parker's mangled madness. She wouldn't give up on preventing him from harming the people she loved.

Brittany cleared her throat, shaking and staring at the floor. "Remember when I said I might know why Parker's family might be after me?"

"Yeah. What's wrong? You can tell me anything."

She started crying, and Blake gulped. Until this week, she hadn't seen her sister cry since Granny Mason had died.

"Please tell me what's going on, so I can help you," Blake said.

Brittany drew a deep breath and steadied her hands. "You know that weekend we came to the cottage when you guys first started dating?

Blake nodded and tilted her head to one side.

"You weren't feeling great, so you went to bed early. Parker, Elaina and I stayed up late drinking and playing cards. After Elaina crashed on the couch, Parker and I got pretty wasted. He crammed his tongue down my throat and tried to grope me. I pushed him off me, but he threatened me, saying he would kill me if I ever told anyone." Brittany wiped her eyes and groaned. "I couldn't bear to tell you, but after you told me Sharon had cheated with him, I called her and told her how unremarkable she was."

Blake gasped and held back tears. "I'm so sorry he put you through that. I wish you would have told me. I love you, Brit. I'll always be on your side."

Needing to clear her head, Blake grabbed a glass of wine, walked to the screened-in porch to sit down. The mystery children were playing on the tire swing without a care in a world.

Chapter 34

Two days later, Blake and Clint were sitting in the hospital room when Nancy suddenly sat up in her bed. "What happened to me?"

Blake's mouth gaped in horror as Clint explained the bookcase incident to Nancy. She pursed her lips together and nodded.

"You don't seem surprised," Blake said, narrowing her eyes.

"No, not exactly." Nancy clasped her hands.

"Could you explain that to us?" Clint asked, furrowing his brow.

"I don't have the energy to go into the details. You need to be on your guard at all times. I'll talk to you soon."

A nurse stopped in to check on Nancy, celebrated the fact she was conscious and went to get Dr. Remington.

"Ms. Parsons, I'm delighted to see you sitting up and talking again. I've told your family, and I want you to be aware you'll need at least six to eight weeks of therapy. However, you're a determined and strong woman, and that is on your side. We'll arrange for transport to a rehabilitation center tomorrow. For now, get some rest."

"Clint, you haven't left Nancy's side this whole time. You should go home to rest, shower and grab some food. I'll stay with her, and I'll call you if anything changes," Blake said, patting his hand.

"Thank you. I'll take you up on it, and when we get Gram settled, I owe you a date." He kissed Blake.

She pulled out her eReader and began reading *Sullivan's Island* by the late Dorothea Benton Frank aloud. After half an hour, Nancy said, "Thanks for reading to me, but my attention span is running low. Tell me about your plans for the wedding."

"We've set the date—September 22, with the ceremony and reception in the garden. Clint and I want to keep the guest list relatively short, fifty to sixty people at the most. We'll hire a photographer, but that's the only vendor we need. I want to carry flowers from Granny Mason's garden, and we'll have your catering crew make a light lunch and cupcakes."

Nancy smiled. "It sounds beautiful. Promise that you will wait for me to be out of rehab to go shopping for dresses."

"Of course, I will. You have to be there with me," Blake patted her hand. "I love you. You've always been part of my family."

Tears began streaming down Nancy's face. "Child, I love you too. I couldn't be happier. Clint is marrying the finest young woman in the world."

When Clint returned to the hospital with dinner for the three of them, Nancy had fallen asleep. "She's in great spirits," Blake said. "I'm so glad the bookcase incident didn't turn out to be worse, but I wonder what she was talking about earlier." Blake rubbed her forehead.

Clint shrugged. "Let's leave it alone for now. It seems to bother her when we bring it up, and I want her to recover with as little stress as possible."

Blake agreed to drop the subject for the moment, but it didn't mean she would forget what was at stake.

"Would you mind if I went home to be with my parents and sister for the rest of the evening? I should probably send them home now that Nancy is doing well."

"Sure. That makes sense. The guests checked out this morning, and no one is due to check-in for two weeks. If it's okay with you, let's not take any new bookings for the next few weeks. We all need a break. Like I said earlier, let's get Gram settled and spend some time together. I love you."

"Love you too, and I'm excited to have some time with you." Blake kissed him goodbye.

She went back to the Mason B&B and asked her family to join her in the second story rec room. "You guys have been a tremendous help here. Thank you for everything. Now that Nancy is alert and moving to a rehabilitation center tomorrow, you don't need to stay here," Blake said. "Clint and I don't have any guests arriving for a while, and we're looking forward to having some downtime."

"Is downtime what you young people are calling it these days?" her dad asked. Blake gasped and slapped her dad on the shoulder again. "Easy. Easy. I was teasing. I'm happy you and Clint are back together. He cares about you and would follow you to the ends of the earth."

Her dad was right.

Chapter 35

Once again, Blake helped her parents load their car. They would drop Brittany off at the airport on their way to Knoxville so she could return to school.

"Be careful, everyone. If you hear or see anything out of the ordinary, please keep me posted. I don't trust that the weird events are over." Blake handed them a thermos filled with coffee and a basket full of banana nut muffins. "I love you guys!"

They waved as they drove away. Blake went back into the house to put the rest of the muffins into a basket to take to the rehab center for Clint and Nancy, and she poured some kibble and water into Willow's dishes.

"Hey, cutie pie," Blake said to the sweet dog, patting her head. She took her for a quick walk, and when they returned, she went back into the house to grab her purse and keys to drive to the rehab center.

When she arrived, Clint groaned while signing the admissions paperwork, and Nancy was napping.

"I brought you guys some breakfast. Do you want to go to the beach with Willow and me while Nancy is in therapy today?" Blake asked.

"Can I have a rain check on the beach day? How about tomorrow?" Clint asked. "As soon as I get this paperwork finished, I need to spend the rest of the day at the station. Tonight, I have something special planned. In case you're wondering, it's an elegant occasion."

"Sure. I'm intrigued. See you tonight." She smiled. *What does he have up his sleeve?*

Blake went home, changed into her swimsuit and grabbed Willow.

She spread out a beach towel on the nearly empty beach and began reading. Willow pranced around for a few minutes and barked at a few birds that landed near the shoreline. Satisfied the birds had received her message, she plopped down beside Blake.

For the next half hour, Blake lost herself in her book, but a cry for help broke the silence. She looked up. A man was struggling to stay afloat in the ocean. There wasn't a lifeguard on duty. Blake dove into the water, and as she got closer, she recognized the man's face.

"So, Parker, we're playing this game again?" she asked aloud as the waves swelled. But he had disappeared.

"Parker? Where are you?" Blake asked. "Don't hide. I want to talk to you."

A massive wave crashed down over her head. The current was too rough to stay in the water. She swam parallel to the beach to break free. Finally, she did, and when she stepped onto the sand, Willow ran to her, wagging her tail. Blake scanned the surrounding area, but no one was in the water.

Should she worry about her mental and emotional wellbeing? It was one thing to see Parker when he materialized to wreak havoc on her life. What did imagining him mean? Had he pushed her over the edge?

Blake didn't want to bother Clint, but with Nancy being at the rehab center, she didn't have anyone else to confide in on the island. She took Willow back to the cottage and left for the police station.

Walking into the station, she asked Latonya, the station desk officer, to tell Clint she was there.

"He's not here, but you're welcome to wait in his office," Latonya said.

Blake sat down at Clint's desk and checked his desk blotter calendar. Maybe he had noted the time he would be back. A note, *Meet Ashley at Charleston Place Hotel*, caught her attention.

Her heart sank. Who was Ashley? Why was Clint meeting her at the swankiest hotel in the area? Could he be interviewing a witness for a case? Was she a relative Blake hadn't met? She should trust him, but after Parker's indiscretions, that was easier said than done.

Against her better judgment, she began driving downtown. She got stuck in traffic just before the Ravenel Bridge and started questioning if she should check up on her fiancé. He was the police chief. Most likely, he was conducting official police business. Blake should turn around and go home, but once she reached downtown, she convinced herself it wouldn't hurt to drive by the hotel.

There were no signs of Clint's police cruiser, so she went home and get ready for their date. Otherwise, Clint might call looking for her. She didn't want to tell him she had been stupid enough to invade his privacy and spy on him while he was working.

On her drive back, the guilt overwhelmed her. She needed to let go of this notion of Clint cheating on her. He wasn't the type.

She parked her car at the cottage, took Willow for a quick walk around the garden and soaked in her clawfoot tub. Afterward, she curled her hair and put on some makeup and a new little black dress she had been dying to wear. She finished her look with Granny Mason's pearl earrings.

Clint's car pulled into the driveway. *Yes!* She had made it back home and gotten ready before Clint made it home.

"Oh my! You're a knockout." He handed her a bouquet of lavender roses.

"Thank you." She smiled. "Now, go get ready so we can go on this special date you planned."

Clint went to get in the shower, and his text notification sounded. The text came from a contact listed as Ashley—*It was great catching up at the hotel today. Should I meet you at your place tomorrow? When will Blake leave?*

For the third time that day, tears stung Blake's eyes. She couldn't tell Clint she had been looking at his phone.

He came into the bedroom and started getting dressed.

"You don't need to get ready. I'm not feeling well, and I want to go to sleep," Blake said, changing into her pajamas and walking into the bathroom to wash the makeup off her face. She climbed into the soft bed.

"That was sudden. Are you okay? Do you need some medicine or something to eat?" Clint asked. Blake didn't answer, out of fear she would begin crying. Instead, she lay there, pretending to be asleep.

Clint's phone began ringing, and he ran out of the room to answer it.

"Hi. Yeah. I should be able to get rid of Blake somehow, around two p.m. tomorrow," Clint said in a hushed voice.

Blake's heart sank. Clint had a date with "Ashley" at her family's cottage while she sent her on some random errand.

Luckily, he did not return to the bedroom. Blake screamed into a pillow and kicked the mattress. She wanted to confront him, but she needed to investigate a little further and say her piece once she had the facts.

Chapter 36

Blake cooked breakfast early enough for them to sit down together and talk. She made crab-stuffed omelets with a side of bacon and avocado and brewed a pot of coffee.

Clint's jaw gaped. "Wow. What did I do to deserve this?"

"We've been so focused on our family, and I wanted to make sure we had some quality time to talk. What's new with you? Is everything going okay at work? Any new interesting cases?"

"Everything has been pretty slow. I'm relieved since I've needed so much family time lately. I need to focus on getting my face back into the community, going to events and doing my part to serve the people on the island. That reminds me, the mayor came by yesterday and asked if we'd be willing to host a Halloween open house. They want Marshal Law to play a few sets. Otherwise, we'll provide treats to everyone who stops by. Volunteers will decorate and be here Halloween night to run various activities. What do you think?"

"That should be fine. We don't have B&B guests on Halloween. I won't accept any bookings," Blake said. "We'll be super busy in November with all the historic home holiday tours going on in downtown Charleston. Jessica from the Chamber of Commerce has connected us with several couples who want to check out the tours but stay closer to the ocean.

"Halloween sounds like fun, but I'd rather hear what's going on with you. Have you hung out with any of your friends lately?" she asked.

"No. I need to make more time for friends. So do you. You've met some cool people through networking for the business. You should have a fun girls' night out."

Blake pursed her lips. "Is there anything else exciting you want to share with me?"

"Not really. I'm just focused on Gram getting better, work, planning the wedding and hopefully, having the date we missed last night," Clint said.

How could he cover up this indiscretion so nonchalantly? Then came the question she was expecting.

"Will you check on Gram around two p.m. today? I have an important meeting."

"Sure. I'll stop by the rehab center this afternoon," Blake said, careful not to show her anger.

Clint thanked her again for making breakfast, kissed her and left for work.

She busied herself, cleaning every surface of the cottage and carriage house. Nausea overcame her, and she had to lie down. A better distraction was in order, so she took Willow for a lengthy walk on the beach, letting the waves rolling back and forth calm her nerves. Afterward, she took the dog back home and went to pick up lunch at Acme for Nancy and herself. Her hands shook as she checked the time on her cell phone—one p.m. She drove to the rehabilitation center and went into Nancy's room, which was empty. *Nancy must be in therapy*. Sighing, Blake put Nancy's lunch in the mini-refrigerator in her room and left a note, saying she would come back to visit.

It was only 1:30. She didn't want to get back to the cottage before Ashley made her way there, so she drove to the IOP County Park and sat down at a picnic table to eat her lunch. She stood on the sand long enough to inhale, exhale and say a prayer for the best outcome possible.

At 1:55 p.m., she asked herself if she wanted to go back to the cottage and what her reaction would be if she caught yet another lover cheating. She wouldn't be the one leaving this time. She lived in her family's prized beach house, the location of her new business.

She got into her car at 2:05 p.m. and drove home. As Blake pulled into the driveway, she had to admit of all the things she pictured "Ashley" driving, a work truck with a welding rig on the back was the last thing she expected. Reading the side of the truck, *Ashley Plumbing and Restoration*, Blake laughed at her overactive imagination. Businesses within a ten-mile radius of the Ashley River loved borrowing the name.

Relieved, she walked into the house, but Clint wasn't inside. She peered out the kitchen window. Clint was in the garden with two male construction workers who were kneeling beside Granny Mason's elaborate stone fountain, which had stopped working a short time after she died. A knot formed in Blake's throat. *What a thoughtful surprise*. She vowed never to distrust Clint again.

She left the cottage, returned to the rehabilitation center and found Nancy in her room, listening to the local news on the radio and enjoying her shrimp and grits.

"Hello, hon. Thanks so much for the delicious lunch. The therapists have kept me busy, but they say I'm progressing faster than expected. They said I might get to cut my time here by a couple of weeks, but we'll have to wait and see," Nancy said.

"That is great news, and I can't wait to tell Clint. I hope you're back home in time for the Halloween open house," Blake said.

"What open house?" Nancy asked.

"The mayor asked if we'd host the event. Clint and I figured it was an opportunity for him to get his face out in the community again. Plus, we can introduce more people to our beautiful B&B."

"You've been experiencing a lot of odd things lately," Nancy said. "Be careful and on your guard at all times. We don't fully understand what we're dealing with here. Unsettled spirits come out of the woodwork on Halloween."

The hairs on the back of Blake's neck stood up. She had experienced enough unsettled spirits to last a lifetime. Celebrating Halloween was an awful idea, but they had already promised the town event planners they would participate. She would do her best to stay on the fun side of the holiday and forgo the ghoulish side.

Chapter 37

Blake returned to the cottage full of questions. The construction truck was gone.

Clint handed her a bouquet of blossoming yellow roses. “I have a surprise for you. I’d planned to wait until closer to time for the wedding, but I found the right contractor to do the work, and we’ll enjoy it throughout the year. Come with me,” he said.

The fountain flowed as if it had never stopped working, and it brought tears to Blake’s eyes. The fountain hadn’t been in working condition since her grandmother’s birthday party right before she died.

“This is the nicest, most thoughtful gift anyone has ever given me.” Blake threw her arms around him. “Thank you. I love you!”

“I’m glad you love it.” Clint smiled. “We were supposed to go out last night, but I figured you would rather have our special date here tonight. I ordered dinner, and it should arrive soon. When it gets dark, I can share the rest of your surprise.”

“I can think of some things we could do in an hour.” Blake laughed, pulling Clint over to the hammock. She had spent her life jumping to conclusions and being impulsive. She needed to focus on trusting her loving fiancé.

During dinner, Clint asked Blake about her visit with Nancy.

"She was upbeat. Her therapists said she might get to come home early if she keeps making progress," Blake said. "However, she isn't happy about us hosting the Halloween open house. She told me to watch out for unsettled spirits."

Clint chuckled. "Gram has been superstitious my whole life, and I'm pretty sure she was before I came along. You know how these older Southern ladies are. You'll probably be the same way one day."

"Hey, watch it!" Blake said, tickling Clint's neck.

"Stop it! Now that it's getting dark, I can show you the rest of my surprise." He clicked a few buttons on his cell phone.

Suddenly, every inch of the garden glowed. Clint had installed new lighting inside and outside of the fountain and strung strands of globe lights from one end of the garden to the other. The sight left Blake breathless for a few moments.

"Wow! This is beyond romantic. Not only will it be wonderful for our wedding but also for the other events we hold at the B&B. Thank you for all the hard work and love you put into this." Blake grabbed his hand.

"You're welcome. It's the least I could do for the woman I love," he said, picking her up and carrying her to her bedroom.

She threw her head back and laughed, grateful for the opportunity for a second chance with her first love. Not everyone was lucky enough to experience this kind of love.

That night, Blake allowed herself to break down any remaining emotional walls between her and Clint. She was back with her soulmate, living in her grandmother's beautiful cottage and running her own business. She couldn't ask for more.

In the middle of the night, she rolled over to put her arm around Clint. Her hand landed in a warm and sticky substance, which covered part of the fitted sheet. Her stomach lurched. She turned on the light. A pool of blood filled the bed where Clint had been lying. She screamed, grabbed her cell phone and followed a trail of blood from her bedroom to the garden. Clint was lying in the fountain, unconscious.

"Oh my God, Clint!" Fearing the worst, she walked over to him to feel his pulse. She was thankful he was breathing and that he had turned the water to the fountain off before they went to bed.

Her head swimming, Blake called the police station and told Shane, the commanding officer on duty. Shane said he and his partner, Dan, were on their way, and his partner had already called for an ambulance.

She kneeled next to Clint and held his hand. "Clint? Wake up. Please, honey. I'm so scared. I don't want to lose you. Stay with me," she said, shaking and crying.

A shadowy figure stood near the gardening shed. "Who's there?" she asked. "Show yourself."

The figure froze, turned to Clint and Blake and began moving toward them. She panicked, unable to move or call for help. Fortunately, Shane's patrol car headlights lit up the garden at that very moment, and the figure turned and ran behind the shed.

As Shane and Dan made their way to Blake and Clint, she motioned for them to check behind the shed. Dan began creeping that way as Shane checked Clint's pulse and looking for open lacerations or wounds on his body but didn't find any.

Dan walked back to them. "There were footprints behind the shed, but whoever left them was long-gone."

"Blake, I thought you said there was a trail of blood from your bed to the garden," Shane said.

"Over here." Blake pointed to a dark maroon splotch on the ground near the fountain.

"I'll take some samples while you wait for the EMTs to get here," Dan said. "Do you mind if I follow the blood into the house?"

"Sure. Do whatever you need," Blake said, absently staring at the fountain.

"What happened to Clint tonight, Blake?" Shane asked.

"It's like I said on the phone—I went to put my arm around Clint, but he wasn't in bed, and my hand fell into a pool of blood. I grabbed my cell phone and followed the trail of blood, which brought me out here," she said, gesturing toward the fountain. "I called you, and while I was waiting for you, I saw a shadowy figure over by the gardening shed. The figure started walking toward us until you and Dan showed up, and then they ran away."

"If he wasn't wounded, where did the blood come from? Why is he unconscious?" Blake asked, putting her palm on the side of her head.

"I'm not sure. We'll run tests on the blood back at the station," Shane said. "The EMTs and the doctors at the hospital will figure out what is wrong with Clint. His pulse and heart rate are normal, considering he has been through a traumatic situation. We'll certainly be keeping tabs on his condition. Call me if you need anything."

The ambulance pulled in, and two EMTs pushed a stretcher toward Clint. They quickly loaded him into the ambulance and began checking his vitals.

"His blood pressure is slightly elevated, but everything else seems to be normal. We can't find any cuts or a source of blood, like a nosebleed. We're taking him to East Cooper."

"I'll be right behind you in my car." Blake handed a key to Shane and Dan to lock up. "Take your time."

Chapter 38

When Blake arrived at the hospital, she asked to go to Clint's room.

"They're still getting him settled back there, but we'll call you back within the hour," the front desk worker said.

Blake chewed her fingernails. She flipped through her social media feeds, trying to focus on anything else, but a three-year-old memory of a trip to Spain with Parker popped up on her phone. She screamed into what she thought was an empty waiting area, but someone cleared their throat. A nurse, clutching her chest, stood in front of Blake.

"Ma'am, are you alright?"

Blake nodded and followed her to the examination room. The nurse walked backward out of the room, staring at her.

When Blake saw Clint, her heart ached, and she trembled with fear. He lay in the hospital bed, still unresponsive, his skin pale. According to his nurses, his vitals were elevated but not to an astronomical level. What had happened to him?

Blake checked the time, 4:30 a.m.—too early to reach anyone at the rehab center to get a message to Nancy. Patients couldn't keep their cell phones on overnight. She would have to wait to tell her what had happened, not that she had answers herself.

Someone called her name, pulling her out of the trance. "Blake?"

Dan and Shane were standing at the foot of Clint's bed. They asked for the doctor's prognosis and explained the blood found at the cottage did not match Clint's blood type, O-positive.

"So, if it's not his blood, whose is it?" Blake frowned.

"We were hoping you would tell us. Do you know anyone who has B-negative blood? It's a rare blood type. Any information you have might help us find a connection to the perpetrator," Shane said.

"Only my late fiancé, Parker."

"Does he have any family members with the same blood type?" Shane asked.

"I don't know." Blake sighed.

"It's at least a start. We can talk to Parker's family. Hopefully, they will provide medical records to us." Dan said.

She couldn't picture any of Parker's family attempting to harm anyone, so that left the asshole himself. But how could a ghost produce a drop of blood, let alone pints, and move a muscular, broad-shouldered man like Clint down a flight of steps, through the first story of the house and out to the garden?

Dan shook her out of her trance by saying, "Blake, you and Clint are in our prayers. You've been through more than your fair share of worry and sorrow this year. We're committed to helping put an end to this madness."

Blake thanked them. Nancy might have her phone turned on by now, but she didn't want her to find out alone. Blake couldn't bring herself to leave Clint by himself. So instead, she called his brother, Landon, who lived two hours away in Columbia. He agreed to come to break the news to Nancy. Blake called her family. Her mom offered to return to the island, but she told her to wait until the doctor provided a diagnosis.

A few minutes later, Dr. Remington walked into the room. "I hate to keep seeing you like this, Blake."

"Me, too." She turned away from him.

"I can't find any signs of external injuries. We're running toxicology tests to see if someone may have drugged Clint," he said.

She thanked the doctor and stopped by the nurse's station to tell the on-duty nurse that she needed to step away for a moment.

Blake searched for the hospital's chapel, but before she found it, she stumbled across a beautiful courtyard with park benches. This would be an even better place to pray and reflect. She began sobbing, and between the tears, she silently prayed for Clint's recovery and her family members' safety.

The door leading to the courtyard opened. Blake frantically searched her purse for a tissue, dabbed at her eyes, and grabbed her compact to check out the state of her face, red and puffy. Along with her reflection, she saw Parker standing behind her. She dropped her compact and turned to get a better look at him, but Parker had vanished.

"Excuse me, did you see a man come out here?" Blake asked a group of nurses who were talking about their plans for the weekend.

"No. We're the only ones out here," a young nurse said. "Are you all right, ma'am?"

"Yeah. Thanks. I'm just a little weak. I think I'll head to the cafeteria for breakfast," Blake said.

Chapter 39

Going back inside, Blake ran into Landon, pushing Nancy in a wheelchair.

"You two are a sight for sore eyes. I'm so glad you're here." She filled them in on the doctor's plans. "They have taken him for testing, so I'm going to the cafeteria. Do you two want to join me?"

"I left pretty abruptly this morning, so I need to fill Claire in on what's happening and make sure she picks up the kids from school today," Landon said.

Blake gave him Clint's room number and told him they would meet him there after eating breakfast. When they sat down to eat, Blake asked Nancy how her treatments were coming along.

"The doctors let me out to see Clint, but I have to go back this evening."

"There's no rush. Just take your time." Blake patted Nancy's hand. "I'm so happy you're on the mend." She began tearing up again. As hard as she tried, she couldn't prevent the waterworks from flowing.

"Hon, I'm confident Clint will be okay."

"How are you so calm right now?"

"I have faith in God, and well…"

"What are you not telling me? There *is* something you are holding back!"

Landon came running toward them, smiling ear-to-ear.

"Clint woke up!"

"Thank God!" Blake pushed Nancy's wheelchair toward the elevator. "Let's continue our conversation later."

When they arrived in Clint's room, he was pale, and his eyes were black-rimmed and weak. Blake ran to him and threw her arms around him. He tried lifting his arms to hold her, but he was too weak.

"Don't rush things, Clint. You've been unconscious." She explained everything that had happened to him. "What's the last thing you remember?"

"I was reading in bed, drinking a cup of tea. You came to bed; we talked for a few minutes. My head was heavy, so I shut off my lamp and went to sleep. I had horrible nightmares."

"What were they about?" Blake asked.

"Parker was trying to kill me," Clint said with a wide-eyed expression. Blake shivered.

Dr. Remington walked into the room and shook Clint's hand. "We're glad you're awake. We're still trying to determine what caused you to become unconscious. The toxicology report came back as inconclusive, but I have some other tests I want to run. Do you have a history of sleepwalking?"

"No. I don't, and I'm not on any medication. I can't think of a plausible explanation for what happened."

Dr. Remington reassured Clint he would provide a proper diagnosis. As he left the room, a group of medical assistants and nurses came in to read Clint's vitals and take more blood.

"Landon, do you mind staying with Clint?" Blake asked. "I need to run home to let Willow out, and I'd like to take Nancy with me so we can catch up."

"Sure. Could you pick up some food while you're out?"

She giggled. *He wanted some Lowcountry food.*

"We've gotcha covered," Blake said, winking. She kissed Clint on the forehead and made Landon promise to call if anything changed.

After she helped Nancy into the Thunderbird, Blake climbed into the car. The chill of the wind grazed Blake's shoulders, and she got out of the car to pull up the convertible top. They drove to the cottage and found a distraught little dog wagging her tail.

"Oh, how I've missed you!" Nancy said to Willow, ruffling her fur. Blake scratched the dog's chin and put her in the garden to play. The laughter of the two mystery children playing on the tire swing caught her attention. Where did they come from? Were they there when she'd stepped outside? No matter-—their playfulness lightened her mood. Willow ran up to them, licking the girl on the leg. She giggled.

Nancy laughed and appeared to be smiling at the children. She had been quick to change the subject when Blake mentioned these children's families in the past. Who were these children? Why did they show up when Blake or her family were in distress?

"In the famous words of Nancy Parsons, 'spill it,'" Blake said.

Chapter 40

"Do you really not recognize the two children who have played on the tire swing since you came here?"

Nancy retrieved the wooden box from the living room bookcase. She pulled out a family photo album and opened it to a page with a picture of Blake's grandparents when they were children.

Blake's jaw dropped. "Let me get this straight; my deceased grandparents have been appearing to me as children for the past several months?"

Nancy nodded. "They didn't want you to recognize them. Your grandmother was confident she had passed down her gift of communicating with the Other Side to you. When Julia Caroline found out she was dying, she vowed to watch over you. She prayed for God to help her find a way. This is the solution she found. I'm happy she reconnected with your grandfather."

Her grandmother had grown up in the cottage, and her grandfather's family had lived next door. The two were childhood sweethearts.

Tears welled up in Blake's eyes. Papa and Granny Mason had the sweetest love story of all time. Their unconditional love for each other and their family had been powerful enough to save generations of Masons.

Nancy put her arm around Blake.

"I'm so sorry if I've put you and Clint in harm's way," Blake said, teardrops glistening on her cheeks.

"Hon, I've loved you as one of my own for your entire life. It has been my honor to help protect you. I hate that your heart has gone through so many difficult times over the past year. And I know Clint feels the same way. He was beside himself when you left for college, and pieces of him died that day. When you two got back together, he became the happy Clint I remembered from his youth. We have no regrets when it comes to you; we never will."

Willow ran playfully toward them, sitting at their feet with her tail wagging. Blake laughed. "Let's check on Clint. If he's doing okay, I'd like to take a quick walk on the beach with Willow. I can take a chair for you to sit and enjoy the view, too."

"I'd like to take a nap. Today has been full of excitement, and my body is still building back up to normal," Nancy said, stretching out on the couch and placing a pillow under her head.

"Sure. I'll be back soon." She grabbed Willow's leash, and the two crossed the street to the beach. She closed her eyes and allowed the salty air to fill her lungs.

After a brisk walk, rejuvenated by the ocean's calming qualities, Blake and Willow began making their way back to the cottage. When Blake opened the front door, Nancy moaned in agony.

"Nancy? Are you okay? Where are you?" She ran through the house looking for her. When she walked into the kitchen, Nancy was lying on the floor. Parker stood over her, pulling her head backward.

"Leave her alone!" Blake screamed, clutching her throbbing head.

She grabbed Parker by the neck, but he shifted. Her arms slipped right through him. The mystery children, *her grandparents*, drifted into the room out of thin air and shot a beam of white light from their hands to Parker.

Unable to process the current events any further, Blake stumbled backward and passed out in the living room foyer. She dreamed about walking on the beach with Clint and him promising everything would be okay, but she woke up in the hospital with her mother holding her hand. Blake sighed.

"Mom, what happened? Why am I here? Where's Nancy?" Blake asked in a panic.

"Blake, you hit your head really hard...you might have an actual concussion this time. The doctors want to monitor you. It's not normal to have so many blows to the head in one year. It puts you at risk for several neurological disorders." Susan grimaced.

"Where's Nancy? Did someone drive her back to rehab?" Blake asked.

Her mother began crying and reached for her. "Honey, Nancy passed away during her nap. She died peacefully." Susan choked back her tears.

Weeping, Blake thought back to the incident at the cottage. Through her tears, she explained the frightening events that had taken place. "No! No, she didn't. Parker killed her. I saw him pull her head back. Papa and Granny Mason were trying to save her," Blake said in disbelief.

Her mom gasped. "Oh, my God!"

Blake clutched her churning stomach and reached for a wastebasket. She dry-heaved.

How could they live without Nancy?

She sobbed uncontrollably, and her mom held her, consoling her. "Clint is still a patient, and Landon has been back and forth to check on you a million times. I'm pretty sure Clint has sent him. They are both extremely upset, and they are worried about you. Call Clint's room. Then I want you to relax. I'm going to call your dad and siblings."

Blake dialed Clint's room. When he answered the phone, she began sobbing again.

"Clint, I'm so sorry about your Gram. What are we going to do without her? She was a friend to everyone she ever met. The island will never be the same without Nancy Parsons."

He took two deep breaths. "Blake, she loved you like a daughter." His voice crackled. "We'll all miss her."

She could tell he had been crying but was trying to put on a tough face for her. "The only positive news to come out of everything is you're okay, and because I'm in mourning, Dr. Remington will let me leave the hospital. Whatever is in my system is untraceable, or at least it is proving difficult for the labs to find. All my vitals have normalized, but I have to wear a heart monitor for the next few weeks to make sure nothing changes.

"Your mom and I talked. We'll take turns staying with you while the other stays with Willow at the cottage. My cousin Kate has been with Willow the past couple of hours.

"Kate said you left the front door to the cottage open when you screamed and fell. Willow went to the front porch and barked. A neighbor called the animal shelter. Luckily, Kate took the call. When she called all our phones and couldn't reach us, she drove to the cottage and found Willow in a pitiful state. She saw you on the floor and called 9-1-1. Blake, I'm glad you're okay! Did something happen to Gram? The doctors said it was an aneurysm, but I want to make sure we're not overlooking anything."

"Clint, I can't fully explain this over the phone. I'll have to talk to you in more detail later," Blake said. "I love you."

"I love you, too."

Blake closed her eyes and buried her head in her hands. Her cheeks and eyes were puffy.

"Blake, I thought I told you I wanted to stop meeting you like this." She raised her head. Dr. Remington was standing in front of her bed, her chart in hand.

She sighed. "I would love nothing more, doctor."

"First of all, I wanted to say how sorry I am about your loss. Nancy Parsons was an icon in these parts. Her departure will have ripple effects on this area for years to come. No one could find a better friend or Southern cook. Now, I would like to focus on you. What caused you to pass out?"

Tears stung her eyes, but she kept them at bay.

"I thought I saw someone standing over her, but it couldn't be so." Her voice quivered as she spoke.

"Why is that?"

"The person who I saw standing over her has been dead for months."

"I've had patients describe stranger happenings, but as a medical professional, I can't admit I believe in such things. However, I'll say some things occur on this earth that we simply do not understand."

Chapter 41

When the hospital released Clint, he stopped by Blake's room. The couple embraced, crying over the loss of someone who had shaped both of their lives. He sat down beside her and held her hand.

"I need to get out of here and clear my head," Clint said. "If you're okay with it, I would love to go take a shower and sleep in our bed tonight. I want to love on Willow, too. I'll come first thing in the morning." He caressed Blake's cheek with his hand. "I'll text you before I go to bed to see if you're up to talking."

"Wait, is your brother going back to the cottage with you?" Blake asked. "Will you have someone watch the cottage tonight? I don't like you being there alone, or even with other people."

"Blake, everything will be fine. Landon is going back with me, and Shane is patrolling the area tonight." Clint kissed her one more time before he left.

Susan entered the room with some magazines, a fuzzy robe and Blake's iPad. "Hi, honey. I brought some comforts from home. Do you want to flip through these bridal magazines?"

Forget looking at pictures of wedding dresses. She needed to research a way to fight back with Parker and end his reign of torment on her family. However, her mom wasn't in tune with her spiritual side. Blake couldn't sit there around and search for *what to do when being haunted by your former fiancé*. She had to get rid of Susan for a while.

"Mom, I'm starving. Would you mind picking up some non-hospital food for dinner?" Blake asked.

"Sure. What would you like?"

"Soup and sandwiches from Page's. Oh, don't forget to order a piece of cake." She could taste the sugary frosting and spongy cake melting in her mouth.

"Sounds delicious. I'll leave now so that I can beat the dinner rush," Susan said.

"Thanks, Mom." Blake figured she had at least thirty minutes to search for information, maybe more if rush hour traffic had begun.

Blake searched for general information on hauntings, with no luck. *Why hasn't someone developed a better how-to guide on getting rid of ghosts?* She turned her attention to researching the history of the Mason homestead. She combed through dozens of old newspaper articles about her family hosting events at the house and Granny Mason winning gardening awards.

On the verge of giving up, she stumbled across an article promoting a Halloween event the mayor had hosted at the house when Granny Mason and Nancy were teenagers. They were wearing witch costumes in the photographs. Paulene wore a fortuneteller costume, equipped with a crystal ball and tarot cards. The reporter called her a clairvoyant and said she would perform a séance during the event.

Blake groaned. With all the terrible events, she had forgotten to cancel the Halloween open house. She called the mayor's office, hoping someone would answer. Thankfully, one of the island's special events coordinators was still in the office.

"Hi, Chelsea. I'm so sorry, but we can't host a Halloween event at Mason B&B." Blake filled her in on all the difficulties her family had faced.

"Oh, my goodness. How can we help support you and Clint? If there's anything you need at all, please consider it done."

"Thank you so much. We're grateful for the offer. For now, we just need to make sure no one shows up at the cottage tomorrow. Please keep us in mind for any Christmas events the town hosts."

"Of course. I'll talk to you soon." Chelsea said.

After the call ended, she quickly dialed Paulene's cell phone number. When she picked up, Blake told her Nancy had passed away.

"Oh, no! I'm so sorry to hear that! What happened?"

Blake explained the bookcase incident and how Parker had killed Nancy. Paulene cried. Blake's heart sank; Nancy Parsons had left her mark on the world. Blake sighed and said she would make sure Paulene had the details for the funeral.

Paulene cleared her throat. "I'll be there. Please call me if I can do anything for your family."

Blake thanked her and hung up the phone just moments before Susan came into the room with their dinner. "Were you talking to someone on the phone?"

"Yep. Just a friend."

As the women ate dinner, Blake fidgeted in the bed. "Mom, I'm sorry if I've caused you an inordinate amount of grief over the past year."

"Not at all, Blake. None of this is your fault. I'm concerned about your well-being, but your life is here with Clint. Plus, I love the fact you're taking such great care of our family's home. I didn't want the house to fall into disrepair if we couldn't afford to keep the groundskeeper on the payroll indefinitely."

"I love living here with Clint, and we have enjoyed hosting guests. It won't be the same without Nancy." Blake's eyes filled with tears. "I'm hoping we find a new normal soon."

Blake remembered Nancy saying she would be safe after her wedding day. She had an idea. "Mom, I haven't talked to Clint yet, but we don't have any weddings or events scheduled until spring. What if Clint and I got married right before Christmas? Everyone has been planning to get together at the cottage over the holidays, anyway."

"Blake, that sounds beautiful. I won't say anything to Clint until you two have talked."

"Thanks, Mom. I need to rest again. You can go back to the cottage. I'll be fine, and you'll sleep better there."

"No. Let me take care of you. I haven't always been able to take time to help you, but I can now. I want to be here for you."

Blake's eyes widened. All the chaos seemed to have changed her mom as much as it had transformed her.

Chapter 42

Blake woke up to the sound of Clint and Susan whispering outside her room.

"You guys—I'm awake. You can stop whispering," Blake said.

They walked back into her room and sat down. "Sorry if we woke you. I'll go pick up breakfast for you two, bring it back here, and then I'll go back to the cottage to check on Willow," Susan said.

"That would be awesome. We'd appreciate that. Hopefully, the doctor won't keep me here too much longer," Blake said.

"Text me if the doctor comes while I'm gone." Susan winked at Clint.

"What were you and my mom talking about earlier?" Blake asked.

"Nothing. I asked if the doctor had come yet. Oh, she said you had something important to ask me."

Blake rubbed her temples. "Unbelievable. I asked Mom not to tell you until I was ready. Oh well, it doesn't matter. I want to talk to you."

"Are you okay?" Clint asked.

"Yes. I want to move our wedding to December, right before Christmas," Blake said.

"Are you sure, Blake? I mean, I'm ready to marry you right now, but you had your heart set on a fall wedding. Will we have enough time to plan?"

"I'm positive, and a simple wedding in the garden with family and a few friends would be perfect."

"Great! Let's get you better. Then, we can start planning." Suddenly, the light in his eyes dimmed, and he hung his head, looking at his feet.

Blake's heart ached. "It won't be the same without Nancy." She began crying. "We have another family event to plan first." She reached out for Clint, pulling his body close to hers. "What can I do to help?"

"For now, just focus on getting better. I need you to be back at home with me. Landon has made plans. We wanted to give my family plenty of time to plan to travel." Tears formed in Clint's eyes. "She was an incredible lady. No one can fill this void she has left in the world."

Blake cried and held him. "I'm glad we have each other."

"Me, too. If I didn't have you…" Clint trailed off, and a tear fell from his eye onto her shoulder. It hurt her heart to see him in this much pain. She reached out for him.

Clint curled up in her hospital bed with her, and after a few minutes, they dozed off.

"Well, this is too adorable for words," Susan said as she walked back into Blake's room with their breakfast.

"I didn't realize I'd fallen asleep." Clint stretched and yawned.

"Did you guys talk?" Susan asked.

Blake narrowed her eyes and pursed her lips. "Yes, Mom. We're getting married in December. I thought you were going to let me break the news to him."

"I did, but I just helped it happen a little quicker than it would have otherwise." Susan winked.

"We need to pay tribute to Nancy's life before we plan the wedding," Blake said. "I mean, we can ask family members to save the date, but I don't want to send invitations yet."

"Clint, does Landon need help planning her service?" Susan asked, placing her hand on his shoulder.

"Gram requested to have her ashes scattered along the coastline, from Isle of Palms up to the coast to Wilmington, North Carolina, where she was born." Clint rubbed his red eyes. "We were thinking about having a brief service on the beach and my brothers and me taking the trip immediately afterward. We need to rent chairs for the service and a large boat for the journey."

"I can get some rental prices for you, and I can plan a small reception back at the cottage for her friends."

"That would be perfect, thank you."

"How's Willow, Mom?" Blake asked.

"She's lost without her people there." Susan frowned.

Blake clutched her heart. "Oh, my gosh. Poor Willow. I hadn't thought about how she was dealing with Nancy being gone. Plus, I've been away, and Clint was in the hospital until yesterday. She probably thinks we've all abandoned her."

"Don't worry. She'll be okay. Just give her lots of love when you're released. In the meantime, I'm on top of it," Susan said.

Dr. Remington knocked on the door. "Good morning, all. Blake, we have reviewed the results from all your tests. Aside from your migraines, you are healthy. Somehow you've avoided permanent brain injuries after severe blows to the head this year. Please follow up with me in a few weeks during my regular office hours." He paused and drew a breath. "You have had some traumatic events in your life lately. I would like for you two to take a break. If you can, take a vacation. If you can't leave town, have a staycation and do nothing for two weeks."

After the doctor left, Susan turned to Blake and Clint with a thoughtful expression. "Are you two going to follow the doctor's orders, or do I need to kick you out of the cottage for a couple of weeks?"

"Well, after Nancy's service, we could take a break and visit Wilmington for a week," Blake said.

"That sounds nice," Clint said, staring at the wall.

The nurse on duty brought Blake's discharge papers. "Good news. You can go home now." She smiled.

Clint squeezed Blake's hand. "We're all thankful for that."

Chapter 43

Willow greeted Blake as she opened the front door to the cottage. She bent down to pet her, and the dog's tail wagged.

"I've missed you, sweet girl." Blake continued to rub her ears.

Landon walked out of the den just in time to witness the reunion. "She has been missing you," he said.

Blake stood up and looked at her future brother-in-law. "How are the plans for Nancy's service going?"

"Everything's ready for Saturday. Susan has a reception planned. We're so glad to be part of your family, and soon it will be official." Landon paused, tears streaming down his splotchy, puffy face. "I miss Gram. I know you and Clint do, too."

A wave of tears flowed from Blake's eyes. Nancy wouldn't pop into the room unannounced ever again.

The cottage was quiet for the rest of the day. Everyone walked around in a zombie-like state, barely speaking. Emotionally drained, Clint and Blake went outside for some fresh air and to nap in the garden hammock. Just as Blake drifted off to sleep, Willow began barking.

"What's the matter with her?" Clint stretched and yawned.

Blake looked up, but she didn't see Willow. She got out of the hammock and began searching the yard, but the pup was nowhere in sight.

Her heart raced. *Where did my sweet girl go?* "Clint! She's not in the yard. She must have gotten out. Come help me find her!"

Blake began running down Palm Court, looking into their neighbors' yards and calling for her furry friend as she made her way to the main road. *Please, God, don't let Willow get hurt*. Blake's heart ached. She should have been watching her better or at least chained her harness to the lead, but the dog had never run away. Typically, she found contentment chasing birds and squirrels around the garden. When she'd had enough exercise and excitement, she'd enjoy the shade of the expansive canopy. Something must have scared her. Blake didn't need two guesses to figure out Parker was to blame.

After running almost three miles with no sign of Willow, Blake cried. Life without her sweet sidekick wouldn't be the same. Out of breath and covered in sweat, she returned to the cottage. Along the way, she stopped to ask a few neighbors if they had seen her. No one answered the door at the first two houses.

In her state of panic, she hadn't checked the time. It was noon. Most people with traditional office jobs would still be working. She opened her social media accounts and started writing a lost pet post on the local animal shelter pages. As she attached a picture to the first post, she bit her lip, and tears spilled out of her eyes. Something had to give. Willow just had to be okay. Today, out of all days, she needed this to be true. She had just lost her confidante and one of her best friends; she couldn't bear to lose another.

She looked up from her phone. Clint was running toward her, smiling. Considering he was grieving the loss of his grandmother, she took this as a sign of hope.

"Roger, one of my deputies, found her in the yard at Gram's house! She's okay, just a little scared. He's still there with her. C'mon, let's go get our girl!"

Tears of relief sprung from Blake's eyes as she ran to Clint's Jeep.

"Thank you, God!" she yelled and threw her hands up toward the sky.

Pulling into the driveway, she cried tears of joy. Willow was sitting on the front porch with Roger.

The second Clint put the Jeep in park, she jumped out and ran to the dog. She kneeled on the porch and squeezed her.

"I'm so glad to see you, girl!" She kissed Willow's head. In between the folds of Willow's fur around her neck, she found something that didn't belong. She pulled a gold chain necklace with a gold and tarnished silver cross pendant. Who would put a necklace around a dog's neck? What a strange thing to do.

She removed the chain from Willow's neck and continued to examine the pendant. It looked old, but she wasn't a jewelry expert. It was smooth except for one spot where dirt had collected, probably while the dog romped around wearing it.

"What is it, Blake?" Clint asked.

"Someone must have thought it was funny to put a necklace on a dog." She held up the chain, and Clint examined it.

"That is one of the strangest things I've seen, and I've been a cop my entire adult life."

She scraped a clump of dirt off the pendant to read the inscription on the back—*From JCM to NLP, In Love and Light.*

"Clint, was this Nancy's pendant? It must be, look at this inscription! JCM, Julia Caroline Mason, to NLP, Nancy Lynn Parsons?"

He shook his head. "I don't remember her ever wearing it, but that doesn't mean it wasn't hers. We're at her house, after all. Do you think *she* put it on Willow?" Wide-eyed, he turned around as if he expected his grandmother's spirit to emerge from the front door.

"I wish I had the answer to your question. Whoever did this wanted us to find the pendant, that's for sure. I guess we'll wait to find out who is behind this and why they did it." Blake gulped. Perhaps Parker was not behind Willow's disappearance. From what she had read online, evil spirits didn't tolerate touching crosses. Could Nancy be helping them from the Other Side? With Parker's relentless antics, they needed all the help they could get. She put the chain and pendant around her neck for safekeeping, ready to use it against Parker the next time he showed his devilish face.

Over the next two days, Blake and Clint's family members started arriving on the island. They held their emotions together until Clint's three-year-old nephew, Ethan, opened the door to the cottage and began calling for Nancy—"Gram, Gram, where are you?"

Ethan's sister, Claire, who was a year older, said, "She has gone up there," pointing to the sky. Ethan looked up and nodded. The adults looked at each other, wide-eyed. Blake was on the verge of tears, and she was sure the others shared this sentiment. They'd agreed earlier that they didn't want the children to see them in a raw emotional state.

Clint's and Nancy's coworkers and friends kept the house filled with food. The owners of the Sea Biscuit Cafe offered to cater the reception for free; Clint bit his lip and whispered his thanks.

When the time for the service arrived, Clint's brothers carried framed photos of Nancy out to the beach, along with one long-stemmed white rose. Clint wore a white rose pinned to his linen button-down shirt. His black guitar strap stood out in contrast.

Standing in front of their family and friends, he hung his head, closed his eyes and picked through a verse of *Amazing Grace* before he broke down crying. Shaking, Blake ran to him, took his guitar and helped him to his seat.

The pastor from Nancy's church read Romans 8:38-9 from the Bible.

> *"For I'm convinced that neither death nor life, neither angels nor demons, neither the present nor the future, nor any powers. Neither height nor depth, nor anything else in all creation, will be able to separate us from the love of God that is in Christ Jesus our Lord."*

Nancy and Granny Mason were together again. Selfishly, Blake wished they were alive, but at least they had each other.

The Parsons brothers each took a moment, recalling their happiest memory of their grandmother. They walked to the water and dropped their roses into the waves, watching the tide carry them away.

When the brief service had ended, her mother called her name. "Are you okay?"

She shook herself back to reality, sighed loudly and teared up. "Yes. Just missing Nancy and Granny Mason."

"Me, too," Susan said, dabbing her eyes with a tissue. "I need to make sure the catering team has everything they need. If you want to talk, I'll be in the kitchen."

"Thanks, Mom. I need to go find Clint and ask him when he is planning to leave for the marina in the morning."

"I'm right here," Clint whispered, with his hands in his pockets. "My brothers and I decided we couldn't leave without spending some time at the reception. We'll leave for Wilmington around eight tomorrow morning. Are you still planning to meet me there?"

"Definitely. You should spend some time with your family and friends. I'm going to find mine and thank them for coming," Blake said.

"Sorry to interrupt you…"

Blake turned to see Paulene standing behind her, clutching a tissue. Blake put her arm around her.

"This must be a hard time for you," Paulene said. "I was torn up to hear about Nancy's passing. We were so close as girls, and we were just starting to build a friendship again right before the *accident*. I've been praying for your family, and I hope you'll call if I can do anything for you."

"Thanks so much for everything. Nancy was glad to reconnect with you. We appreciate you coming today." Blake smiled weakly.

"That's sweet of you to say. I overheard you talking about your trip to Wilmington. There are some excellent antique bookstores along the Riverwalk. I've called around a few times looking for your Granny's book, but, in the used book market, inventory turns over so quickly. Anyway, it's worth taking time to browse in person."

"I appreciate the tip. I'll call you if I find it," Blake said.

Paulene hugged her and said she needed to leave. "I'll see you soon. Call me if you need anything."

After Paulene walked away, Blake found her dad and siblings sitting with a group of her high school and college friends. She thanked everyone for making the trip to support her.

"I'd better go check on your mom. I am sure she has the entire kitchen crew under her spell by now." Jeremy laughed. "However, I'll go, just in case they have turned on her."

By the time Blake made it back to the kitchen, the catering crew had already set up the buffet in the garden. She followed her mom and helped replenish a few trays of food. Guests were dining and taking in the coffee table books Susan had filled with photos of Nancy and her boys on the island. On each table, she had placed a stack of postcards with the information on how to download the pictures.

After two hours, guests began leaving the cottage. Remaining were the closest family members and friends, most of whom were staying overnight. Clint's siblings and their families filled the carriage house to the brim, and the cottage was full on this grief-stricken night at the Mason B&B.

Blake walked into her bedroom. Tears rolled down Clint's cheeks as he stood near the window.

She wiped his eyes with a tissue. "I love you. I thought you were in bed."

"I can't sleep right now. Gram didn't deserve to die; it's so unfair. We should have had a lot more time together."

"I'm so sorry. I'm missing Nancy, too." Blake's eyes brimmed with tears. "Let's go to bed."

When Clint lay down next to Blake, he began crying again. "She was the best grandmother any of us could have asked for."

Blake held him, letting him vent to her and cry for the next three hours. Finally, his body had enough, and he fell asleep.

Chapter 44

Clint and his brothers met for breakfast in the main house's kitchen at 6:30 a.m. He had cooked enough for an army, two-dozen eggs and three pounds of sausage.

"Something smells delicious. That should keep your energy levels high during your trip," Blake said as she entered the kitchen. Clint turned from the stove to kiss her and offered her a plate.

She sat down at the kitchen table with the Parsons brothers, who were reminiscing about their childhood on the island. Nancy would have loved to be there with her boys. They had cared for their grandmother as much as she loved them.

Blake's heart ached. Today Clint and his brothers would honor Nancy's last wishes by scattering her ashes along the Atlantic from Isle of Palms to Carolina Beach, just outside of Wilmington. Afterward, Blake and her future sisters-in-law would meet the Parsons men for dinner at Nancy's favorite restaurant in Wilmington, the Boathouse.

When Blake got ready to leave the house, Susan curled up with Willow on the couch.

"Aww! You two are so cute together," Blake said. "Thanks for taking care of each other while we're away."

"You're welcome, sweetie. This is a hard time for you; it is for all of us. But when you get back in town, would you want to shop for a wedding dress and start getting plans underway? We don't have much time," Susan said.

"Yeah…I'm worried about the short timeline. We'll figure it out, though. We always do." Blake grinned.

"Isn't that the truth." Susan laughed. "Have fun!"

Blake threw her luggage into the trunk of the Thunderbird. She grabbed her cell phone to queue up her '80s dance hits playlist. Sliding on her favorite sunglasses, she made her way to Highway 17 North. Drunken Jack's Seafood in Murrells Inlet called her name. Blake glanced at her watch. She had plenty of time for a leisurely lunch at Drunken Jack's, a family favorite. After finishing her seafood, she strolled along the boardwalk. The scent of the salty water filled her lungs, and the vibrant green spartina grass sparkled in the sunlight.

After lunch, she continued heading north, passing through Myrtle Beach and finally making her way across the North Carolina state line. Childhood trips up the coastline in the Thunderbird flashed through her mind. She could almost hear Granny Mason's laughter as they made up silly songs about their family and friends. During one especially fun drive, when Blake was 13, they'd written a song about Clint.

You stole my heart when we were four. I'll love you forever, even if you snore.

Blake snorted. Her grandmother had made typically boring activities exciting. Childhood memories of Granny Mason were her favorite.

Just outside of Wilmington, a rustling sound came from her backseat. With the convertible top down, she hadn't placed any bags or luggage in the backseat. Her throbbing browbone confirmed she had picked up an unwanted passenger. She checked her rearview mirror. Parker flashed his smug, assuming grin she recognized all too well.

"Well, hello there. Took you long enough to notice me." Parker gave Blake an icy stare. "So, how are you doing today, beautiful?"

Blake let out a high-pitched scream and slammed on her brakes. Luckily, there wasn't another car in sight. She pulled over onto the shoulder and threw the gearshift into park.

Ripping off her sunglasses, she slammed them down on the passenger seat. She turned, locking eyes with Parker. "What in the hell are you doing in my car? Haven't you have caused my family enough grief?"

She reached out to punch him, but her hand went right through his body. He laughed in amusement. "That was a classic move. Don't hurt yourself," Parker said in a condescending tone.

"Why won't you give up on torturing us and just move on already?" Blake demanded, reaching out as if she wanted to strangle him.

"Dearest, Blake, I'm just getting started." Parker flashed a devilish grin and faded away as if he were a mist in the breeze.

Blake's blood boiled. Parker was to blame for Nancy's death, Clint's injuries, not to mention her own, and many strange happenings that had occurred at the cottage. Since Parker had died, interfering in their lives had become his full-time job. He needed to move on to his next destination. She would find a solution as soon as they returned to the island. Parker would have his day of reckoning.

Trying to get her mind off him, she pulled into a parking space in the historic downtown district and wandered through some shops Paulene had recommended. Browsing the windows of a cute boutique, she wandered in to browse the jewel-toned hardbound books on the bookcases that lined the walls. For a book lover, this was heaven, but she didn't see a copy of Granny Mason's book.

Blake searched through five more stores, but she didn't have any luck. Still hopeful, she scanned the stores along the Riverwalk. She had a powerful urge to go into a charming antique store, filled with beautiful solid mahogany furniture, oil paintings, jewelry and odds and ends.

Rummaging through all the artifacts, she pushed Parker's recent appearance out of her mind. A book fell off a shelf, and she jumped. Bending over to pick it up, she read the title—*The Curse and*

Blessing of the Other Side and the author's name, J. C. Mason. The copyright in the book read 1962. She gasped, trembling. "J.C." as in "Julia Caroline?" This had to be the book.

"Find something that interests you?" A tall man with a white beard and glasses approached her.

"What do you know about this book and the author?"

"Ah…yes. The author wrote the book in a different time," he said, puffing on his pipe. "The topic of seeing spirits, especially among refined young women, was taboo. She was a new bride when this book debuted, and she received quite a bit of criticism for her so-called 'outlandish' behavior. However, I had the opportunity to meet Mrs. Mason when she visited the shop. She seemed like a lovely woman."

"Mrs. Julia Caroline Mason?" she asked.

"Yes. How did you know?"

Her heart burst with pride. "She was my grandmother. I'd heard she wrote a book but hadn't been able to track down a copy."

"You should be proud of her accomplishments. She truly was a trailblazer. Please accept the book as a gift from me," he said with a warm smile. He placed the book in a shopping bag and handed it to her.

Eager to tear into the book, she thanked him and walked outside to find a park bench to read the book, and, hopefully, learn how to get rid of Parker's unseemly presence in her life.

A breeze stirred all around her as she read through the first two chapters of the book where her grandmother confirmed the story Nancy had shared. Her father-in-law haunted her, leading up to her wedding. Her powers came into fruition the day before her wedding, and once the nuptials took place, he left her alone. However, her connection to the Other Side didn't end.

Granny Mason had spent her young adulthood exploring the paranormal world and trying to find ways to protect the living from being attacked by spirits. She had discovered other people, with similar gifts, who had ended a haunting by a major life event—a graduation, wedding, baby being born or buying a new home.

Lost in the pages, she received a text from Clint saying they had arrived at the marina and were preparing to dock and moor the boat.

She stuffed the book into her tote bag and began walking toward the restaurant. *Should they move up the wedding yet again, despite not having a dress or plans for their Christmastime ceremony, a mere eight weeks away?* In the chaos, while setting the wedding date, she had forgotten one crucial detail Nancy had mentioned—the lunar eclipse. She did a quick Internet search. Crap…the next one would occur the weekend after Thanksgiving. After that, they'd have to wait another for six months. They couldn't take a chance that Parker would cause more pain in their lives.

Deep in thought, when she arrived at the restaurant, she couldn't help but shift her focus to Clint and his brothers. They were sitting close to each other and laughing. Their boat ride together had been therapeutic. Nothing could replace their beloved grandmother, but they had grown even closer.

If Parker's goal was to cause sadness to rip apart the family, he had failed to accomplish what he had set out to do. She wouldn't let him hurt anyone else in her family.

Chapter 45

After Clint's siblings went on their way, he and Blake checked into a charming bed and breakfast in a turquoise-and-pink Victorian house.

Once they were in their room, Blake told Clint what she had discovered. "Are you okay with moving up our wedding to the Saturday after Thanksgiving?"

"As I said before, I would gladly marry you now. Whatever we need to do it to get rid of Parker, I'm good to go. But for now, we're in this beautiful room. I'm determined to focus all of my energy on you."

Clint kissed her.

Blake threw her head back and sighed. "I've missed this."

"Well, you'll never have to miss it again. I'm all yours."

The couple spent their mornings in Wilmington soaking up the sun while exploring quaint cafes and boutiques along the Riverwalk. Thank God for vacation, an escape from life's problems.

One morning, Blake woke before Clint, so she wandered out to a cute bakery to buy some treats and coffee for them to enjoy in their room. When she returned, Clint had built a fire and had a gleam in his eye.

"I've been waiting for you." He pulled her closer.

She pouted. "Not too long, I hope."

"Long enough. So many horrible things have happened over the past month. I'm ready to put it all behind us and focus on us."

After two delightful hours in their room, Blake kissed Clint and got up to pour a bath and a glass of wine, soaking until the water lost its warmth. She slipped on a robe and walked back to the bedroom to curl up with Clint again. She dozed off in his arms, and the two didn't wake for the next few hours.

"Let's just have something delivered for dinner and stay in tonight," Clint said, pulling her closer to him.

"Mmm…sounds great to me."

When their dinner arrived, Clint took it outside to their riverfront balcony. The scents of the food and hints of salt air from the nearby Atlantic Ocean swirled together to create a tantalizing aroma. Blake retrieved a bottle of wine from the mini-fridge, pouring each of them a glass to enjoy with dinner.

Clint brushed Blake's hair out of her face. "I enjoy every day I spend with you, but this has been my favorite so far. I'm lucky to have many more days like this one to look forward to throughout our lives together."

"Definitely—I'm ready to get married. You're the one I belong with."

A text came in from her mother, and a picture of Willow, grinning ear to ear, popped up on her phone screen. "Oh, I miss her! Let's go home in the morning."

"I miss her too, but for now, we're right here with no distractions or responsibilities. I can think of some intriguing ways to finish out the evening."

"So can I." Blake flashed him a seductive smile.

"Well, what are you waiting for?" Clint pulled her back into the bedroom.

A tingle went down her spine, and she couldn't help but giggle like a teenage girl. She loved the man who had swept her off her feet more than once. No one could measure up to him, not that she was tempted even to try.

The couple spent the rest of the evening snuggling in bed, wrapped up in each other's arms.

"Where should we go for our honeymoon?" Clint asked.

"Christmastime will be chilly here," Blake said. "I want to go somewhere tropical where we can sink our toes into the sand with a frozen drink. What about the Bahamas?"

"I love that idea. It sounds heavenly."

They lay in bed reading in each other's arms until they dozed off.

Dreams swirled through her mind, starting with the morning of her wedding. Granny Mason stood by her side every step of the way until the moment Clint kissed her at the ceremony. Then she vanished into thin air. Blake hit her knees, crying.

She shot straight up in bed with tears streaming down her face.

Laughter filtered into the room from outside. Blake looked out the window. The children, *her grandparents,* were there. The girl turned and waved at her, and Blake waved back and smiled. At that moment, she was confident her grandmother would make good on her promise to always be part of her life.

Chapter 46

The couple took one last walk along the Riverwalk and then returned to the bed and breakfast to check out of their room. They loaded their luggage and left for Isle of Palms. As Clint drove, Blake rolled the windows down and shuddered when the cool, crisp air brushed against her skin.

Everything they had been through since she'd come back to the island flashed through her mind. Would they be safe after their nuptials? She hoped Nancy's theory was right.

If it were up to Blake, she would have planned a simple elopement for her and Clint. But in addition to the specific timing of the wedding, there was a strength in numbers. Having help with the cleansing ceremony and support during the wedding itself would help foolproof her attempt to get rid of Parker. Also, she wanted to get married at the cottage with her friends and family present.

She needed to finish reading Granny Mason's book before she made too many decisions. If their vows would bring an end to the series of tragedies, she needed to prioritize planning the wedding. The bed and breakfast could be put on hold until the spring. They had canceled existing reservations and stopped taking new ones when Nancy got hurt. Each subsequent event had further delayed the reopening of the business.

Fortunately, Blake had built a healthy savings account. Clint had been with the police department his entire career and had great paid leave benefits. He had worked as much as possible in between each devastating incident. Blake appreciated his dedication to his career, the island and, above all, his family and friends.

The drive back to the island seemed to take less time than usual. No matter how many times she drove across the IOP Connector, the familiar sights of the marshy creek, the gorgeous beach homes and, in the distance, the Sullivan's Island Lighthouse. She craved a walk on the beach and the warmth of the sun, but first, she needed to hold her lovable dog.

When they opened the door to the cottage, Willow greeted them. Blake kneeled to pet her. The dog wagged her tail and licked Blake's face.

"Hi, sweet girl! I've missed you!" She grabbed a treat from Willow's cookie jar and ruffled her fur.

Susan walked into the living room. "I'm glad to see you both. Willow has been pouting today. She missed you."

"I'll take her for a walk on the beach," Blake said.

Clint grabbed Willow's leash. "I'll come with you, and I have a surprise for you in the garden. Your mom said it arrived while we were away."

Blake walked outside. A white and turquoise-striped SUP board and paddle leaned against a tree. She smiled at Clint. "You remembered! Let's go now!"

Clint offered to carry the board for her, and they crossed the street to the beach access. The moment the water came into view, the tension in her shoulders melted away. The ocean was part of her everyday life now, not just a seaside getaway.

They walked into the water, and Clint stayed with Willow while Blake tried out the paddleboard. She started on her knees, and after 20 minutes, she worked up the nerve to try standing on the board. She fell off a few times, but after some more practice, she had better control of her core and balance.

A massive wave came crashing down, knocking her off the board and slightly bruising her ego. Blake looked over her shoulder.

She laughed as Willow chased seagulls, pulling Clint across the beach in the process. The two seemed to be getting smaller as they ran farther away from her. Clint stopped walking and, although she couldn't make out the words, he was yelling. He motioned as if he were trying to tell someone to get out of the water.

Who was swimming? Were they having trouble fighting the current? Maybe she could help.

Clint kicked off his shoes, tied Willow's leash to the pier and ran into the ocean, swimming quickly. Blake craned her neck, but she was too far away to see why he had dived into the water in such a hurry. She jumped out of the water, set her board and paddle on the sand and began running. Someone was struggling in the water. She pulled her phone out of her pocket to call for help, but dialing the numbers, she froze.

"Clint, no! Don't bother. It's Parker. That son of a bitch is already dead! He pulls this kind of stunt on me every other week." Blake screamed, but Clint had shifted into his first-responder zone, focused on the matter at hand. Panicked, she needed to get into the water quickly and stop his rescue efforts.

No! Please, God—spare Clint!

She dived in, but she had lost sight of Clint. Then she spotted Parker, who was holding him underwater. Clint tried to break free but couldn't. Blake swam, kicking her legs furiously, but the current kept sweeping Clint further away from her.

Her stomach churned, and tears stung her eyes, but she had to keep going to save the man she loved.

Finally, she caught up with them and screamed at Parker. She lunged at him, but a wave swelled and pulled her underwater. When she resurfaced, she began yelling again.

"Leave him alone! He is none of your concern. If you have a problem with me or how things ended between us, take it up with me." Adrenaline pumping through her veins, Blake pulled Clint out of Parker's arms.

Clint was unconscious. Blake swam, struggling to keep his head above water. After fighting the current, she pulled him to shore and gave him CPR. Thankfully, he began breathing during the first set of compressions, but he needed to get to the hospital immediately. She pulled her phone out of her pocket, hoping the waterproof case had protected it. She dialed 9-1-1 and gave the dispatcher directions to their location on the beach.

While she waited, she called out to Parker and hit her knees. “I know you’re out there, and I want you to listen to me. You’re the one who cheated on me. I was faithful to you. What good did that do me? Now you’ve tried killing Clint and me multiple times, and you murdered Nancy. You have threatened my family. After you died, I realized I never loved you. I beg of you: please let me go. Leave us alone.”

By the time the emergency crew arrived, Clint had opened his eyes. They asked him a few questions as they loaded him into the ambulance, and he responded. Blake pulled herself together as much as possible and told the driver she would meet them at the hospital, untied Willow and ran back to the cottage.

“Mom! Clint has been in an accident, but I think he will be okay. I don’t have time to explain. I’ll call you when I get to the hospital. Here’s Willow.” She grabbed her keys, jumped into her car and sped to the hospital.

Her mother yelled, “Go! Go!”

When she got there, the emergency room staff pointed her to the room where Clint was waiting. She couldn’t help but hug him.

Dr. Remington came into the room, shaking his head. “I was trying to avoid seeing you two like this again. Please tell me this will be the last time.”

“Hopefully, we’ll be able to arrange that very soon.” Clint winked at Blake.

“I’m beyond grateful you’re okay.” Blake wept tears of relief.

“It will all be fine.” He patted her back.

“Clint, you appear to be alright, and you’re in good hands. You two can leave. I need you to try a little harder to avoid the hospital,” Dr. Remington said.

While Clint signed some paperwork, Blake texted Susan to share the news. *Thank you, God, for sparing Clint.* She couldn’t imagine life without him.

Chapter 47

"It was a battle of the snores in here last night." She closed her eyes, pretended to snore and laughed.

"Oh, no. Did Willow and I keep you up?" Clint asked.

"I'll be okay." She laughed.

"Well, let me cook breakfast to make it up to you." Clint kissed her. "Why don't you go soak in the tub and relax?"

"You just got out of the hospital. You need to rest."

"Seriously, I'm okay. I want to cook for my fiancé. What's the harm in that?" Clint winked at her.

"Okay. If you feel up to it…" She began walking upstairs to her bathroom.

Blake pulled her hair into a bun, poured a warm bath and dropped a honey-scented bath bomb into the water. Sliding into the tub, the tension in her shoulders melted away. She pulled her grandmother's book off the tray she kept near the tub and lost herself in its pages.

Granny Mason's paranormal research was fascinating. She shared case studies of young men and women who had struggled to get rid of an evil hitchhiking spirit. Chapter Nineteen focused on the details of the cleansing ceremony, which intrigued her until the heavenly scents of breakfast cooking wafted upstairs, making her stomach rumble.

"I guess it's time to eat," she said to herself, pulling on a sundress that had been lying on her dressing table. She made a mental note to go back to that section in the book after she finished eating. When she turned back, something in the mirror caught her attention. A young woman who resembled her appeared in the mirror. Blake stood, paralyzed with fear.

"Don't be scared," the woman said. "It's me, Granny Mason, Blake. I don't look the same, but surely you recognize yourself in my appearance. I've wanted to talk to you for a long time, but I wanted to give you time to come to terms with your gift. Nancy agreed to help ease you into the idea." Julia Caroline smiled. "Please listen to me carefully. I know you have a copy of my book, and you're planning to marry your true love. I'm so happy for you. Don't deviate from the directions in my book, or you risk the cleansing ceremony not working. Do you understand?"

In shock, Blake forced a nod.

"Papa and I are trying to keep this devil away from you, but our schedules aren't always predictable. If you need help, my friend Paulene Sisk still lives on the island. Find her." She paused. "Blake, I want to tell you how proud I am of you, and I love you." Granny Mason smiled as her image faded away from the mirror, revealing Blake's reflection.

Blake numbly walked downstairs to tell Clint what had happened, but Susan was sitting at the kitchen table, breaking beans for dinner. Blake must have made a strange facial expression when Clint handed her a plate filled with scrambled eggs, bacon and cinnamon toast. He raised his eyebrows at her, but she shook her head and pointed at her mother.

Blake furrowed her brow but tried to smile. "Mom, you don't need to stay here to take care of us."

Susan threw her hands down. "Oh, sweetheart, don't worry about me. I'm planning to go to Mount Pleasant to shop and get my hair cut later today. But are you okay? You are as pale as if you've seen a ghost."

"But you don't like talking about supernatural beings," Blake said.

"I didn't say that, but I haven't personally experienced them. Granny Mason had a gift—or as she called it, a blessing—to see and communicate with ghosts and other supernatural beings. She was an accomplished researcher and author on the subject when she was younger. When you were little, she always told me she suspected you would grow up to have the gift."

Blake narrowed her eyes. "I found one of her books in an antique store in Wilmington. Why haven't we talked about this before?"

"I asked her not to say anything until you were old enough to decide for yourself. I had no way of knowing she would die so young." Susan wiped a couple of tears off her cheek.

After her mom regained her composure, Blake continued their discussion. "Mom, I've told you how Parker attacked Nancy, Clint and me, but I haven't shared the extent that I've seen spirits ever since Granny Mason died. Just now, I saw Granny Mason as a young woman. She appeared in my bathroom mirror. She and Papa have appeared to me many times as children playing on the tire swing in the backyard."

Susan winced.

"Mom. Say something."

"Sorry. It was a lot to take in, but I think I've processed what you said. What did Granny Mason say? What does all of this mean?"

Blake started by sharing what Granny Mason had told her and didn't stop talking until she had caught Susan up to speed.

"Oh, my goodness, honey. You have been through so many devastating events this year. I'm so sorry." Susan hugged her. "Well, tell me how I can help."

"Thanks, Mom. I'm getting ready to go finish reading the book. By the way, this is short notice, but we're planning to move our wedding to Thanksgiving weekend."

"The sooner, the better, right?" Susan asked. "It's the perfect time."

"Yeah, all of our family will be in town for the holiday, so it makes sense," Blake said. "We can invite friends, and those who can make it are welcome. I'm ready to put Parker behind us and never look back."

"What do we need to do first?" Clint asked.

"I'll help you contact guests. I'll send a group text to all the family members. Can you two text your friends and any of Clint's extended family beyond his brothers?"

"Thanks for helping, Mom. I appreciate it so much. You've been so busy taking care of us. Who has been running your boutique in Knoxville?"

"Cecilia, my assistant manager, has everything under control. I'm planning to promote her next year. I'll still be the owner and be active in the store's operations, but it will give me more time to visit my children—and, eventually, grandchildren. On second thought, scratch the eventually part. Go ahead and start trying for the first baby."

Blake almost choked on the coffee she'd been sipping. "Mom…let's get this wedding planned before we discuss grandchildren. And before we get too far into planning, I'd better go finish reading Granny Mason's book."

She poured a second cup of coffee and went outside to curl up in the hammock and begin reading. Willow came bouncing through the yard and begged to join her.

"Sweet girl. I'm so glad you came to curl up with me." Blake scooped up Willow and set the dog beside her in the hammock. She held the book to her heart, ready to read the words her grandmother had written so eloquently in her young adulthood.

Chapter 48

Blake read Chapter Nineteen at least ten times to make sure she fully understood Granny Mason's words.

Those who can communicate with spirits will develop the ability to send them to their final resting place. Most people are blessed with this gift the night before their wedding, the birth of their first child or moving into a new home. A new beginning is essential; as one door opens and another closes, the hitchhiking spirit will not be able to follow.

To get rid of the spirit, plan the cleansing ceremony around one of the life events mentioned above during a lunar eclipse, and follow these directions:

Write a letter to the deceased to tell them why they need to move on to their next destination. Find a photo of them and, with a group of your loved ones, bury it and the letter in the ground near the last place you saw them. Plant a tree over this spot. As its branches grow toward the light, so will their wandering spirit. Say three kind things about the deceased. On the eve before your event, say a prayer for their soul by candlelight. Blow out the candles when the clock strikes twelve.

You will have confirmation of your success if you hold up a mirror and see the reflection of the deceased standing behind you, holding a candle with an extinguished flame. Tell the spirit to go on to their next destination and have no fear; they can no longer harm you or anyone dear to you. However, they can cause chaos until time for the event. You must go through with the cleansing ceremony, and your loved ones need to be present. There is strength in numbers.

Energized, Blake jumped out of the hammock, picked up Willow and set her on the ground. "Come on, girl! We have a wedding to plan."

They ran into the cottage. Clint was in the kitchen doing dishes, and Blake leaned into his body. "I can't wait to marry you."

"I'm excited to marry my best friend and the only woman I've ever loved. Come upstairs with me for a little while."

"That sounds great, but wait, where's my mom?" Blake asked, looking over her shoulder.

"She went to her hair appointment and to go shopping," he said.

"Well, what are we waiting for?" Blake began running up the steps.

Clint came into the bedroom behind her. "You're so beautiful."

She ran her hands through her hair and shook her head. "I look terrible. My hair is frizzy. I'm not wearing makeup, and I have my baggy sweats on right now."

"You're perfect. You're the one I want," Clint kissed her softly.

"I feel the same way about you."

The couple lay in bed, wrapped in each other's arms and making up for time lost due to the painful occurrences that had taken their lives hostage.

"Let's get up and start dinner. When Mom gets back, we can start making plans for the wedding and sending Parker on to his next destination."

"Sounds like a plan. Susan has all those beans simmering in the slow cooker. We just need to fry the chicken, bake some biscuits and make the gravy."

"Yum. I'm getting hungry," Blake said.

Susan walked into the kitchen and dropped several shopping bags on the table. "Don't be mad, Blake—I was shopping for a dress to wear to your wedding, and I found this champagne-hued Vera

Wang hand-beaded gown. I know how much you love her dresses. It very well may be the only one in South Carolina, and the price I paid was unbelievably low. I figured it was worth taking a chance and returning the dress if you don't like it." Susan pulled out a simple A-line wedding gown with a short train and beaded bodice.

"I love it, Mom. I hope it fits." Blake grabbed the hanger from Susan and ran into the downstairs bathroom. She slipped the dress over her head and zipped it halfway.

Susan waited outside the bathroom, making Clint swear he would stay in the kitchen.

"Come out and show me." Susan poked her head around the corner. "Clint can't see you."

Blake came out, and Susan helped her finish zipping the dress. "What do you think, Mom?"

She twirled around, and her mother held her face in her hands.

"You are so beautiful." Susan smiled and dabbed at her eyes with a tissue. "You need to make sure you're happy with the way it fits. We could always have some minor alterations made if needed."

Blake walked into the living room to look in the full-length mirror in the foyer. She stepped back to get the full effect and smiled at her reflection.

"I feel like a fairytale princess." Blake twirled around, and her mom laughed. "Thank you so much for buying this gorgeous dress. I was worried I wouldn't find one in such a short time frame. The dress fits like a glove. I won't need any alterations…thank God!"

"So, what else do we need? Just an officiant, cake, flowers and a photographer? Oh, and what did Granny Mason's book say?" Susan asked.

Blake ran through the directions outlined in her grandmother's book.

"Sounds easy enough. It should be therapeutic for you," Susan said.

"I agree. I want to keep everything very simple for the wedding."

After making some phone calls to vendors to hold the date, she called her sisters and asked them to wear navy cocktail dresses. And

Clint texted his brothers, asking them to wear khaki dress pants with white button-down shirts. Blake needed to order matching bow ties and bracers for them to wear. She smiled and let out a sigh of relief. Everything was coming together.

"I love seeing you smile," Clint said. "Judge Stephenson, who has been a family friend for years, said he would officiate the wedding. I have a question for you, though—would you be okay holding off on our honeymoon until after Christmas, as we had originally planned? I've already put a deposit on the trip to the oceanfront resort in Nassau. I can try to change the date if you'd rather go right after the wedding."

"No. That will be great. We can unwind from the wedding here at the cottage and enjoy the holidays with our family. We'll go on our exotic honeymoon when the time comes."

Chapter 49

For the next week, Blake and Susan busied themselves with wedding preparations while Clint worked.

When he came home, they made it a point to have dinner together each evening. Afterward, Susan made herself scarce, saying she needed to check in with her boutique management staff. It was clear she was trying to give the couple some space to enjoy the last few moments of quiet time before family members started arriving for the wedding. Blake and Clint happily took advantage of their alone time, taking moonlit walks on the beach, binge-watching their favorite shows and spending romantic moments lost in each other's embrace.

Blake's sisters would arrive on the island in two days. They had a relaxing spa day planned. The rest of the immediate family members would be in town the day before Thanksgiving. Most of their out-of-town friends had made plans to be there Friday afternoon in time for the rehearsal dinner.

When Elaina and Brittany arrived, they threw themselves into finalizing wedding plans and helping with anything else she needed. While driving to the spa, Blake told her sisters how Parker had haunted her and their family. Brittany sat up front so she could read

Blake's lips. She knew bits and pieces of the events involving her but not much else.

"I need to tell you something, and I'm not sure how to start. After Parker died, a lot of strange things started happening, and his spirit appeared to me several times. He is responsible for Nancy's death. I'm certain he is the one who pushed the bookcase onto her, and the day she died, I saw him reach his hand into her head and twist it. He has threatened this family for the last time."

"Blake, that is horrible. Wasn't it enough that Parker hurt you while he was alive?" Elaina asked. "I like your positive attitude, but how can you be sure Parker has finished tormenting you?"

"Before Nancy died, she told me Granny Mason shared that I have the family gift for seeing and talking to spirits. I am pretty freaked out, but Nancy said Granny Mason and Papa have been watching over us.

"They have appeared dozens of times as the cutest, sweetest children. Apparently, they are protecting us from evil spirits. The other day, Granny Mason appeared to me in the bathroom mirror and gave me specific directions on how to send Parker to his next destination."

Brittany sat with her head hanging down.

Blake bent down to get her attention and signed, "Brit, you okay?"

Brittany stared off in the distance. "So, he was the one who threatened me at school? Why didn't you tell me?"

She looked back at Blake, who shook her head. "I didn't want to worry you," Blake signed. "He'd moved onto Nancy, so I thought you were safe. I mean, if I had called you and said, my dead ex is trying to murder me and everyone close to me, what would you have thought? I'm telling you now because I need to enlist your help in carrying out Granny Mason's directions. I want to make sure we follow them to a 'T.'"

"We're in," Elaina said.

Brittany nodded emphatically and waved her fist in the air. "Let's take this asshole down. No one gets away with messing with our sister!"

"Thank you! I'm so glad to have my sisters here with me. Now that I've caught you up to speed on the ridiculously crazy part of my life, we can relax and enjoy the rest of the morning." Blake parked the car, and they began walking toward the beautiful stone day spa building.

Spa staff members greeted the sisters with a glass of champagne and shown to the ladies' dressing room, where an attendant handed them white plush terrycloth robes and slippers. After changing, the attendant guided them to the dimly lit relaxation room, where calming music and herb-scented aromatherapy oils filled the air. They each sat down on a soft, oversized chair, and a server stopped by to offer a selection of fresh-cut fruit along with pineapple-infused water.

Blake melted into the chair, happy for some time to unwind with her sisters before the madness of the holiday and wedding activities started. She had opted to start with a hot stone massage, and her body let go of its tension. Next, a sugar scrub facial cleared out toxins and impurities in her skin. Finally, she and her sisters enjoyed spa pedicures and manicures, complemented by another glass of champagne.

"Thanks for recommending the spa day, Brit. I needed this," Blake said.

"It has been nice, and I'm glad we had a chance to celebrate you," Elaina said as Brittany reeled them in for a group hug.

Pulling away from her sisters, Blake signed, "I have a strange pre-wedding errand I need to run. One of Granny Mason and Nancy's friends volunteers at the library. Paulene has connections to the spiritual world. Since this is our first foray into banishing spirits, it might be helpful to have an expert. Wow. I never thought I would say those words."

After they arrived at the library, Elaina spoke up. "We'll stay in the car. It might be overwhelming if all three of us go in at once."

Blake entered the coastal-style concrete building with a tin roof and walked up to a middle-aged woman with black hair. "Hi. Is Paulene Sisk here today?" Blake asked.

The woman nodded, pointing to the children's library. Blake took in the colorful reading nook displays, decorated with cutouts of characters like Winnie the Pooh and the Cat in the Hat. Her eyes went from a bookcase filled with best-selling children's books to the hunched-over woman with silver hair shelving books.

"Hi, how've you been?" Blake asked.

"Hi! I've been busy with a lot of after school reading programs, but I'm doing well. How are you? I'm so sorry I haven't stopped by to talk to you since Nancy's funeral. I've been searching high and low for your grandmother's book, but I haven't had any luck. Have you?"

"A lot has happened. I found a copy, and Granny appeared to me. She recommended that I talk to you if I had any questions. For the most part, I want to be certain I'm successful in sending Parker to his next destination. It's short notice, but would you be willing to come to our cleansing ceremony at seven p.m. on Friday at my grandmother's house? I'd love it if you would attend my wedding on Saturday as well. Granny Mason would have wanted you there."

"Let me know if I can help." Paulene said.

"Thanks so much. I'd best be going. My sisters are waiting for me. I'll see you around five on Friday."

She walked back to the car and climbed in with a smile on her face. "That went pretty well. Let's get some lunch. I'm starving!" Blake said. "Where do you guys want to go?"

"Page's!" Brittany and Elaina said in unison.

"I should have known." Blake laughed.

They agreed to split three entrees—the shrimp and grit cake, fried seafood platter and the chicken and gravy biscuit. Too full for dessert at the restaurant, they ordered three slices of coconut cake to take back to the cottage and share with Clint and Susan.

"I definitely need to walk. Do you want to go to King Street to shop for your honeymoon?" Brittany asked.

"What a fun idea! I don't make it downtown as often as I would like."

The three women piled into the Thunderbird. After Blake parked, the sisters walked down King Street, making their way through boutiques, picking out lingerie, swimsuits and sundresses, all sure to make Clint's eyes pop out of their sockets. As they left the lingerie shop, an intricate pearl headpiece in the display window of the nearby antique store caught Blake's eye.

Elaina gasped. "Blake, you have to get that to wear with your dress. The vintage style is perfect for a wedding in Granny Mason's garden."

Brittany and Elaina followed her into the shop, where she asked to try on the headpiece. The owner removed it from the display and pointed her to a mirror.

"That is beautiful on you. I agree. You need it." Brittany snapped a photo with her phone.

Blake found her wedding day jewelry, some simple pearl studs and a delicate silver chain with a single pearl pendant. After paying for the jewelry, the sisters headed back to the island to enjoy the tacos, black beans and margaritas Susan had made.

"Let's watch some of the movies we loved as kids," Brittany said.

Blake pulled out a few animated fairytale films. "You guys pick which one you want to watch and make some popcorn. I want to go talk to Clint for a few minutes," she said.

She ran upstairs and found him in the den, watching a football game with Willow on his lap. "Hi! I wanted to see you before we settle in for a girls' night. I love you," Blake said.

"I love you. Did you have fun today?"

"It was the perfect day," Blake said.

"I'm glad," he said, smiling. "My brothers and their families will be here in time for dinner tomorrow. What time will your dad get here?"

"Probably around the same time," Blake said. "Mom has placed a catering order with Acme. She figured everyone would want seafood their first night on the island. By the way, there's some coconut cake from Page's in the kitchen."

"Ugh. I ate way too many tacos at dinner. I think I had six," Clint said.

Blake laughed, patting his stomach. “I may not see you before you go to bed. So, goodnight.” She kissed Clint before she walked back downstairs.

Elaina walked into the living room with a bowl of popcorn and a bag of chocolates. Blake grabbed a handful of both.

“I probably shouldn’t eat like this before the wedding, but I figure Thanksgiving is in two days, so there’s no use in dieting,” Blake said.

“I’m not worrying about calories,” Brittany said. “I want to eat this whole bag of candy.”

The three sisters settled in for the movie with their mother. Afterward, they played a couple of rounds of dominoes and drank a bottle of Moscato on the screened-in porch.

“I’m exhausted,” Susan said. “I’m so glad to have all of my girls here together. Have fun, but don’t stay up too late. We have a busy week ahead of us. Goodnight.”

After Susan had gone back into the house, Brittany turned to Blake with a devious grin on her face. “So, how are things?” She raised her eyebrows.

“What do you mean? Oh...everything is awesome. I have no doubts we’re meant to be together. He is the kindest, most giving partner I could imagine having.” Blake smiled.

“I’m glad to hear it.” Brittany winked.

Blake shook her head and laughed. She had missed Brittany’s incorrigible nosiness and Elaina’s approach of taking everything in and rolling with the punches. They were different yet alike at the same time. Blake guessed most sisters could say the same.

Chapter 50

"Blake, what are you doing?" asked Clint, who had walked into the kitchen as she scribbled notes in her wedding planner.

"I'm thinking about how many people will be in the two houses by the time Friday afternoon rolls around."

"It's overwhelming but exciting."

She nodded. "I agree. I wanted to make sure we have everything covered as far as bedding and food. Thank goodness, we're ready."

"Yep. It's time for you to kick back and take it all in. You only get married once," Clint said.

"I hope so," Blake teased. "We still have to get through Thanksgiving tomorrow, the rehearsal and the cleansing ceremony."

"Everything will go great, Blake. This is the reprieve from Parker you have been needing. We'll make it happen."

Blake kissed him softly. Applause and whistling filled the air. Brittany and her father were standing a few feet away, laughing.

"You guys are hilarious." She blushed but smiled.

"I'm glad you guys are still hitting it off," Jeremy said. Her dad had always made the corniest jokes. She and her sisters had cringed as teenagers, but as adults, they had learned to appreciate his sense of humor.

When they entered the cottage, Susan asked everyone to calm down and clean up. "You guys, Clint's brothers are due to get here soon. Please clear out all the luggage and your extra belongings, so they aren't tripping over everything."

Everyone snapped up their belongings and cleared out the living room and kitchen—the rumble of cars driving over the shell-filled driveway filtered into the cottage.

"Clint, one of your brothers just arrived," Blake said, and he went running outside. She peeked out the window. Clint pulled the hood from Chris' hoodie over his head. She laughed—no one outgrows torturing their siblings.

Susan smiled. "Seems like everyone is having fun already."

"Definitely. We don't need entertainment. We push each other's buttons. What time do we need to pick up our dinner order?"

"Your dad just left to pick it up. Do you think Clint would mind hosting one of his famous outdoor movie nights?" Susan asked.

"That sounds like fun," Blake said.

When dad got back, they helped set up a buffet line in the garden. Everyone else started helping set up tables and chairs. Susan and Blake carried pitchers of sweet tea and lemonade, and for the adults, buckets of beer and carafes of wine, outside.

After dinner, Clint set up the projector. The children began falling asleep halfway through the movie. Clint smiled at his nieces and nephews and raised his eyebrows.

"I'll tell you the same thing I told Mom, let's not get ahead of ourselves," Blake said.

"We're almost married. We already have a house. So, it's the next step, right?" Clint laughed.

"Not necessarily. I'd like to wait a few years before children come into the picture. But I'm happy to have your nieces and nephews here for a visit anytime you want."

"Speaking of my nieces and nephews, we should probably help get them to bed." Clint walked over to the older kids and helped them walk to their beds while his brothers and their wives carried the little ones.

"That is a sweet sight," Blake admitted to her mother. "I need to clean up the garden. Can you send Clint out after he gets the kiddos settled?"

Her mom nodded, and Blake made her way outside.

Dusk blanketed the garden as she helped the catering crew break down the tables and chairs and take them to Granny Mason's potting shed, which they had repurposed for storage. They had tracked mud and sand onto the floor. Blake told the others she would sweep if they wanted to move on to the next task on their post-event to-do list.

She queued up her '90s playlist and danced around the shed with the broom. The heaviness of someone's eyes weighed on her. Blake trembled, drawing a deep breath before turning around.

"I thought you were cleaning up." Clint laughed.

She dropped the broom and gasped, "Oh, my God, Clint! You scared me to death!"

"Let me make it up to you by dancing a slow one with you." He put his arm around her waist, and she melted into him as they twirled around the potting shed.

When the song finished, Clint held her in his arms.

She smiled. "How did you know I needed a dance partner?"

"Well, the broom was all over the place and completely offbeat," he said with a straight face.

"You're so full of it." She laughed. "But I'm glad you came over to dance with me. You can go on inside. The caterers have already accomplished so much. I'll actually sweep the floor, and I'll be right in."

"I hope so. I have plans for us tonight." He raised his eyebrows and winked at her. She giggled. He kissed her and walked down the garden path to the house.

As she retrieved the broom from the floor, she accidentally backed into a row of small porcelain planters, knocking them off a shelf.

While picking up the pieces of the broken planters, the doors to the shed slammed shut. It wasn't a particularly windy evening, so Blake suspected Parker was to blame. She tried opening the doors, but they wouldn't budge. Rubbing her head, she turned around. The jerk, in all his glory, had her granny's book in his clutches. A few months ago, he would have frightened her, but now, she was just angry.

"Put the damn book down. I'm tired of this stupid game we're playing," Blake said.

"Oh, you mean the one that I'll win? Come on, be a good sport."

Blake snorted. "You sure are winning; you're dead and alone. Congratulations on getting everything you ever wanted!" She pulled the vial of holy water she had bought from the spiritual store and sprayed it on him.

"Is that supposed to be holy water? Let me guess; you bought it online for $5.99. It's not going to work. You'll have to do a lot more than that to get rid of me."

"It's just a matter of time. I'm working on it. Don't you worry your silly little head about it," Blake said.

Parker's face turned purple and then red. He waved his arm in her direction, and a gardening trowel and shovel set, followed by a rake and a hoe went flying toward her, pinning her shirt and hair to the wall. Everything happened so quickly that Blake didn't have time to react. Her first impulse was to scream, but she didn't want to give Parker the satisfaction.

Her alarm turned to sheer terror when he stepped outside. *What was he doing?* She needed to take advantage of his absence to devise a plan. Wriggling one of her arms out of her sweatshirt sleeve, she dug around her pocket for Nancy's cross pendant. She put it into her hand and slipped her arm back into the sleeve.

He returned, holding a bouquet from the garden and presented it to her.

Faking a smile, she batted her eyes at him. "Hey, Parker, I haven't given you a fair shot. Let's try to make this work. What does it matter if you're dead? We talk every day, anyway. I can see you, so really, we could have a pretty full life together."

He narrowed his eyes. "What's with the change of heart?"

"I've been reminiscing all the fun times we had, like that trip to the Amalfi Coast in Italy. I'll never forget staying in that sweet village. The seafood, the people, the romance…it was the trip of a lifetime."

"Yeah?" His expression softened. He almost looked like the man she had fallen for all those years ago.

"Definitely. I'd be willing to give up everything I have with Clint as long as you can still kiss me passionately without an ounce of hate in your heart."

"I guess I had better give it a try, then." He smiled and swept Blake's hair out of her face with his icy hands.

As he leaned in to kiss her, she slipped the chain with the cross pendant over his head.

The book slipped out of his hands and, along with the pendant, crashed onto the floor. Fading into nothingness, he screamed in agony, "It's not over yet!"

She sighed. Parker was right. According to Granny Mason's book, putting a blessed cross onto an evil spirit was the equivalent of a living person getting stung by a whole swarm of bees. It wouldn't kill you, but you might wish it had. Nonetheless, Blake was relieved for even a temporary reprieve.

Unsure of how much time she had, she needed to free herself and get inside. Blake scooped up the book and pendant and ran to her bedroom, placing them along with a Bible under her pillow. She had picked up this advice from Granny Mason's book. Should Parker show up again, she would read verses to weaken his powers and slip the chain around his neck.

Clint had fallen asleep with Willow curled up beside him. She couldn't bear to disturb their sleep. Instead, she went to the widow's walk to lie back and enjoy the stars sparkling through the lush canopy, the cool ocean breeze and the sound of the waves crashing along the shore.

Adrenaline raced through Blake's veins. She had narrowly escaped Parker's clutches. He'd return, but she would be ready.

Chapter 51

Chaos ensued on Thanksgiving. The family split into two groups, cooking in both kitchens.

Making matters worse, the children had found a stash of candy bars in the carriage house. They were running continuous loops between the houses. Eventually, their energy burned out, and they took Susan up on an unlimited movie and popcorn marathon in the second-floor den.

After spending the entire morning cooking, everyone was quiet as they sat down for dinner in Granny Mason's garden. Even the children were too tired to talk.

Brittany stood up and turned to Blake and Clint. "I'd like to make a toast to you guys. Clint has always been part of our family, but now I'll finally have a brother to help me torture my sisters. Seriously, though, I'm happy for both of you. I couldn't imagine a better husband for my sister. I love both of you."

Blake giggled. "Love you, too, little sis."

"Love you, Brit," Clint said, forming the "I love you" sign with his hand. Brittany beamed, and Blake's heart swelled with joy.

When everyone finished eating, they took a walk on the beach.

"I want to walk Willow!" Clint's niece, Shelby, grabbed a leash just as the small dog skittered around the corner. Willow possessed that special ability all dogs share, hearing words like "treat," "walk," or "bath" from a truly remarkable distance.

As the family walked to the beach, Clint pulled Blake aside. "I've wanted some *alone time* all day. We'll catch up with them in a minute." He softly pressed his lips against hers.

"I love you," she said.

"I love you. I'm counting down the minutes until our wedding. I know we're holding off on taking our official honeymoon until after Christmas, but I booked a room for two nights in Kiawah. I figured we'd stay here Saturday night after the wedding and go there for two nights. I'm planning to go back to work on Wednesday. Does all of that sound okay?"

"It's more than okay." She kissed him again. "Now, let's go to the beach to catch up with everyone."

The children were wading and splashing each other while the adults enjoyed the beautiful weather. Elaina walked over to Blake. "You're truly blessed to live this close to the ocean. I'm beyond jealous."

"You're welcome here anytime."

"Visiting isn't the same. Plus, I wouldn't want to disturb the newlyweds."

Blake rolled her eyes and laughed. Part of the group started wandering back to the garden to play lawn games, but Susan and her daughters stayed behind.

"I'd love to get some casual pictures of us here on the beach," Susan said.

"Consider it done. I'm the selfie queen," Brittany said, setting up different poses for the ladies.

The sun started going down, and Blake announced she needed to go back to the cottage. "There's so much to get done before our other friends and family arrive tomorrow. I want to make sure I'm ready for the cleansing ceremony."

"We'll come back and help," Elaina said.

The women changed the sheets in the bedrooms and gathered up the items Granny Mason's book recommended for the ceremony.

Afterward, they sat down in the living room and talked about the wedding.

Half-hour later, Blake began yawning. "I hate to say it, but I'm worn out. I need to go to bed. Goodnight, you guys."

Clint hadn't returned from the carriage house, so she texted him, *Goodnight. I love you.* Then, she fell asleep right away.

When she woke up, he was in bed next to her, and she kissed his cheek before she got dressed and went downstairs to cook breakfast for both households. Susan came to help her in the kitchen, and Clint delivered breakfast to the carriage house.

At lunchtime, out-of-town friends and family began arriving. Unfortunately, they didn't have space for everyone to have a private bedroom, but they took advantage of every pullout sofa and air mattress they had. A few friends had opted to extend their vacation and rent a beach condo or stay at a hotel in downtown Charleston. Clint and Blake had invited everyone to join them for the rehearsal dinner, all the festivities on Saturday and brunch Sunday morning.

Chapter 52

One of Blake's college friends, Lauren, reached out to hug her. "We're glad to be here to celebrate with you and Clint. I remember you talking about him for all those years. I was so surprised when you got engaged to Parker. I'm glad it's all working out. Also, you need to hurry and have a baby, so little Jackson has a friend."

"First of all, why is everyone so obsessed with us having a baby? We haven't even gotten married yet. Second, Jackson—you're having a boy? Congratulations!" Blake said.

"I agree! Don't rush to have kids. I need someone to go to Bonnaroo with me." Brittany winked.

Blake didn't have long to catch up before needing to change for the rehearsal. She ran upstairs to find a beautiful, emerald green silk dress hanging on her closet door. She read the attached card—*I can't wait to see the way your eyes sparkle while wearing this dress. I'm so lucky to be marrying you tomorrow. Love, Clint.*

Slipping on the dress, Blake gasped. It fit like a glove. She freshened up her makeup and put on a simple silver chain and seashell pendant. Blake looked at her reflection and smiled.

As she walked downstairs, Clint whistled, staring at her. "How did I get so lucky?" She kissed him and thanked him for the dress.

They walked outside to start the rehearsal. Judge Stephenson was standing in front of the garden trellis, with most of the wedding party standing nearby.

"Clint, you're one fortunate man." Judge Stephenson said. Blake blushed.

"I was just telling her the same thing." Clint grinned.

"Let's get this rehearsal started," Blake said, eager to turn the attention off herself.

The judge guided them through the walk-through. Everything went off without a hitch, and the catering crew brought out stockpots filled with corn, sausage, potatoes and sweet Lowcountry shrimp. Paulene strolled into the garden. Blake waved her over, inviting her to join them for dinner. After everyone had eaten their fill, Blake and her sisters went inside to change into casual clothes and gather the items they needed for the first part of the cleansing ceremony. Paulene followed them into the cottage and pulled Blake aside.

"I recommend that we perform a séance before the cleansing ceremony. It will help strengthen the effects of your letter if you can include the reason the spirit hasn't crossed over," Paulene said.

She was wearing a simple black dress. Her wrinkled hands were covered in rings, containing oddly shaped, brilliantly colored stones. Dangling from her neck was a singular silver chain embellished with a large, rough-edged purple crystal.

Blake tried not to stare and nodded. "Sure. We can use the dining room. Make yourself at home."

They walked into the dining room, and Paulene set a large black leather bag on the table and pulled out jagged chunks of crystal and pink Himalayan salt. She appeared to be putting a lot of thought into placing these items on the table. It was as if she were putting pieces of a puzzle together. When she seemed satisfied with the setup, she added sleek white candles to each open space. Blake was unsure of the significance, but Paulene was an experienced medium. Both Granny Mason and Nancy had recommended asking her for help.

"Who will talk to the spirits tonight?" Paulene asked.

"I'm not sure. Why?" Blake winced.

"We need to form a circle of protection. Anyone who might speak to the spirit needs to come in here now."

Blake walked to the kitchen to collect her mom and sisters.

When they entered the dining room, Paulene was seated at the head of the table. She had placed jewels on her temples and closed her eyes. Her head leaning back, she was holding a bejeweled dagger over her head. Blake mouthed the word "wow." Her family stifled a laugh. At that moment, Paulene's eyes opened, but only the whites showed.

"Those who are talking to spirits tonight should make a small cut on the palm of each hand." Paulene handed the dagger to Blake.

The other women's jaws dropped.

"Do it now!"

Trembling, it took Blake a moment to steady her hands and make the incisions. She gasped and jumped slightly with each cut. When she finished, she handed the blade to Brittany.

As each woman cut her hands, Blake stared at Paulene. How could this demanding person be the meek woman who volunteered in the children's library?

After everyone had finished with the dagger, Paulene looked around the table.

"Sit palm-to-palm. Your blood must flow from one to another. Do not break the circle regardless of what happens. Do you understand?"

They nodded, but Blake's stomach began flip-flopping. Throwing up seemed inevitable, but she forced herself to take several deep breaths to calm her nerves as much as possible. It helped some.

Ready or not, Paulene began her efforts to reach out to the Other Side.

"Spirits, if you're here tonight, make your presence known. Within the sacred circle, you can't harm this loving home."

The women sat in silence, staring at each other, waiting for something, *anything*, to happen. A cool breeze from an open window filled the room.

"Does anyone else see that, or am I imagining things?" Brittany vocalized and motioned with her head toward a large pewter platter flying in their direction.

Blake turned her head and started panicking. She wanted to run away, but she couldn't.

"No one can break the circle. If it's intact, the spirit can't cause harm," Paulene said forcefully.

Blake gulped and nodded, her arm hair standing on end and her nerves raw. *What an odd way to spend the night before my wedding!*

Suddenly, the tray spun around in the air and crashed straight into the wall.

"Hi, Parker." Blake rolled her eyes. This was precisely his style. Her head ached in an all too familiar way. "Stop showing off for my family."

"How do you know it's him?" Susan asked. "You will have to tell me what is going on since I won't be able to see or hear him like everyone else in the room, but I'm here to support you, honey."

"He thinks he's so funny. He's been doing that sort of crap to me since the beginning."

Parker joined them at the table. "That's what I love about you. You get me so well. Why don't you guys drop your hands already? I want to show Blake something. I need her to come with me."

Blake narrowed her eyes. "I won't be going anywhere with you, Parker, but we want to talk to you. Why are you still here? What is your unfinished business?"

"Does a guy need a reason to hang out with his fiancé? Seriously, wouldn't you be worried if I didn't want to be around you?" He cackled.

"You're dead, Parker, and even if you were still alive, you ruined our relationship when you cheated on me. I would never stay engaged to a cheater."

"Clint has never had a wild night with another woman? I seriously doubt that. Women love a man in uniform, or so I've been told. If he hasn't done anything yet, it's only a matter of time."

"Clint is a hundred times the man you ever were. And since you've been dead, you killed Nancy, and you have hurt Clint and me numerous times. It's time for you to go on to your final resting place. Pack your bags. We'll be sending you on your way tonight."

"That's where you're wrong, Blake!" Parker screamed as he disappeared into a mist.

The lights flickered, and the power went out. Candlelight illuminated the dining room.

"What should we do now?" Blake's ears burned. *Grr...For a dead person, Parker's so childish!*

Paulene whispered in a spooky tone, "Try to coax him back out and get him to say why he is haunting you."

Blake brainstormed and devised a plan. She would have to use what little acting skills she had to convince Parker she cared about him. The concept disgusted her, but it was a necessary evil. She called out his name.

"Sweetie, come back. I was wrong. I shouldn't have been so unkind. You were so good to me when we were together, and all my friends were jealous that I had a handsome, successful fiancé. I was mad when I saw you cheating with Sharon, but I've forgiven you. Can we let bygones be bygones? Please forgive me for leaving you so abruptly. We can still be friends."

"Well, that's more like it." Parker smiled his devilish grin and put his hands into his pockets. He lay his icy hands on Blake's shoulder and kissed the back of her head.

"That's so nice," Blake said, trying not to become sick.

"It's like I've said before—it's not too late for us to be together. If you're willing to die, I'll help you find a fast and painless way. I want to be with you."

"Is that why you haven't crossed over to your final resting place?" Blake asked.

"Yes, but you've resisted so far. And I decided if you didn't want to come on your own terms, I'd take away one person you loved at a time until you were so miserable you wished you were dead."

Blake let out a sigh of relief. She had the information she needed for the letter. She couldn't pretend any longer. "Screw you, Parker!" Blake screamed. "I can't do this anymore. What's next, Paulene?"

Paulene closed her eyes and began chanting, “It’s time for us to close this conversation with the Other Side. Spirits must separate from the living and give us the required three hours of sanctuary.”

She turned to the other women and told them to begin preparing for the first steps of the cleansing ceremony. Blake’s knuckles turned white as she wrote a letter to Parker, including a paragraph explaining that his so-called unfinished business would not to come into fruition, whether she was dead or alive. She closed out the letter—Rest in Peace. She hoped he would, allowing her to find respite and enjoy her new life with Clint.

Chapter 53

The glow of the blood moon cast a red hue on the women as they walked outside. Paulene instructed them to dig a hole, burying the letter along with a picture of Parker.

They replaced some of the dirt, planted a small dogwood sapling, filled the hole with the rest of the soil and watered the roots. Blake wiped the sweat dripping from her face.

"What do we need to do now?" Brittany asked.

"I have to say three nice things about him." Blake frowned and turned to Paulene, who nodded. "Here goes. Parker was handsome, he had beautiful eyes, and he was successful in his career. Now, we wait until close to midnight to say a candlelit prayer for him."

"Well, that doesn't sound creepy at all." Elaina shivered, rubbing her arms.

Blake groaned. "Granny Mason is protecting us. She will make sure we're safe. Let's watch a movie to take our minds off this super weird night."

When they walked into the living room, Willow was curled up on Susan's lap, while she drank a glass of wine.

"How adorable! Willow's loving on Grandma," Blake said.

"What kind of movie? Romcom or action?" Susan smiled at Paulene. "Oh, I'm sorry I didn't get a chance to talk to you earlier. You look familiar. Were you a friend of my mom's?"

She nodded and introduced herself, shaking Susan's hand.

"Wanna watch some home movies of us here with Granny Mason?" Elaina asked.

Blake dug out the box of VHS tapes her grandmother had recorded in the '80s and '90s, filled with moments from holiday gatherings and birthday parties. Everyone's favorite video was of Blake's fourth birthday. Tiny four-year-old Clint hugged her so hard, they both fell. The women giggled.

"You are destined to be with Clint," Brittany said.

Susan glanced at her watch. "You guys, it's time to resume the cleansing ceremony."

"Hurry. Gather a bunch of candles and a hand mirror," Blake said.

"Wait, what are the candles for?" Susan laughed. "I didn't fully understand what I was getting into tonight."

"Come with me, and I'll explain while we look for candles." Elaina winked at Blake.

They ran outside, and Paulene instructed them to gather around the sapling they had planted earlier that evening. Brittany lit candles and handed one to each of the women.

"Brrr...did it just get 10 degrees colder out here?" Blake rubbed her arms for warmth. The other women nodded, shivering. "Let's get this over with so we can go warm up."

"What's your hurry?" Parker asked as he appeared beside Blake. "You're not going to get rid of me so easily. We're supposed to be together forever, my love."

"Funny how that changed when I caught you screwing my boss," Blake yelled.

The candle flames appeared to snuff themselves. A blanket of darkness enveloped the garden.

"Honey, who are you talking to?" Susan asked. "Is it Parker? What is he saying?"

Someone was beside Blake. Brittany's perfume filled the air. She found her sister's hand and grabbed the matches to begin relighting the candles. After her eyes readjusted, she gasped. One of her family members was missing.

"Mom? Where did you go?" Blake asked. "Mom?"

"Oh, don't worry, I put her away for safekeeping." Parker cackled.

"Leave my mom alone! She can't harm you. I'm the one you want!" Blake screamed.

Parker ignored her. "You're going to stop this ceremony at once. We'll resume our game of cat and mouse, and if you get away, so will your mom. Sounds like a delightful plan to me, what do you think?"

Before she responded, Granny Mason appeared as her younger self, motioned for her to begin the ceremony again. "Keep going! Don't stop, or you will risk the safety of the entire family. You've come too far to stop now, Blake. Don't worry about your mother. I can sense she is okay."

Blake nodded. Her hands shook, but she trusted her grandmother's advice wholeheartedly.

"Don't listen to her. I'm going to kill your mom if you don't stop this right now," Parker said.

Suddenly a burst of light hit Parker in the chest, and he fell to the ground, stomach first. Granny Mason's stretched out her arms, with a colorful beam extending from her fingertips to his body.

Blake looked at her sisters, whose mouths were gaping.

Paulene pulled them into a close huddle. "It's time to begin praying, Blake."

"Okay, here goes—dear Lord, I've forgiven Parker. Please bless our home and our family and allow him to cross over to his final destination. We want to cleanse our home from any evil spirits that are in our presence. Amen."

"Amen." The other women echoed and blew out their candles.

"Please hand me the mirror," Blake said. Elaina handed it to her.

Just past her reflection, Parker sneered back at her. "I have one last thing to say to you—you're not the only one with family connections. Wait until my twin sister, Maggie, pays you another visit. She might not be so passive next time."

Blake's hands turned red as she squeezed the mirror handle. "You need to go on to your next destination. You can no longer hurt my family." But his face remained.

A decking board on the screened-in porch creaked, and Blake turned her head. Susan was standing on the porch, wearing a vacant expression. Blake choked up.

"Mom! You're okay!" Blake exclaimed. "What happened? Where did you go?"

"I'm not sure. Everything went dark. The next thing I knew, I was standing here watching you look into the mirror."

She held up the mirror again. Parker's sneering face remained.

"Where did Granny Mason go?" she asked.

"My mom was here?" Susan asked.

"She was, but she disappeared when Parker appeared in the mirror," Brittany signed, the streetlight illuminating her hands.

Blake shuddered and clutched her stomach, her dinner swirling upward. After thanking Paulene for her help, Blake handed the mirror to Susan. Clutching her stomach, Blake said, "I don't feel well. I need to go inside."

She climbed into bed, unable to forget Parker's menacing face. She tossed and turned all night. When Clint came to bed two hours later, Blake snuggled against him, hoping she would find some comfort and be able to fall asleep.

They had followed Granny Mason's instructions to the letter. Supposedly, by following these steps, she had banished him from her life. Could it be that easy to get rid of someone who had plagued her life with terror?

On this eve before her wedding, she prayed for a sign that would prove they had successfully sent Parker to his final resting place.

Chapter 54

The next day, no one, including Parker, could dampen Blake's spirits. Everyone helped make sure the couple's day was perfect.

Susan sent Clint to the carriage house so he wouldn't see Blake in her wedding dress before their planned first-look meet up with the photographer. Clint's brothers were outside, setting up tables and chairs, and vendors were setting up a dance floor and flower petal aisle runner. The catering crew set up breakfast in both houses.

After eating, Blake and her sisters took turns doing each other's hair and makeup.

Blake twirled around, grinning ear to ear. "I'm so excited! This day is finally here. I mean, we pushed the date up, but I've been waiting my entire life to marry Clint."

"You guys are such a great couple. I'm thrilled for you," Brittany said.

"Neither of you are too far behind me," Blake said to her sisters.

"I'm in no rush," Elaina said.

"Me either," Brittany shook her head.

Blake laughed.

A commotion stirred outside. Blake craned her neck toward the window. "Oh, my goodness. More of our out-of-town guests just arrived, but I need to get dressed so I can meet Clint and the photographer. Can one of you go outside, shuffle people to the right house and show them where the caterers have lunch set up?"

"Sure. I'll take care of it," Elaina said.

"Thank you! Brittany, can you stay and help me zip up my dress?"

"Absolutely. Let's go upstairs and finish getting you ready."

Blake stepped into her dress, and someone knocked on her bedroom door. "Who's there?" she asked.

"Just me, Mom. I wanted to help you two finish getting ready."

Her mom zipped up Blake's dress and helped her with her jewelry and the pearl headpiece. Susan wiped a tear from her face but smiled at Blake. "I'm so proud of you. You look stunning."

Tears threatened to spill out of Blake's eyes, but she refused to allow them. "Stop it, Mom. I can't cry. I'm getting ready to have my picture made. The photographer told me to stand on the front porch, and she would take me to Clint," she said.

"Well, I'm not missing this," Brittany signed. She and Susan followed Blake to the porch.

The photographer led Blake to Clint, who was standing in the garden with his back to the cottage.

"Clint, count to five and slowly turn around to see your gorgeous bride," the photographer said. She and her assistant got into their places. "Okay. Now, open your eyes!"

Clint's smile was priceless; his love for Blake more than apparent. Nothing else mattered. She ran to him, holding him and trying her best not to cry, but tears of joy streamed down her face. He put his hand under her chin and tilted it upward.

"You're beautiful, and in just a couple of hours, you will be my wife." Clint pressed his cheek against hers.

"I love you. I'm happier than I ever thought possible," Blake said.

Clint embraced her from behind and kissed her bare shoulders. Both photographers quickly captured the tender moment, but Blake couldn't take her eyes off her sweet fiancé.

Blake called over the rest of the wedding party and immediate family members so they could finish all the posed photos before the ceremony. "Come on! I want to party down after the wedding!"

Blossoms covered the dogwood tree they had planted during the cleansing ceremony. Typically, these trees blossomed for only a short time during the spring. So, with it being late November, something magical had to be afoot.

After the photo session wrapped up, the rest of the wedding party went inside to take a break before the ceremony, but she wanted to inspect the tree. The delicate pink flowers reminded her of Knoxville, where the trees flourished in March and April. A shimmery ribbon hung from a bottom branch. Struggling to bend over in her wedding dress, she finally untied it. A note was attached.

Blake, you have banished that evil man from the earth. He shouldn't be able to return. Your blessing is at its full potential. I hope you never need to use it again, but if you do, use it wisely.

I wish you the best for a blessed life with Clint. I'll always be with you. Love, Granny Mason

Blake held it to her chest, and her eyes misted over. She was free to marry the man who she had always loved. Together, they would find the peacefulness that only the island and the Atlantic Ocean provided.

She went inside to find Clint, who reached for her.

"Is everything going to be *okay* now?" Clint asked.

Blake nodded and smiled with more warmth and happiness than she had mustered the entire time she had been on the island. The terror was over. In mere minutes, the incredible man next to her would be her husband.

Judge Stephenson opened the kitchen door to tell Clint it was time for him and the groomsmen to line up. "Ladies, you're up next. Blake, I just sent your dad this way. He should be right behind me."

Jeremy entered the room and wiped a tear from his eye. "You're so beautiful. I'm so proud of you."

"Thanks, Dad. I love you." She kissed his cheek. Her heart began fluttering. Marrying Clint was a dream come true, but standing in front of a crowd during the ceremony was a nightmare. *It will be over soon, and our life together will begin.*

After the bridesmaids had made their way down the aisle, her dad smiled. “Blake, I’m so happy for you and Clint. Neither of you could ask for a better partner.” Jeremy squeezed her tight. “Are you ready to do this?”

Unable to speak, she held back her tears once again and nodded. He walked her down the aisle, and all eyes were on her, but she stared at Clint, who smiled ear to ear. Guitar in hand, he played and sang the song he’d performed at the Windjammer.

“I wrote this song the night I heard you’d returned to the island. I call it *A Piece of My Soul*. Now that we’re getting married, I’ll never have to worry about feeling whole again. Thank you for marrying me and making each day more incredible than the last.”

Blake dabbed her eyes with a tissue and kissed his cheek. She was fortunate to get a second chance for happiness with Clint. Some of life’s lessons made more sense with age.

They exchanged their vows, and when Blake said, “I do,” there wasn’t a dry eye in the garden.

“I now pronounce you husband and wife. You may now kiss your bride,” Judge Stephenson said.

Clint smiled and gently kissed Blake. Her heart overflowed with joy; this was the happiest moment of her life. She kissed him again and turned to face their family and friends. Their applause filled the garden. In the back of the crowd stood Granny Mason, smiling and glowing. Blake blew her a kiss. Her grandmother pretended to catch the kiss and waved before disappearing.

Somehow, good had come out of the hell Parker had put her through. She had rediscovered the love of her life; for a short time, her grandmother had come back to her. And that was worth everything.

Books By This Author

Pearls of Wisdom: An adult coloring book
Did you love Nancy Parsons' colloquialisms? Get better acquainted with her sass in Pearls of Wisdom, an adult coloring book full of Southern charm.

Coming in 2021: The Return to Palm Court
New college grad Brittany Nelson moves to the South Carolina Lowcountry to help her sister manage the family bed and breakfast and care for her three-year-old niece.

Soon after, strange occurrences begin taking place. Brittany can't shake the feeling that perhaps the ghosts of their family's past haven't been laid to rest after all.

Visit stephedwardswrites.com for purchasing details and information on Stephanie Edwards' upcoming books.

CPSIA information can be obtained
at www.ICGtesting.com
Printed in the USA
LVHW022252130721
692589LV00014B/1760

9 781735 169118